Praise for *The Vi...*

Tony Vicar is back at full throttle, ...d ....me round, using the same brilliant language and acerbic wit we came to adore in *The Liquor Vicar*, our star brings his own share of wild baggage.

— PETE MCCORMACK, Oscar nominated filmmaker and author of *Understanding Ken*

The Vicar's Knickers is a delightful humour noir novel. Vince Ditrich generously lends his trademark wit and cleverness to the characters of fictional Tyee Lagoon, with laugh-out-loud turns of phrase on every page.

— SARAH CHAUNCEY, author of *P.S. I Love You More Than Tuna*

I don't remember the last time I smiled so much while reading a novel. Vince Ditrich's vivid descriptions and colourful characters are the perfect escapism.

— MARTIN CROSBIE, bestselling author of the My Temporary Life trilogy

They're back! All the beloved characters from *The Liquor Vicar*, plus a baby, two deliciously evil villains, a moose with a passion for golf balls, and a mysterious entity. How I would love to spend an evening in The Vicar's Knickers, pint in hand, chatting with the fine folk of Tyee Lagoon!

— ALISON KELLY, author of *Granville Island ABC*

The greatest sequel since *The Wrath of Khan*, if Tony Vicar was William Shatner.

— GRANT LAWRENCE, author and CBC Radio host

Praise for *The Liquor Vicar*

The Liquor Vicar is an energetic romp through a closet community on the Island, populated by well-drawn characters and strewn with more references to pop culture and euphemisms than you can shake a stick at.

— *Winnipeg Free Press*

Funny, silly, lighthearted, sentimental, snarky, and often hyperactive with comic energy, Vince R. Ditrich's novel tells a tall, quirky tale of redemption in snack-sized chapters.

— *Vancouver Sun*

Ditrich presents a fresh, gonzo voice in his debut novel, a quirky tale of the down side of life and a promise of redemption in a narrative that is entertaining.

— *Booklist*

The Liquor Vicar is beautiful chaos. Ditrich's characters come alive with all the complexity of a Shakespearean comedy and a uniquely Canadian dry wit. Colourful characters carry this story like a current, moving seamlessly from side-splitting humour to tenderness as it explores our human desire for relevance and purpose.

— MELANIE MARTIN, author of *A Splendid Boy*

A very entertaining read, with a cast of characters that feel like you've met before. *The Liquor Vicar* is full of the troubled and broken hearted, but Ditrich finds depth and honesty, and most centrally the humour in these intersecting lives. A great debut.

— AARON CHAPMAN, author of *Vancouver After Dark*

THE
VICAR'S
KNICKERS

THE MILDLY CATASTROPHIC
MISADVENTURES OF TONY VICAR

The Liquor Vicar
The Vicar's Knickers

Book 3 coming in 2023!

VINCE R. DITRICH

THE VICAR'S KNICKERS

THE MILDLY
CATASTROPHIC
MISADVENTURES
OF TONY VICAR

DUNDURN
PRESS

Publisher and acquiring editor: Scott Fraser | Editor: Shannon Whibbs
Cover designer: Laura Boyle
Cover image: Man at bar istock.com/A-Digit

Library and Archives Canada Cataloguing in Publication

Title: The Vicar's knickers / Vince R. Ditrich.
Names: Ditrich, Vince R., 1963- author.
Description: Series statement: The mildly catastrophic misadventures of Tony
   Vicar ; 2
Identifiers: Canadiana (print) 20220216991 | Canadiana (ebook) 20220217025
   | ISBN 9781459747289 (softcover) | ISBN 9781459747296 (PDF) | ISBN
   9781459747302 (EPUB)
Classification: LCC PS8607.I87 V53 2022 | DDC C813/.6—dc23

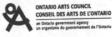 

We acknowledge the support of the Canada Council for the Arts and the Ontario Arts Council for our publishing program. We also acknowledge the financial support of the Government of Ontario, through the Ontario Book Publishing Tax Credit and Ontario Creates, and the Government of Canada.

Care has been taken to trace the ownership of copyright material used in this book. The author and the publisher welcome any information enabling them to rectify any references or credits in subsequent editions.

The publisher is not responsible for websites or their content unless they are owned by the publisher.

Printed and bound in Canada.

Dundurn Press
1382 Queen Street East
Toronto, Ontario, Canada M4L 1C9
dundurn.com, @dundurnpress 🐦 f ⊚

To Louis.
Welcome to the world.
Sorry we didn't tidy the place first.

alentine was drunk. It was payday and his envelope had been full of cash. He had set aside a chunk and stuck it into a sock that he had hidden in a hole at the bottom of the closet. No one would find it without a major search.

He went downstairs to join the boys. There were loggers everywhere in the beer parlour and his whole crew was over in the corner. He called the waiter over.

"Cover the table," he said, with false bravado.

"Yes, sir. Right away."

Valentine liked being called sir. He wasn't quite old enough to drink yet, but no one out here gave a damn. Pierre, the waiter, with his Continental tie and long white apron, starched white shirt buttoned neatly at the wrists, departed and came back quickly with a giant tray filled with tapered glasses of draught beer.

Valentine leaned back and let him completely cover the table in twenty-four of them.

He casually passed him a ten-spot and told him to keep the change. Pierre looked down at Valentine doubtfully and asked, "Are you sure, sir?"

"Yes, yes. No trouble." Valentine tried to look casual, but his eyes still flicked toward Burt, his foreman, as if looking for reassurance. Burt gave him a little wink. There was an audible murmur from the gaggle of co-workers surrounding him. *Big tipper — young man.* They knew they were about to witness a christening of sorts, a declaration of independence from a kid who, after the better part of a year out here, felt he knew the ropes.

By 11:45 p.m. the beer parlour was closed and they had to shoo a drunken Valentine to his bed. He wobbled upstairs and practically fell into his room.

My God, I am starving. He saw the large box his parents had sent and peered into it. For some reason they had set a huge box of baked goods on top of a bucket of chicken, which had been hastily surrounded by leaky ice packs inside a light wooden crate, ice packs melting soon after shipping. Ravenous, he pulled everything out of the twine-wrapped box and feasted on busted cookies, rock-hard hot cross buns, and some shrivelled yet remarkably greasy chicken. It had partially warmed up on top of the radiator for a while. He didn't care. He would have chewed the arse out of a live hyena at that moment. He gorged on the chicken until there wasn't a speck left — he even dumped the crumbs from the bottom of the barrel down his rapacious maw. Ray Stevens sang "Everything Is Beautiful" on the transistor radio, and he heartily agreed as his stomach gurgled happily. Then he lay back against the headboard, drifting off to sleep, his belly growling and rumbling like there were creatures inside him having an argument. He was half-embarrassed, but it was just one of those nights. He needed some food to soak up all that beer.

PART I

One / Present Day with a Side of Apocalypse Then

f Vancouver Island could be imagined as the index finger of a right hand, bent hard over and pointing toward its own elbow at four o'clock, the town of Tyee Lagoon lay on the palm side, near its middle knuckle. Ramshackle town planning had allowed for one paved road spur that led to it, along which were a couple of dreary plazas containing a handful of shops, none easily accessible on foot. Around here you drove, or you stayed put. There were a couple of gravel goat trails that let drivers access the old highway, which in turn could access the new one. Those routes offered enough inconvenience to make them a last-ditch option.

Near the Strait of Georgia but set back from the water just a little, the town once supported coal mining, logging, fishing, and even a little farming. Mining had vanished decades ago, and after flattening the immediate area, logging had moved away to denser and more remote stands of timber. Against their better judgment, the logging companies had left a few trees standing, which surrounded the town like a high, green picket.

The fishing industry was now a mere shadow of its former self, but the sport fishery was non-stop and kept the marina in business. Nothing short of the total evaporation of the oceans would prevent the keenest keeners from wallowing around in small craft to hook a spring salmon and putt around in their well-worn boats. A few souls owned ostentatious floating condominiums, but the old heads never had much patience for shiny yachts steered inaccurately by weekenders from Calgary. But whatever their opinion, the area's main push had now become lifestyle and tourism.

The locals called the place "the Island," as if it were the superlative form and all other islands would need to specify. Residents knew that they sometimes had to say "Vancouver Island" as a courtesy to the unwashed, but that was as weird as saying "ice hockey." So many had come here to retire and, once ensconced in their giant homes, they'd advise everyone else that they should stay away. They, too, had become beguiled. But no one listened.

From Victoria Day to Labour Day, the town and its surroundings crawled with tourists, mostly older couples in matching shirts and Velcro-lashed walking shoes, sallying forth creakily from their ginormous motorhomes, the bane of swift summer travel and on-time ferry trips. Tony Vicar's beautiful new pub, the

Vicar's Knickers Public House — "the Knickers" to
most — was open for business and awaited their arrival.

Through a freakish sequence of events, he had found
himself the heir to the hotel and property that housed
the pub, a gift from a sweet centenarian named Frankie
Hall. A few small acts of kindness by Vicar were repaid
by Mrs. Hall ten thousandfold.

More bizarrely he also had become a celebrity of a
strange type. A few things had happened in the last
couple of years that were so odd that most folks just
attributed them to the paranormal, the supernatural,
or simply the telling of tall tales. It had either been an
astonishing run of luck or a heavy dose of magic. Vicar
wasn't sure himself and stumbled through life with
a stupid grin pasted to his face, trying his best to be
friendly to all his new "pals." But in fact, he felt like
a postapocalyptic Walmart greeter girding himself
against approaching zombies.

As successful as the Knickers renovation had been,
the old Agincourt Hotel, in which it sat, was nowhere
near complete. After two years spent on the pub, Vicar
was slightly depleted. Life was gaining speed, his world
changing; when he looked back, he barely recognized
the man he so recently had been. A minute ago, it
seemed, he had been a young, footloose bachelor, un-
tethered but hilarious, a musician and self-proclaimed
tastemaker, with that taste frequently questioned by
more conventional minds.

He, a guy named Ray, and Farley Rea — still his
close friend now — had rented the most awful old

house and lived fully immersed in a brand of stag-party squalor that had to be seen and smelled to be fully appreciated. Their days had all been a running gag, and their life bore no resemblance to the tidy and totally civilized way he currently lived: in a huge, lovely, rambling old house with an ocean view, alongside Jacquie O, a woman way out of his league. They lived quite happily together and shared everything — his pub; her house; crisp, clean linens; even fully functional appliances, some still under warranty.

The freakish, smelly bachelor trio of his youth, serious up-and-coming rock stars if you had asked them, were at least colourful. Man, they were sure they'd write a hit or two and fly to the top of the charts, their star qualities and dazzling musical talent lofting them into the stratosphere of fame. But of course, they did not. They had possessed neither talent nor focus, but to his mind there was just something *off* about the band's collapse. He had been heartbroken yet somehow relieved. He hated the mixed message. But the issue just wouldn't quite scan.

He nurtured a blind spot about the viability of prog rock efforts — passé by the time they'd even started. Their magnificent trio was, he had said preciously, a "*power triangle.*" He recounted the stories of their adventures again and again to anyone who'd listen. They had been great, great days. But … Vicar knew they had been living like musky quadrupeds.

Farley, for example, had claimed that he washed his sheets only on New Year's Day. This awful factoid was true, so a ceremony involving pizza, beer, and faux-Gregorian chant was devised to celebrate the annual de-cheesing, but despite all the fun, Vicar had been a little grossed out. By year two the grand performance felt forensic.

That old place was not only their bachelor pad but was infamously "*THE* Bachelor Pad" to the locals — a notorious, exhausted cottage that dated back at least to the 1920s, as drafty as a wind tunnel, arctic in winter, hotter than the surface of the sun in summer, jumping with fleas in the spring, and a year-round fire trap — but it only cost them each a hundred bucks a month. It sat in the front corner of a large farm and had been the original homestead in the years before fancier digs were erected farther back on the property.

The old joint had carried with it the crazy aroma of some unidentified spice, dark and overpowering, that intensified near one cupboard. Inside it was nothing save that pungent aroma and a single packet of prehistoric mac and cheese, marked in felt pen *Apocalypse Rations*. They had discovered it there when they moved in and the packaging made it look at least a decade old, probably more. Vicar knew he'd only tuck into it if an atomic war started, leaving them irradiated and starving.

Ray had smoked a vast quantity of pot one night during a rocking party, delivered via Farley's massive bong, assembled from discarded PVC pipe. It was Farley's one contribution to science and engineering, his so-called "experimental model" — about four feet tall, and merrily dubbed the Douche Bassoon. Using it was a two-person operation but by God it was effective. Vicar had been terrified of the contraption and wouldn't go near it but watched in horrified fascination as Ray hoovered greedily while Farley knelt below with a little butane torch.

Squinty and famished, his long dreadlocks in a headband, dishevelled and upended, looking like radio antennae, Ray had rooted around in the fridge, pawing at its contents, muttering incoherently. Finally, in desperation, he'd grabbed the mac and cheese packet from the smelly cupboard, cooked it up, and gobbled it down. Minutes later, he'd staggered out to the backyard, higher than a condor's cloaca, now nauseated, and became violently ill. An angular allegro of lurid retching could be heard, and then *pfft* — no more sound effects.

They had gone outside to see if Ray had popped his clogs, but he was nowhere to be found. They could track a trail of orangey goop on the pathway to the front gate and then it dribbled to a stop. At that point the trail, mercifully, went cold.

Right about then, one of the partiers had lit nag champa and put on an antique half-speed master LP of *Dark Side of the Moon*, so everyone forgot about Ray. No one knew where he had ended up that night, but he was never the same afterward.

Vicar and Farley eventually found him asleep face down on a couch that was perched on a porch located nearly two miles away.

He had lain there as if left for dead, at the most unappetizing house Vicar had ever seen ... And, for fuck's sake, he lived in *the Bachelor Pad*. The house was painted a distressing gonorrhea green, deliberately rendered that way it seemed. *No one except a total skinflint would choose a colour that horrible*, Vicar had thought, as he spied Ray from the roadway. *They probably got the paint for free — more likely someone paid 'em to cart it away.* Anyone that cheap would be *mean*. He'd shuddered with revulsion at the sight before him and feared being caught on the property.

The yard surrounding the infection-coloured bungalow had been mowed bald of all flora, flattened right down to the battle-scarred dirt where three gnarly trees stood in a rigid line, looking like wounded POWs standing at attention in front of their hut. Just by looking at the house, Vicar had known he'd hate the artless turds who owned it — he couldn't believe they hadn't already discovered Ray's unconscious body on their ugly porch and attacked him with a shovel.

Ray's clothes had been inside out. Still half in a dream state, he'd believed that he had been abducted by aliens, examined, and then returned to this random alfresco chesterfield. Man, he had been fucked up. Soon afterward, he took up sitar.

Everyone began calling him Cosmic Ray. He disappeared one day, just vanished, never again to be seen or heard from — there were some whispers that he had gone to India. Vicar thought that might be a possibility, but then again, he might have gone off with the aliens he kept talking about …

Yup, Vicar mused wistfully. *The good old days. The good old days?*

Two / Kiss Me, Hardy

Wearing an old paint-stained work shirt and with her mahogany-coloured hair in a ponytail to keep it out of her face, Jacquie O held the phone to her ear with her shoulder while she jotted notes on the back of an old bill.

"Yes, it's a hotel. Yup, we are the new owners …"

She'd spent at least twenty minutes just trying to get the billing information changed on the Hydro account. The phones and the internet were equally time-consuming. Glancing in a mirror, she tapped the end of her pen on the counter irritably and then forced herself to stop. *Oh God, I look just like my mother.* That was a route she didn't want to explore; surely there was more awaiting her than vinegary impatience, early widowhood, and canasta Thursdays.

Miss C. Jacqueline O'Neil, whom everyone knew as Jacquie O, was a young woman who was still growing into her power. As with most people she had begun her adulthood with too little direction and too many amusing distractions. She was bright, inquisitive, grounded, and flat-out gorgeous, and had dropped out of UVic one year shy of a bachelor's degree. If asked why, she blamed it on the untimely death of her boyfriend. The grief of his death had made her course of study seem pointless, just an endless list of requirements that screamed, *This shit is worthless if you die tomorrow*. She was determined to have a life, not just a job.

Jacquie had been a little older than most in her classes and had seen a lot more of the world even by that early point. She had, after all, supported her educational career through exotic dancing, but she never prettied up her job description. She had been a stripper.

By day, she had hung around innocuous, out-to-lunch kids and held her tongue while they parroted parochial opinions about equality, morality, propriety, all theatrically delivered with overweening pride; by night, she lived in the world of the frazzled, the misguided, the addicted, the closeted, the unrealistic — *the desperate*; souls who were occasionally noble, but not for long. Hypocrites, too, but without the brittle rich-girl outrage.

Jacquie innately had a strong sense of right and wrong, but she also knew that what her prudish classmates looked down upon without ever having tried, she sometimes liked very much. On the other hand, her compatriots in the dark, semi-clad nighttime world oversimplified any philosophical riddle and often made arguments in favour of self-destruction. Jacquie could see that she lived in a middle ground; she was wise enough to pursue her own path quietly.

Her former dancing cohorts could open any door with their beautiful bodies, their wiles, and their strategically deployed fantasy underwear. But once the door was opened to them, few had anything to bring to the table. They had never been anywhere, had never really read any books, knew of life only from TV. Jacquie saw it happen again and again. Beautiful young women with no plan beyond what outfit they might sport for the evening, who still believed that being a stunning ornament would suffice in life. Naïfs who serially fell in love with muscle-bound meatheads and then wept when they were invariably cast aside. They aimed for *The Real Housewives of Beverly Hills* but ended up third on the bill at some dump in Red Deer.

Far too many of them turned into heartbroken cynics, mothers whose children had multiple fathers, grimly trying to keep all the plates spinning. What had once been glamour and romance was now more like basic survival; the years lumbered on, but the rent, it seemed, was perennially due.

Jacquie made efforts to keep her sense of self well protected in this convergent social riptide. She told herself she could hold it all in balance, but after boyfriend Prentiss's bizarre demise on a bicycle in light evening traffic, she lost her marbles, unplugged from everything, and hid out — went off the grid, in what she thought would be quiet and uneventful Tyee Lagoon.

It was by sheer kismet, not to mention the need for a hookup on an early spring evening after a gloomy, long winter, that she had gotten mixed up with Tony Vicar and plunged right into the midst of an adventure that she didn't even try to describe to strangers. It was just too weird.

Three / Knickers Innards

"*That* has *got* to go," proclaimed Vicar the day he and Jacquie had committed to the reno on what would become the Vicar's Knickers. He pointed contemptuously at the industrial-style bar that had, in the 1980s, replaced the original, glorious wooden one; it was a pile of neon-festooned scrap metal. He thought it had all the elegance of a crushed shopping buggy and dragged him kicking and screaming back to the era of Duran Duran's diabetes-inducing synthesizers. Every time he laid eyes on it, he heaved it an insult.

The mere sight of it chafed at him like a nasty itch. What the place needed was a throwback to a golden era, *fin de siècle*, or its Vancouver Island equivalent; a grand, traditional, elegant bar — a tip of the hat to the days of loggers with axes, and coal-powered trains. It should be long and hand-made of fir and cedar, maybe a little piece of arbutus here or there, finished with brass. Bas-relief on its lower panels. Filigree at every corner. It should be made by a local woodworker, just like all the best bars have been through the ages. Standing at it should fill a customer with delight, make them thirsty, and inspire them to get on the blower and bring all their friends down, too. *Let's get this show on the road.*

Later that week, Vicar had wandered into the old beer parlour to really look the place over with no one else there to distract him.

It became apparent that someone had done an upgrade of sorts to it in the 1960s that brought in a buzzing fluorescent light fixture over a dilapidated pool table, as well as a few more electrical plugs, run with aluminum conduit, rough-hewn and unsightly. Gruesome reddish shag carpet was laid in one corner for unknown reasons. The revolting metal bar came in the 1980s, and then followed video games, vending machines that clunked and buzzed, a mechanical cigarette dispenser that eventually took four brawny men to move, and a mismatch of chairs from various eras.

Worst of all, there was a road sign that read *Margaritaville*, a brash reminder to patrons that they simply *must* launch into a heinous singalong of what amounted to "The Wheels on the Bus" for forlorn drunks. *Break out another bottle of tequila, Madge!* The sign alone tinged the place with desolation.

The archaeological layers that showed the evolution of the old heap lay before him, waiting to be observed, interpreted, and then unceremoniously heaved out. Jacquie seemed to tense up whenever she entered, and Vicar knew she just couldn't quite envision the endgame. So, Vicar wanted to start gutting the place before he could be demoralized and change his mind. He pushed to get the renovation underway, and it began ahead of schedule on a winter day, occluded sun low in the sky.

Once the workers had started pulling the old beer parlour's insides outdoors, Vicar felt worry dissipate. There was no going back now — and with amazing speed, the place was just an empty shell, reduced to bare framework. Soon, they'd rip the roof off, too, and truck the old one away. Steel beams would reinforce the inner structure; a crane would gently lower them into place from above, readying the whole schmozzle for a new and very stylish roof. Welders, electricians, and plumbers crawled around the place from morning to night. It was taking shape, and when Vicar stopped to think about it, Frankie Hall's final wishes had quite readily become his wishes. A seed had been planted. A single comment she had made completely changed the trajectory of his life. He'd always fancied the thought of having a pub, but Frankie had put it on his radar. She had asked, "What kind of town doesn't have a beer parlour?" Vicar had replied, "It's not a town without a pub."

He believed it; he wasn't just being agreeable to a little old lady. He just knew there was a place for the

Vicar's Knickers Public House, a brand-new pub backed by a thousand-year-old tradition.

The process had begun with a brief visit to Frankie Hall's lawyer.

"Sign here, here, here, and ..." He flipped the page. "Here." The tweedy barrister had offered his pen.

Vicar had signed, then looked up at him and asked, "Is that it?"

Indeed, that was it. A few signatures affixed to a few documents and, boom, he took possession of nearly a whole block of downtown Tyee Lagoon, land and a hotel that Frankie Hall had owned for decades. This inheritance had been a surprise but was only one of many so-called miracles to have descended upon him of late.

With the hotel's main entrance located on Dumfries Road, Vicar's new property faced east, toward the morning sun. Dumfries intersected Gull Street, running east to west, where the entire north side of the building lay. The whole structure backed onto an alley, beyond which was the more distant Jersey Road, home to a couple of restaurants that incessantly changed hands, every one of them having begun with the highest hopes and then quickly dying from extreme lack of interest a few months into their overly optimistic leases. There had been one that specialized in things like kale salads, eggplant parmigiana, and some bitter grass clippings called *arugula*, a name better suited to a vegetarian vampire. Ostensibly they served food, but it was made entirely of plants. Vicar, always satisfied with reheated chicken strips and a bucket of institutional gravy, would rather have eaten the Apocalypse Rations than dine there.

The other side of Jersey Road also featured a succession of pointless village boutiques, as well as Balmer's Funeral Home at the southern terminus of the long, sad avenue, which seemed wryly appropriate. The most memorable to Vicar had been a place called Konnie's Kountry Kottage, that specialized in bland souvenir apparel for aged tourists bereft of style or taste — much of it spackled with gold lamé. Its proprietor, Konnie Kemper, a cheerful but out-to-lunch middle-aged lady with absurd glasses, was blind to the fact that the entire world, other than she, called the place Klan Headquarters. Mockery of the poor woman and her shop was knee-jerk and much protracted, yet she smiled though it all, blithely oblivious, never for a second picking up on the glaring error in her choice of name. In the window of her shop, Vicar once spied a mannequin in a beige T-shirt with a whale-shaped logo that said in a flowy font, *Come Back Soon t' Tyee Lagoon.*

Sheer fuckin' poetry. He groaned. When he had clapped eyes on the heinous garment for the first time, he had turned to his friend and said, "If you ever need me gone, just dress me in that and I'll die from shame." This from a man who still occasionally wore pleated jeans.

As a *special attraction*, appealing to God only knows who, they also sold "Hand-Knitted Sock Puppets." The sight of the shop made Vicar feel despondent; he was secretly relieved when it closed. The respite, however, had been only temporary — it had been immediately replaced by an ill-fated millinery shop. He had never once in his life seen anyone in the town wear a lid such as they displayed, nor had an event ever occurred where someone might need one of their otherworldly fascinators. Fascinating, all right, leaving a guy staring as if transfixed by a sixth finger on an outstretched hand.

In downtown Tyee Lagoon, there were only four streets north to south, and five east to west, so owning almost a whole block of real estate made Vicar practically a mogul. The inheritance from Frankie Hall had been, in fact, a mind-blowing windfall.

The amount of money he could have jammed in the bank by simply selling the property would have been huge, although nearly any amount of dough would have seemed huge a couple of years ago. The future had suddenly felt limitless for the first time, and his mind boggled at the options before him. He had for a while imagined himself in Tahiti or Peru or Morocco, or nearly anywhere exotic, strumming his guitar on a beach, wandering the untracked desert, traipsing over mountain passes with a walking stick and a backpack, utterly at peace. Then he remembered he fucking well hated hiking. His colon clamped shut at the thought of funky international toilets, too.

But, more than two years later, he stood inside what would soon become the Vicar's Knickers, a place born of his imagination and about to be brought to life by his efforts, not to mention a line of credit for twenty times the cost of his mother's first house.

One thing was certain: this place was going to have the most gorgeous bar, made to exacting requirements, costs be damned. Then he'd drive hard for enticing taps, new windows, a saloon-style plank floor.

The two floors above the old beer parlour, formerly an entire wing of the hotel, were blown completely out, and a construction crew ringed the inside of what used to be the second floor with a balcony that looked downward into the main pub below and gazed at the ceiling above. The interior would feel almost tower-like and the exterior would be crowned with a mansard roof, making it look like the Empress hotel in Victoria.

To boot, they had somehow managed to make it look "antique"; homey, broken-in, comfortably worn. It was Jacquie who had the eye for that stuff. But Vicar was relieved to discover that he had been useful during the design process, too. The construction of his new bar had determined the look and flow of everything else that remained to be done inside. After all his work, Vicar gazed at it with a feeling close to love, as if it were a living thing.

"See, Jack? I can practically hear it calling me." He waved his arm at the mammoth bar and pantomimed drinking a pint of beer with sensuous pleasure, cupping his ear as if listening to it whisper.

"All I hear is the bookkeeper from the lumberyard gleefully rubbing his hands together." She shook her head.

Thanks to Jacquie's insistence, they doubled the size of the main floor ladies' room and added a second one, also very spacious, up in the balcony that ringed the whole inner structure.

It was said that the ladies' rooms sent a ripple of excitement through the female population of Tyee Lagoon. That's where Jacquie's ideas went over the top. She had made certain that the facilities were of the finest standards, agreeably lit, and pleasant to the nose, at least at the start of the day — Vicar had been quite shocked to discover how bad they could get after alcoholic refreshments had been introduced.

On the Sunday morning after opening weekend, when they had been absolutely slammed with so many customers that they were stretched to the maximum, he went into the ladies' bathroom to help the janitors with the cleanup. He was nearly knocked over by the smell emanating from inside. It reminded him of childhood, when his mother had taken him to visit one of her old grande dame friends, a frail woman partial to Murchie's No. 10 Blend and cucumber finger sandwiches, whose bathroom honked of Jergens lotion and a partially flushed poop.

▪ ▪ ▪

Vicar, increasingly famous with each passing day, legend of his so-called powers now ballooning in magnitude until the claims should have been patently unbelievable but were not, was constantly being asked his opinion, hit up for favours, approached by friends and strangers, and gawked at openly.

More happily, he had been asked to sponsor a kids' baseball team. He knew that many of the local businesses coughed up a few bucks, and really, loving kids as much as he did, he happily donated some money. He knew that Lagoon Hardware had done it and had sponsored a hockey team, too. It really didn't amount to much money, and he imagined a child of his own playing on the team someday. *Probably just a pipe dream, Vicar*, he thought.

The team had decided to call themselves the Tyee Lagoon Vicars as a thanks for his generosity, which made Vicar delighted and embarrassed at the same time. He had an open invitation to any of their events.

The coach left a message on Jacquie's phone early in the season asking them to attend.

"Tony, the baseball team wants us to come to their thingy on Wednesday night."

"Uh, okay. Is it a gig or just a rehearsal?"

"You mean game or practice?" she asked, amused.

"Uhh ... you practise at home and rehearse with the band, Jack."

She snickered and said, "I think it's a rehearsal ..."

"Great! Do you think they'll be wearing their new costumes?"

"Uniforms, honey. Uniforms."

They arrived at the school field a little late and there was a wave of excitement that ran through the crowd. *It was Vicar!* The kids had heard so much about this guy. Why, if he started coming to their games, they couldn't possibly lose.

Jacquie was aware that this kind of thinking was coursing through the crowd, but Vicar was a bit out to lunch about it at that moment, far more interested in watching little ones swinging haplessly at the ball, running like kittens to first base if by some miracle they connected with it. He loved it. Surveying the diamond, he realized that the outfielders were lying down, taking a nap on the grass. There wasn't the slightest chance that a ball could get out there. He thought his ol' buddy Farley might be good at that position.

One very small boy, much shorter than his teammates, stood at home base, with a bat in his hands so small it looked like a billy club. He could not hit the ball, even with all his teammates and all the parents shouting out words of encouragement. Finally, at two strikes and three balls, he put his bat on the ground, ran to the mound, and took the ball from the pitcher's glove. He had heard all the stories about Vicar's abilities — his parents talked about them all the time. He had heard his dad say, *"Why doesn't he magically make our mortgage vanish?"* He ran directly over to Jacquie and said, with the most endearing sweetness, "Do you think Mr. Vicar could get me a hit?"

Jacquie melted. Omigod, it was so cute. She misted up, and Vicar, sitting right beside her, felt under a microscope; he had to do something, but he was almost sick at the thought of falsely getting the kid's hopes up. This was this kind of stuff that he feared the most.

Jacquie nudged him and so Vicar thought, *The hell with it* ... He took the ball from the boy's hand, stood up, and held it high, while putting his other hand on the boy's helmeted head. He boldly pronounced with a fake smile, "You will hit the next one, and it will be a *rocket!*"

The boy grabbed the ball, chirping, "Thanks!" over his shoulder, and dashed back to the plate.

After a moment of preparation, while the parents in the bleachers buzzed noticeably, the pitch came right down the line. The little slugger, four feet tall, connected with it for the first time in his short baseball career. It got some air and then rolled right between second and third, eventually banging into one of the napping outfielders.

The kid stood there, dumbfounded, while his teammates screamed, "Run! Run!"

Jacquie turned to Vicar with a look of amazement on her face, and then realized every parent at the ballpark was doing the same. This, she knew, would be yet another entry into the journal of Vicar's growing ledger of fabulous feats; at this point the smallest event made a splash. *Gawd, a guy brings one person back from the dead ...*

▬ ▬ ▬

A street light shone from Dumfries Road through the lobby windows of the Agincourt, giving its interior a dim orange glow. The front desk, once quite grand, was now little better than a battered old counter, set to be demolished the next week. Behind it was a hutch of pigeonholes where messages, mail, and keys for each room were once stored.

At the side wall were shelves, one of them a tacky adjustable unit with two notched rails. The construction crew had left a few items sitting on it: a yellow electric drill, a box of nails, and a cardboard chicken bucket — a source of amazement to the young workers who were starting the renovations. For decades it had sat in one of the abandoned guest rooms on the seldom used second floor, the last inhabitant clearly having had a good appetite. One of the guys found it and brought it downstairs, holding it as if he'd just found a dinosaur fossil. The construction team just could not believe the old bucket said *Poulet Frit à la Kentucky* on one side and spent a whole coffee break wondering where it had come from. France? They all laughed. The nearest such outlet was probably an hour away, even today.

Had anyone been inside the building at that moment they'd have heard rattling in the pipes upstairs, a knocking sound that moved slowly from the street side to the rear of the hotel, vibrating the whole structure. It stopped, but then only a moment later the shelf collapsed. Nails rained down and sprayed across the floor's chequered tile surface, and the electric drill now hung from its power cable, swinging back and forth like a corpse from a hangman's rope.

The chicken bucket fell neatly onto the centre of the counter, almost as if having been deliberately placed there, and greeted the workers who arrived to find the mess early the next morning.

■ ■ ■

The hotel stood mostly gutted now, junk being removed out every door daily. The pub, however, was complete, serving beer, and contained a bright, clean, modern kitchen manned by a small platoon of people in aprons. By some manner of alchemy, they had managed to make the place grand and elegant while keeping it intimate, especially in the cozy corners. That felt like a bit of a magic trick to Vicar. He had hoped the Knickers would be this sweet, but he had fallen short in so many projects in his life that he almost assumed some unforeseen cock-up would wreck everything in the final stretch. He had driven himself hard to achieve it. Even now he wandered around his lovely new pintery expecting to find a hidden catastrophe coalescing in some dim recess.

On the Knickers's opening day, one of their first patrons had come in, bubbly and effusive, and when his eyes took in what Vicar and Jacquie had accomplished, he was awestruck and began speaking in a hushed tone, as if he'd just entered a cathedral.

"This is the most beautiful pub I've ever seen," the man whispered.

Vicar agreed, without ego. He had pulled out all the stops; it might be one of the nicest drinking establishments ever. He replied to the customer, somewhat amazed himself, as if he had been in no way responsible, "I know, right?"

He still got weak in the knees at the thought of how much they'd spent on that giant fireplace, so large that it felt like a separate little village within the pub's interior. It even featured a nook with little stone benches. The whole place, he thought, looked almost regal, and he was well satisfied — though he did worry that they might have put a twenty-dollar saddle on a ten-dollar horse. Tyee Lagoon was in the middle of nowhere, after all. By this point he could do nothing more than proceed on faith, serene in the knowledge that, if nothing else, they had nailed the look — stuck it like a Nadia Comăneci landing.

Vicar now felt he had to get the hotel finished, too. He wanted people to come here and stay awhile. It seemed obvious that if enough showed up, business for everybody in town would increase, there'd be new shops and restaurants and attractions — and he would be the guy who started it all. Tyee Lagoon might never again be blighted by a hand-knitted sock puppet shop. It wasn't like being a rock star, but, hey, maybe they'd name a street after him.

Four / Pink

Ross Poutine was writing notes onto a pad of paper in cursive chicken scratch as cryptic as his speech patterns and gazing about the space that would become his new liquor store. The space had for decades been the coffee shop of the Agincourt Hotel, and now stood empty, awaiting his redesign.

His original store location, starkly named Liquor, still operating until this new location was finished, was a short drive down the road to the highway and sat in a gravelly pullout. It was an even shorter drive if he opened 'er up with his lovingly maintained and extensively modified '66 Chevelle, his prized possession and personal trademark. Under his care it sparkled and glistened and could output more horsepower than a small commercial aircraft. It was his only love, his only hobby, his only focus outside of Liquor, although the last couple of years saw him bring into the fold Jacquie

O and Tony Vicar, who he now considered to be practically family.

This new space was big and high and perfect for the purpose, so Jacquie kept trying to convince him to pretty it up, make it look all fancy and shit. Wasn't it enough that he was moving to this new location, closer to town? Did he have to spend all his damn loot on window dressing?

Poutine did appreciate the burgeoning sales of pricey wines that increased month by month and had begun to make up the bulk of his profits, yet he still had his feet planted in some distant era where a pyramid of cardboard boxes clinking with stubby brown bottles was a "fancy" display. Artistic he was not. He grumbled and growled about the price of materials and especially about the paint swatches that Jacquie kept dropping off. She had suggested "Cider" or "Sugar Cookie," with a "Ballet Slipper" accent. Poutine had tilted his head like a perplexed pooch and wondered what the hell she was talking about. Turned out they were colours. And shitty ones, to boot.

She was such a cutie, so smart. It was tough, but he managed to talk her out of "Ballet Slipper." And by the way, what the hell was wrong with calling it pink? It was clearly *pink*. That would absolutely, positively never do, not for one second. Not in any joint he owned.

"Uhh, Jacquie, howzabout jes' black 'n' white?"

"Oooh!" she replied, a sparkle of mischief in her eyes. "Just like Chanel!"

Poutine looked like he'd just been slapped and pulled his head and shoulders back in horror. He made as if he was going to whack her with his clipboard. "You git the hell outta here." She giggled and dashed off.

He thought of Jacquie as a daughter, almost, or something close to that; she was young enough. Well, if push came to shove, he'd admit that he once looked admiringly at her arse end, but it wuz pleasant to the eye — she wuz wearing a tight-fittin' jean.

Of all the people in the tiny town of Tyee Lagoon, Ross Poutine was the one who always looked the same. His appearance never varied, except at the odd funeral and one or two weddings, where he put on a shirt that was allegedly white but looked "Spilled Coffee." His life's uniform was a Levi shirt and button-up 501 jeans, engineer boots, a regrettable leather fanny pack turned around backwards, and a chunky belt buckle in the shape of the Chevrolet bow-tie logo. Someone once gave him a Nissan buckle as a gift, merely as a jibe, and he heaved the damn thing as far into the ocean as his arm could throw. His hair was a slightly matted art-rock tonsure, quite a bit more scalp on top now, and a frightening, mangy, silver-grey nightmare at the back.

Accompanying him, for reasons no one had yet been able to determine, was the odour of goat. Not too bad at ten feet but up close you might really choke on the wafting aroma. In-depth detective work by his friends could uncover no goats, no history of goats, not even the slightest hint of goat-adjacent activities.

His friends eventually became accustomed to it, but at any rate, Poutine was completely oblivious to his own pong. Had he been made aware he still probably wouldn't have cared. He was a simple, direct, honest man — and surprisingly capable of tenderness when he was of the right mood. He was not often of the right mood.

Evelyn Weens had been a thoroughly rotten handle for a new arrival to Canadian shores. The hazing, at first, had been so heavy that it took him a month or two to even recognize it as such. He thought that perhaps the social customs in this country were weird. But he soon came to understand the problem. When your first name is Evelyn ... well ... yikes, especially in the 1990s on this woodsy and wild island. He would sink in his chair when his mother would correct school secretaries and dentist receptionists, "It's *EVE-i-lin*, not *EV-ill-in*. He was named ahftah Evelyn Waugh." Like that would help.

His name might have been acceptable in England, but here ... Hell, he might as well be known as Assmunch McFartbreath.

A couple of classmates took a form of twisted mercy on him. After being served beans on toast when they visited his house one afternoon and learning it was his favourite treat, they dubbed him "Beaner" Weens. Not great, but he'd take anything to not be *Evelyn*.

Beaner Weens grew up to be a rather odd duck, prone to wandering from town to town in the area, hard to pin down. He had a bizarre accent, a mix of vaguely upper-crust British and rural hoser. You really couldn't nail down where he was from and his vowels slid around imaginary map coordinates like cooking oil on wax paper. After a few beers, he sounded as if he might be a couple of people stuck inside one body.

He always seemed to have a job, but never a lucrative one, and had spent far too much time as a line cook in this or that restaurant. In fact, he had worked two whole years at that dumpy, old, now-demolished diner that they all called "The Mouldin' Phallus." The place was dreadful, but he stuck it out because it required no effort at spit and polish.

Its sign read *The Golden Palace* and touted both *World-Renowned Chinese* and *Western Cuisine*, but the diner could deliver neither one.

Drab, white, slightly dry hamburger buns that always seemed to make a *muff, muff* sound when chewed perennially held a steamed puck of some type of brownish-grey meat, garnished with a soul-destroying gherkin slice and a squirt of a mysterious condiment made from emulsified sadness and mothers' tears. Beaner was instructed to heat up their woeful crinkle-cut french fries in the microwave, stored frozen in a plastic sack, before serving. The resultant blazing hot, flaccid chips offered all the appeal of generational poverty and the texture of stewed Kleenex.

He also learned about pseudo-Chinese food with multiple varieties of Day-Glo chicken balls, and it was the only place for miles around that still offered tapioca pudding; bowls of it could be seen sitting in beige trays on the spackled Formica counter as customers walked in. The flies loved tapioca, it seemed. If they got mired in the pudding, it was renamed tapioca with raisins.

Beaner didn't have too many career aspirations beyond paying for the basics. He unabashedly collected cans and bottles from the ditches and roadsides, organizing them tidily and returning them to the depot to make a few extra bucks. He discovered to great delight that used golf balls were worth a small fortune, so he spent a lot of time at the local links on his hands and knees in the surrounding bush scooping them up into an old knapsack he always carried with him.

He caught hell from homeowners who saw him rooting through their trash, sifting through their recyclables that sat at the roadside waiting for weekly pickup. They yelled at him from their front door, and in one case a grumpy woman came out to challenge him with a broom, fur-trimmed housecoat billowing in the breeze. He noticed her fuzzy high-heeled slippers, better suited to Zsa Zsa Gabor, and wondered why this millionaire was so territorial about her trash. In the case of the local golf club, where the mother-lode of golf balls was, he was chased off by some tubby goon stuffed into a bulging windbreaker. Strictly private property, he was warned. Trespassers would be prosecuted.

Clearly this posed a problem. He had a system, and he often depended on the extra money it brought in. There had to be a way around all of this.

His discovery of internet shopping, belated but illuminating, propelled by his need to market and sell his "pre-owned" golf balls, allowed him to stumble across a site that sold "realistic animal costumes." They totally looked like real creatures, he thought, but were awfully expensive. African lions complete with bushy mane, horses that had hoof-like attachments at the hands and feet, and even strange ones like mermaids and seals. The website was pretty splashy and got him interested. There was no way he could ever afford one, though. So expensive!

But sometime later, on a whim, he looked up "used costumes" and found one that jumped out at him. A moose costume. But only the head of the moose, not the body. One of the pics showed the seller putting it on. It was totally realistic. The antlers were detachable for easy storage, the ad stated. You could even control the mouth with a wire — and that was the feature that sold Beaner.

The moose head came in a huge box, carried to his door on a hand truck by a taciturn courier.

"Sign here, please."

Beaner had a stupid grin on his face and blurted, "Oh, great! It's my moose head."

The driver looked up at him without expression and said, "Mmhmm."

"Been waiting for weeks!"

"Well …" The driver waved his arm vaguely. "Here it is." And with that he turned and clattered away.

* * *

Merri Crabtree could find the silver lining in an extinction-level meteorite impact. No matter what the situation, she was upbeat, so very, very upbeat. She joyfully described herself as "wacko" and most found it hard to argue the point. Her wittering was fast, incessant, and recondite — but determinedly jolly, fiercely chirpy. Hers was a weaponized cheerfulness.

She was rotund and had accepted her zaftig shape decades ago; her fate was not to be an underfed bauble. She was hearty, energetic, vivacious — a people person.

She had ended up back on Vancouver Island after ten years retired in the Caribbean. Her husband had suddenly had a heart attack one morning and died, right there on the dock, leaving her in a tropical paradise, lonely and without a plan. The situation challenged even Merri's indomitable positivity. With a new grandson back home, she decided to return to Vancouver Island to spend her remaining years nearer to him, her daughter, and son-in-law in the tiny village of Tyee Lagoon, but away from the warm, easy sun.

One thing Merri had brought back with her from the Caribbean was a taste for spicy food. To her palate now, local fare was as bland as a church concert. She began zazzing up her meals with experimental hot sauces based on the ones she had tasted on Eleuthera. To her surprise the concoctions were becoming popular, the talk of the town. Dinner guests, and she had many, raved about her flavourful sauces with the charming bottles and unusual spices.

At first, she made batches of liquid zing and gave it away to friends. It turned out, however, that there was a serious demand for her sauce, so now, a year later, she had decided to open a little boutique and sell it.

Merri's grandson, Wallis, pronounced *sauce* as "thoth." She believed it obvious that this was the *cutest thing ever* and felt that everyone would agree. Though confusing and unpronounceable, her shop, when she found a place to rent, would therefore be called Hot Thoth.

Six / "Puttin' on the Ritz"

Normally Vicar was rapturous about gigs but tonight he was hating it, every tortured note. He was playing at the Tyee Trapper, the competition, under duress, and the band was not cutting the mustard. He glanced at Farley Rea, who was, for all intents and purposes, just rummaging around on his bass guitar, bumbling so badly that Vicar thought he might have had a seizure.

Vicar scrubbed at his guitar, trying desperately to keep up with the chord changes. He and Farley Rea, who had remained his perennial musical sidekick for years, had been asked to do a one-off "concert" with Pat Horrigan — a local who always called his group Horrigan's Heroes no matter the personnel or occasion. Horrigan had played some of these songs for ages. He knew them by rote but wasn't skilled enough to offer a bit of guidance. He just kept ploughing through.

To add to the amateurish vibe, Farley had been left in charge of the posters for the show — a foolhardy idea. Unsurprisingly to Vicar at least, Farley had created two hundred expensive copies of something that read, *Apering 1 nite onely — Horriggans Herpes*. He hadn't said a thing to Farley, saving his energy for what was sure to be a long series of musical emergencies that night, another surely due at any moment. If you loved you some Farley, you had to take the whole package.

He and Farley were turning the gig into a flaming rock and roll dirigible. But in fairness, all three onstage were impressively wretched; each side of the musically challenged trio was compounding the misery of the other two. Oh, the humanity.

Nevertheless, the place was full, and people were beaming. They really didn't give a hoot that it was awful, either couldn't tell or didn't care. They just wanted to see Vicar: the man reputed to have all manner of paranormal, surprising, magical powers. He might make you rich! He could control minds! He brought the dead back to life! That certainly was the widespread opinion, as internet hype and wild rumour had established over the last couple of years. But as the audience imagined him bathed in a mystical halo, all Vicar could feel was the schvitzing of flop sweat.

And what had propelled all this adoration? The Accident, capitalized like The Moon Landing. Now a folk tale so wide of the truth that you could tell it in any random way you wanted and be just as accurate as all the other reports, it claimed that Vicar miraculously brought a dead woman back to life at the scene of an accident and then, later, went on to grant additional miracles to his luckiest acolytes. With seeming effortlessness, he rescued his fair maiden from the clutches of a murderous temptress and conjured a few financial windfalls for himself while he was at it. He had, they claimed, an "aura." When Vicar looked in the mirror, he saw no aura, no glow. Nada, except a crown of disorganized hair quite notably out of style, beginning to grey a little at the temples.

Granted, Julie Northrop had *seemed* dead as she lay beside the overturned car next to the road; Vicar remembered his anxiety and desperate desire to help. But surely it was just a fluke that she started breathing again as he beseeched her not to die. At the time that it happened he had been just as amazed by the whole thing as everyone else; the situation had been sorta mysterious. Every crazy thing downstream of that one event in this wild ride seemed to stem from it, and every one of *those* things pushed him farther down an unmarked road.

It was only a matter of weeks before the report of his spooky ministrations in a grassy ditch went international. Vicar's name now got thousands of hits on a Google search, too many of them at paranormal or religious sites. His every move had been trumped up to sound like pure voodoo, mapped out in advance by an omniscient deity that was sweet on one Tony Vicar. He was shocked to learn that he was an angel, a demon, a saint, a member of the Illuminati, an agent provocateur sent by a vaguely described antipope, a character predicted in a Nostradamus quatrain, a wish-granting djinn, the Mothman, an amoral hypnotist, a Man in Black, a reincarnated healer, and a few things even less believable than these. His iffy deportment, slapdash organization, perennially collapsing musical efforts, and uneven attempts at normalcy did not prepare him for any of it.

That included the dark chapter of Serena, the erstwhile murderous temptress, who remained a sinister and perplexing spectre, lurking in the shadows. She had stalked him, kidnapped Jacquie, and concocted a splashy scenario that could have left all three of them dead. Vicar had come out master of the dangerous situation but could not for the life of him fully understand Serena's motivations, and couldn't believe how a person who crumbled before him so easily had still managed to manoeuvre him into such a surreal, life-and-death plot. His inner narrative entirely glossed over the power of her looks and sex appeal, but no one was immune to her almost supernatural magnetism.

One thing was certain, though: Serena's actions had poured gasoline on the fire of hype that had nearly engulfed him. Every news team from miles around had been on hand at the hostage-taking incident, and coverage had only gotten more intense in the aftermath.

He glanced over at Farley on the other corner of the stage, who was at that moment performing as if he knew the material inside out. He did not, but the more confident he was, the faster he played. Vicar was getting disoriented as he fell in the cracks between Horrigan's ham-fisted pounding and Farley's random scrubbing. *I might as well be grating parmessano.*

But Serena … Serena … Had she been a case of random chance, a glancing one-off, or a foreshadowing of what lay in store for him forevermore? Thinking about it made his gut tighten with anxiety. He didn't know if he could survive another such episode.

Vicar was relieved she was gone from his life — out on bail, though he wished she was rotting in a cell, awaiting trial, far away from any potential future victims. He wasn't sure where she was, didn't particularly care; he just wished her locked somewhere very secure. He knew she had been admonished to stay away from him, from Jacquie, from Tyee Lagoon in general, but he had left it at that; he admittedly lived in deliberate ignorance and denial. Thinking about it stressed him so badly that he began to malfunction. He calmed himself by remembering what the Crown prosecutor had told him: Kidnapping Jacquie meant a long stretch in the hoosegow. They would know Serena's fate "in the fullness of time."

Vicar noticed that Pat Horrigan, his cheesy little keyboard jammed in the corner, seemed oblivious to the musical calamity happening around him. He also clearly did not appreciate the mental state of his guitarist and plodded on with a desperate smile pasted to his mug.

Oh God, enough with the Elton John songs, Vicar thought. He heard an eruption of guttural yelping that on further examination was Farley, briefly confident again, yowling into the microphone, "Saturday,

Saturday, Saturday," as if he were auditioning for *Young Frankenstein*.

After their appalling rendition of the song ended, Horrigan took a quick sip of his drink and looked around at Farley and Vicar, muttering into the microphone something inanely positive, along the lines of "Yeahhhhhh ... Cooooool ... Mm-*hmm* ..." Vicar realized they were merely mouth sounds, like how you try to soothe your twitchy dog, meaning something like, "We *meant* to do that." Vicar closed his eyes and turned his face away from the crowd.

Ah, damn you, Ray. He and Ray and Farley had been such a hot trio back in the day. If Ray hadn't fucked off, they'd probably be huge by now. Vicar had a plan, but they broke up; it was all part of the long muddy trudge of despair he had slogged through for so many years, before he met Jacquie and the pathway finally headed upward again.

He couldn't wait until he built a stage at the Knickers and he could play there, in that sweet space that he'd worked on so hard — rather than for the competition, in this awful heap with no sightlines.

In lieu of rock stardom, he'd be satisfied to play on his own stage in his own pub. A consolation prize, but a pretty good one. Jacquie, though, was strongly hinting that a stage in the Vicar's Knickers would wreck the look, take away from the warmly welcoming atmosphere. He was having a hard time admitting that she might be right, he just wanted it so badly. But she'd said that installing one would be like wearing fuzzy bedroom slippers with a cocktail dress. He'd looked at her blankly.

He had just wanted to be in a super-good band. Live the life. Make grand gestures and put on big shows. Hang out backstage with Mick and Keef. Instead, he was admired for mystical powers he doubted he possessed. He'd much rather be biting the heads off licorice bats for shits and giggles.

To add insult to injury, tonight he was playing like total crap. He wasn't feeling confident enough to just prance around charismatically as a form of misdirection. He couldn't even enjoy being enjoyed.

Like a misfiring engine, they sputtered into another song, but right in the middle Vicar felt one of his dark moods set in. Not good. They had been known to send him spinning. If he lost the thread, and some days he really couldn't locate it easily, he'd be left without a road map, possibly without Jacquie, and without even a shred of credibility remaining. The shallow celebrity could backfire, leaving him stuck in a no man's land, up to his neck in debt, maybe without his beautiful pub, the very same pub that he had finally decided to build after having received encouragement from a dead man. Yes, he had once gotten advice, he was quite certain, from a *dead man*. This astounding tidbit alone drained most of the magic out of playing mangled cover songs with Horrigan's Herpes in a countrified dump.

Just one or two missteps and he'd be even worse off than he had been before all this started. Which is to say, pretty goddamn bad.

■ ■ ■

Jacquie was sure that there had to be a bunch of folks here who had come from far away. There was no way little Tyee Lagoon could supply so many customers to the Knickers on a Wednesday night. She wended her way between tables, chatty, welcoming, and stylish in an ivory silk headband with stitching on it, her hair arranged around it artfully.

In the closet at home, she had all kinds of odds and ends, such as a couple of scarves that she would sometimes use as a sash, a shawl, a wrap, a blanket. It blew Tony's mind; he had recently blurted that she could probably look sexy in the mat from the trunk of his car. She took the compliment — his were only intermittently poetic.

She had noticed that "women of a certain age" seemed particularly interested in him. Their husbands, by that point in their marriage, either acted as if they hadn't noticed all the attention they were lavishing on Vicar, or offered him "the wife" in return for a winning lottery ticket — picking the winning lottery number had been yet another skill attributed to Vicar that he wished he truly had. Weak comedy by the husband always garnered outraged play-acting from the wife, and Vicar had learned, Jacquie could see, how to turn the awkward comment into a good chuckle, make hubby seem *hilarious*, and outrageously compliment the missus. He had discovered that it led directly to a photo opportunity, an autograph, and hopefully a goodbye as soon as they went through the checklist. No terrible harm done, but the spectre of another *grip and grin* lay waiting around almost every corner, even when he was buying bread and milk in his sweatpants. Tony was anything but vain, but jeez, people sometimes just couldn't tell when enough was enough.

She watched a lady near the bar, who sat beside her disengaged hubby. When Jacquie had served her earlier, she'd noticed that she smelled strongly of a noxious bargain perfume that Vicar would have hated — her scent had notes of lilac and Formula 409. Tony Vicar had a very sensitive nose for someone who had to live with Tony Vicar.

If this woman had known how to draw in a man with just a look at one point in her life, she had certainly forgotten it now. Extruding her lips into a grotesque pout, her eyes scrunched half-shut, she looked at Vicar as if she had just ingested a lemon covered in wasabi. Vicar replied with a wan smile, which she took as an invitation, strolling over with a matronly toddle to chat him up.

Jacquie smirked and waited for the look on his face once he got a whiff.

t one point partway through the redesign of the Knickers, they had been delayed in the renovation, resulting in Vicar being increasingly frustrated and short-tempered. Jacquie believed it was a good time to point out flaws in his planning and harped at him about his precious bar. She had unknowingly walked into a minefield.

"The old bar looked just fine," Jacquie spoke up. "Because of your twenty-five-foot-long monster, we're a couple months behind and way over budget. Why spend all that money and sweat on a new one?"

"Looked fine? *Fine*?" He spat out the word like it was the most horrible expletive in the English language. There was a heavy sprinkling of drywall dust in Vicar's sticky-uppy hair, making him look like Einstein's slightly loony nephew. "You think we should open a place that's *just fine*? We tore this old shack down to studs! Now it's like a castle! It's too late to cheap out now."

"Well ... I was just saying that the old bar looked perfectly *fine* to me, and maybe we could have salvaged it."

Vicar rasped out a sigh of exasperation.

"Why don't you downgrade to a hairstyle that's just *fine*? Why be stunning and stylish when you can be *fine*? Easier, cheaper ... *FINE*!"

Jacquie was surprised and took a step back.

"You obviously have a strong opinion, but I honestly don't get it."

"Jacquie, the bar is the centrepiece of the whole pub. It's the main focus. If it has personality and character, then the whole place has it, too. You could fill this place with furniture you found on a rubble pile in Stalingrad, but if the bar is sweet it would get chalked up to 'kitsch.' A grand bar is *integral*. Absolutely critical." He rambled on for a while, speaking to everyone and no one, muttering about the Sistine Chapel, comparing it to the church in the strip mall next to the muffler shop. Speaking of the Sistine Chapel ... *How are we going to finish the ceiling?*

"Okay, okay ..." Jacquie put her palms out and backed away gently. She knew he had a crazy plan, but she really had a helluva time visualizing the ideas he kept presenting. *Jack, Jack ... I found some sconces with a royal coat of arms on them! I think they might be from a frickin' castle or something!*

Yes, they had been from a palace or government building in Bratislava — and shipping would have cost about the same as buying each light fixture its own plane ticket. Jacquie tensed up and applied the brakes, but on that occasion, he just dropped it and moved along to the next crazy thought.

As a kid she had once seen a book filled with cutaway transparencies that showed how a moon rocket was assembled; she wondered if she might just be getting a layer at a time from Vicar's secret, mad plan. Then again, he might have forgotten to link all the bits together. This was possible. She had pulled him back from a couple of bugged-out schemes already. She felt her concerns rising as the money slowly but steadily dripped away.

At least she was confident that the pub, and in fact the entire hotel, was structurally solid and safe; some guy gave them a report that guaranteed it. Even so, it creaked and groaned and sounded alive at times, although a case might be made that some of the sounds were the last agonized moans of the hotel wing, just before death. During a wind it seemed there was a banshee yodelling in the rafters. Its low moans sounded like a cry of loneliness.

▬ ▬ ▬

Looking out to sea from the high kitchen window of 411 Sloop Road, the beautiful, vintage Tudor manse that Frankie Hall had willed to Jacquie, Vicar gazed admiringly at the view. The day was partially cloudy but the Strait still shimmered gold, blue, and green, reflecting like a mirror toward the horizon and darkening to a rich purple at the shady shore. The view was so satisfying that Vicar ungrudgingly did the dishes as he stared seaward. Jacquie had asked him to wash the pots and pans by hand, which of course he couldn't understand. He believed that if it was a "dish" it needed to go in the "dishwasher." Duh, right? She would have none of it and insisted that her good pots get the royal treatment. But she was probably right; their fancy new dishwasher was a piece of imported scrap that malfunctioned as often as it worked.

Yet he had still resisted until she said with a sultry voice and a provocative look on her face, "If you do the pots and pans, I'll make it worth your while …"

He looked at her, immediately circling the bait, but suspicious. "You're lying, aren't you?"

Jacquie extinguished the look like a light bulb going off and cackled. "Of course I am. Just rinse thoroughly, please. There's nothing worse than greasy pots when I'm cooking."

Vicar shrugged, baffled, and filled the sink. Living with her was something like shacking up with a shape-shifter. He simply turned to his task.

As was his custom when doing chores, he talked to himself a lot. He also burst out in song sometimes. This day was no exception.

He listened to the radio that was perched on the window ledge in front of him and sang along, "Yurrrrr so vein, ya prolly think this song is an art'ry …" Pleased as punch with his lyric, he turned and crooned over his shoulder as if wooing Jacquie in the other part of the house, hopeful that she might come 'round and get a little frisky after all. Surely, she wouldn't be able to resist. He went up high to sing the background vocals but had a buzz saw–like falsetto, sounding a lot like a crow someone had accidentally hit with a rock. He threw his arms out in a diva-like gesture of inclusion, spraying soapy foam all over the window.

He had an incessant soundtrack that bounced around inside his skull, but Jacquie hadn't gotten used to it. She stared at him far more often than anyone would stare at a normal boyfriend, but shit, who wants to be *normal*?

His internal dialogue *was* a bit unusual; he had to admit it. When he was walking, or driving, or mowing a lawn, he would babble to himself, solve problems, rehearse arguments, and vibrantly recall events from his past. He flitted around the continuum of his history like a gnat.

Time is an illusion! Farley's bass playing proved it, ha ha! *This pan is filthy — I'll just leave it to soak and find out if Jacquie's in the mood …*

I n 1970, room 222 of the Agincourt had been a long-term rental to a young man who worked for the local logging company. He was from Saskatoon, Saskatchewan, but came west after graduating high school. A "gap year" was not on the radar of Larry Kaminski. He was from a working family who did all right but couldn't fathom romping around the world for months on end, as if high school had been punishment that required R & R afterward. Larry was the first member in his family's history to finish Grade 12, and now, educated, would have to go out on his own and earn a living.

He did. There was plenty of work out west, or so he'd heard. Within six months of having arrived in Tyee Lagoon he was already feeling like a veteran. He knew the ropes and got along with all the men. After a few weeks they had begun to call him Valentine, after

Karen Valentine from the TV show *Room 222*, because his hotel room number had been the same. The nickname stuck; they liked him. He earned a good wage, not great, but enough to feed himself, pay his hotel, and save a little for a truck — something he wanted to buy at the earliest opportunity. And he really didn't miss the long, bitter Saskatchewan winters.

He fell in love with Vancouver Island. Could do without some of the rain, but otherwise he was perfectly happy out here. He was sure Saskatchewan would empty out if word got to them about the splendour of this place. He didn't yearn for home at all. Honestly, the only thing he missed was his mum's cooking, which was starchy, fattening, and plentiful. Stuck to your ribs, the way food was supposed to do.

His mum, in return, badly missed cooking for her son, a kind boy who never got in trouble. To her, family was everything; to her husband, Bogdan, work and steady income were most important.

Before Larry left, she confessed how much she wanted grandchildren, how much that would mean to her, a woman whose family had died in the war and who had come to Canada alone, on a boat, while still a girl. Dead parents and siblings were an aching void in her life that only little ones could fix. Papa could be satisfied that Larry got a good job, but to please her, Lorko, as they affectionately called him, would have to find a nice girl, come back home, and have babies. She said it almost as an injunction. He had promised her that he would. He was young and footloose, but the serious look on her face when she held his hands and made him promise left a deep impression.

When Larry's birthday was on the horizon, she had the inspiration to make him a batch of her special cookies. His very favourite ones — shortbread sandwiches with jam in the centre, shaped like the suits of playing cards: diamonds, clubs, spades, hearts. Someone had given her those cookie cutters for a Christmas present half a lifetime ago and the kids had loved the delicious treats they made, often playing pretend card games with them as the deck got eaten away, round by round. She lovingly wrapped the cookies in wax paper and put them in a sturdy shoebox. They arrived in the mail a couple of weeks later, somewhat worse for wear and stale, but a welcome reminder of Mum. Valentine fairly inhaled the whole box of large fragments with a Thermos of coffee one Saturday morning.

He thoughtfully wrote Mum a note of thanks and gave a brief and nondescript report of life in the backwoods — he was fine and hoped they were, too. But he spent a couple of sentences raving about receiving cookies in the mail.

That comment made his mother determined to send more.

Vicar had not foreseen how long it would take to gut and renovate the hotel part of the project. His concentration had stayed squarely on the Knickers pub, guiding it lovingly from empty shell to world-class thirst-slaking cathedral, and now he felt the heavy slog of phase two.

He decided that he needed to pitch in to help speed things along and arrived at the hotel early one morning to gut the interiors of the second-floor hotel rooms, chambers that were ramshackle and aged. Climbing up the squeaky steps, he smelled the mustiness of the building, which reminded him of the Bachelor Pad. He drifted off in vivid recollection, recalling that, back in the day, he had once returned there, a new-to-him Elvis costume in hand. He had put it on — wig and all.

Ray and Farley were amused, and he had launched into a hilarious but wildly inaccurate Elvis impression. Someone had had a stupid idea and they pawed through the closet. They couldn't muster a teakettle or two matching plates in the malodorous kitchen, yet in their closets they were able to dig out a clarinet, of all things, and Vicar's beat-up old accordion. The rationale for having them in the house was unknown; no one could play them. All the same, Ray and Farley made attempts at accompanying Vicar, and the sound they were making caused Ray's dog to howl. Vicar, always primed to take it one step higher, sang to the miserable pooch while Farley squeaked and honked on the clarinet, urging ol' Shep into canine wails. Surely, Ray's hideous accordion-work wasn't helping, and the cacophony coming from the little house that night was alarming. Vicar shook his head at the memory and snickered.

Reaching the top of the squeaky steps of the Agincourt, Vicar walked to the far end of the south hallway, jiggered with a balky key in the old doorknob of room 222, and entered a space that was strewn with tipped furniture and a bit of garbage.

As Vicar puttered in the dim hotel room, he continued to daydream about the birth of his Elvis impersonation so many years before.

In the living room of the ol' Bachelor Pad, Ray and Farley had laughed themselves silly at Vicar's Elvisian hijinks, and then Vicar had a brainstorm. The Kiwanis Club was having a talent contest in a few weeks. They had to enter!

He had described his plan. The trio would mount the stage, Vicar dressed as Elvis, his buddies in lederhosen, which *of course they owned* for some inexplicable reason — and which they often wore to the laundromat on washday.

They'd include the pooch, too. Clarinet and accordion would accompany Elvis singing to the dog. With any luck Shep would howl madly, and they would win first prize. Seventy-five bucks would buy a lot of beer, man. Vicar had tried to convince the boys to enter the contest, but Farley and Ray were lukewarm, until Vicar had a thunderclap of an idea.

Vicar was snapped back to the present by some movement just behind him and pointed his little flashlight over to the closet, which contained a bunch of hangers, one of them with an old dry-cleaning bag trailing from it. *Overactive imagination*, he said to himself. Working in an old building in the half dark could mess with a guy's head. It must only have been that plastic bag in the dim light, but he was sure he saw a shadow or a black blob.

A little put off by the fright, Vicar tried to resume his recollection of the Birth of Elvis and picked up the story at his Herculean sales pitch to the boys.

Selling it like a Ginsu knife telemarketer he had said, "Guys … guys … Now listen, listen … We're going to name ourselves …" He paused dramatically, hoping to stoke anticipation with Ray and Farley. "Are you ready for this? We're gonna call ourselves … Polka Salad Annie."

Absolutely no response, just an awkward silence. When the dead air got painfully long, Farley finally crossed his eyes and mewled a miserable howl on the clarinet. Then suddenly they found themselves weeping with laughter, collapsed on the rug, and were *all in*. It didn't matter what happened now. In their minds they had already won.

At that moment in room 222, amidst Vicar's renovations and recollections, a violent crash occurred, and Vicar wheeled around. The long wooden pole that for the better part of a century had acted as the hanging rod in the little clothes closet had chosen that exact moment to shear loose from its moorings and crash to the floor, wire hangers falling in a rattling heap. Vicar's eyes were wide, and his heart nearly jumped out of his chest. There was nothing, no one there. But for it to collapse moments after he thought he saw *something* … He tried to tamp down his surging alarm.

He needed to get out. As quickly as he could, he stumbled out of the room, nearly tripping over an old broken chair. He flew to the top of the stairs. Taking his first bound down three of them, he thought he heard a low, menacing growl. Whether real or imagined, he fled as if being chased by a flame-thrower.

Nine / Richard X. Dick

All eyes locked on him as the man swooped into the Vicar's Knickers, scanning imperiously as he divined in a glance if the place and its inhabitants were worthy of his presence. His clothing was completely out of context, big-city suit cut far too tight like he'd had a sudden growth spurt, flashy shoes, expensive tie. He jutted out his lantern jaw and appeared to Vicar a little like a soap opera star or a TV lawyer, slightly windblown from the outdoors but preening on the fly. The fucker looked like he was wearing makeup and was as out of place as a string quartet at a chemical spill. Vicar's flags went up.

Around his neck were doodads and ID passes, ostentatiously displayed and swinging around. He dug around in his pocket and Vicar thought he might be playing with his balls. For all his camera-ready looks, he had an oily, rapey vibe.

"I'm looking for Vicar."

Vicar stood back a half-step, set his jaw, and said with mock formality, "I am he. And who might you be?"

Squinting, the man chucked a business card on the bar and looked up in challenge. "I'm Richard Dick. International reporter for *Glib Re-Post*." He held his gaze as if expecting this to impress Vicar. Dick was in Tyee Lagoon under extreme duress, and he buried his reluctance under a thick, repellent cloak of arrogance. *GRP* had helped him through a terribly tough time — but now he was vulnerable. He owed them and they leveraged this for all it was worth. They wanted him on this emerging story about Vicar, up north in the damned boonies, where no one else wanted to be. When he protested, they reminded him about his "debt." Dick was slimy, but some of it had been dripped upon him from above. Vicar picked up the lavish card that announced, in fancy script, *Richard Xavier Dick, Chief Correspondent / Glib Re-Post / Hollywood, California*, and examined it like an amazed yokel.

Eventually he spoke. "Dick Dick, huh? So nice they named you twice?" With that the battle lines were drawn.

On the walls of the Knickers, Vicar would allow no glossy beer posters, no adverts. Nearly everything was nicely framed and related in some way to the town and surrounding area. He had framed two great old black-and-white photos depicting a small gaggle of men posing with the biggest halibut anyone had seen since the 1950s. It truly was "a barn door," as they called them. Surely, it had weighed several hundred pounds.

Beside those photos were military medals in a long row, donated by the granddaughter of a veteran who had enjoyed a pint or two here, back in the days before it had become too rough for a gentleman and his wife. That old gent never said a peep about his military service to anyone, he just quietly spent forty-two years working for the telephone company; but Vicar could plainly see he had been one of the D-Day Dodgers — the guys that took such a terrible pounding in Italy. It also looked like he had ended up in Holland at the end of the war. Vicar reminded himself to get a framed photo to go alongside the medal display.

He had held back a sheaf of newspaper and magazine clippings, some of which had been mailed to them from places all over the globe, that Jacquie had saved — all of them about "the Liquor Vicar," the car crash, the rescue, the hostage situation, his remarkable and sudden status as a man of fame and heroism.

"Tony, why don't you frame those? The customers can read them and save you explaining again and again."

"Yeah, I guess," he grunted, seeing her point but highly uncomfortable at the thought of displaying stories that he himself didn't quite believe.

One enjoyable thing Vicar had done was seek out and ornately frame a portrait of the Queen. He displayed it prominently, a gesture throwback as all hell, but the right tone for the Knickers, and he just loved it.

Some of the more unruly patrons wryly raised a glass to her after they were half-cut. Vicar had discovered to his surprise that it pissed him off if anyone dissed her. But few took it too far — it felt right up there with insulting your own granny. One guy, a regular, born in Cork, always took a seat as far from the portrait as possible, facing away from it, his left side toward the cavernous inglenook. His buddies supplied snickers at his passive protest. Getting into the spirit of it, Vicar found on the internet a photo of Ambassador Kevin Vickers manhandling an Irish protester into the arms of the waiting Gardaí, and mounted it on the opposite wall where the man would be forced to see it while turning his back upon the Queen. The humour of it was not lost on the patron, who laughed and said in his soft brogue, "Fair play, lad." After that, he came more frequently, and Vicar, delighted with their détente, had a brass nameplate affixed to the place he liked to sit.

In the entranceway there was now a grand and official-looking framed declaration, inked in calligraphy and affixed with a wax seal that Vicar had fashioned with a dinner taper, an old silver dollar, and a ribbon from a box of candy. It was a red paraffin rosette with the image of a flying goose that he'd turned upward at an angle as if heading skyward. It explained in too-flowery language that entry to the establishment was contingent upon willingness to vacate the seat of the VIP ennobled upon the nameplates, should that VIP desire it. Basically, if they showed up, *ya had ta git*. Vicar didn't even know if this was legal, but he wanted it that way, and so he decided that the honourees wanted it that way, too.

Thinking back, Vicar winced at the occasionally rough patches with Jacquie over the reno — he had been a bit of a bulldog with the project. He nearly always had some variety of kooky dream, he knew this about himself; but this time the dream had been real, possible, tangible. She had been on the budget like a hawk from beginning to end and it had started to piss him off. *Do we really need that? Isn't that a bit too much?*

He gave in on some of them, like the brass pole he wanted installed that was supposed to go from the ground floor down into the cellar, through a huge round hole in the planks. He imagined himself charismatically spiralling downward, accompanied by the oohs and aahs of goggle-eyed patrons.

"Jack, Jack … Babe, I'm telling you, no other pub will have a Batcave! It'll be AWESOME."

Jacquie responded with a look of astonishment. Did her ears just hear him say Batcave?

She gathered herself after a minute and painted a horrifying portrait of drunken old men, reliving their glory days, recklessly plummeting to their death onto the concrete far below, while the two of them lost everything to some stupid lawsuit.

Okay, she might have been right on that one, but … When you're handcrafting a grand vision, you can't always hew to the practical. Vicar was being propelled by a dream, damn it, an awesome dream … About an 8.9 on the Lionel Richie scale.

Ten / Exhaust Flames

Three months after the Knickers's opening there were two businesses renting space in the Agincourt's ground floor. Ross Poutine was slowly but surely moving operations from his old shop, Liquor, to his new space, also named Liquor. Jacquie begged him to rename the shop, to give it a tag that went with the vibe of the new location. Something a little fancier. He utterly refused. He would rather be given a Brazilian wax by grabby Vikings than jigger around with the name. *Don't screw with perfection.*

The other shop was Hot Thoth, run by Merri Crabtree. It was tiny, a hole in the wall, and contained a small customer area, a long narrow counter that wrapped around the entire interior of the shop, and three walls full of shelving that housed the countless varieties of hot sauce she conjured up in the tiny backroom-cum-food factory.

After the first week or two, Hot Thoth really left an aroma in the street, drawing in passersby who strolled past the ever-renovating building. It was spicy, vinegary, smoky, enticing, and concocted by the town's honourary grandmother — she was already doing well. As the curious popped in to check out the source of the smell, she nattered with inexhaustible positivity until they withdrew, usually feeling like they'd been half drowned in cheer. Ross Poutine was a fan of hot sauce — he flooded his terrible meals with vats of it. Merri had already perfected "Eleuthera Blend," "Nassau Nippy," and a few other politely titled but flavourful concoctions. He got the idea that he wanted her to make him a vat of custom hot sauce, after he smelled the heavenly aroma wafting into his shop just next door. It was an unusually lavish thing for him to do, but he had always fancied having a private stock of potent stuff.

He liked his hot sauce, well … *hot*. Merri's hottest was around thirty thousand Scovilles — a heat measurement high enough to bring tears to the eyes of most folks, and as far as she dared push it. *It's a garnish, not a weapon!*

Poutine explained that he wanted a big vat of custom sauce that was at least a *million* "Scooby-Doos," as he called them.

"Oh, Ross, dear. You can't be serious. You'll kill yourself. I don't even know if it's legal to make battery acid like that." As usual the statement was followed by her jolly giggle, her tic-like statement ender.

He pulled an empty bottle out of his pocket and showed her what he had been using until recently. A greenish-yellow sauce called "The Grimmest Reaper." Skulls blowing fire adorned its gothic label. Its Scoville rating claimed to be over one million.

"I like this one. Can't feel my tongue after. Can't feel my arse after, either." He yucked out a little laugh.

"Okay, Ross," she said, a warning tone in her chuckle. "But if this burns your innards out you can't take me to court."

"Don choo worry, missy. It'll be perfect, dere." He was grinning, an infrequent thing to see, and rocked his head left to right in a proud swagger.

Vicar ambled into Hot Thoth, a daily visit he made like a doctor on rounds, and breathed in the striking fragrance. It was like opening a gateway into another country. The aged patina of the shop contrasted by the modern cabinetry really looked great to his eye. It was the perfect vibe for the place. In the little hutch in a short hall that led to the kitchen and storage, he saw Merri over her grandson's shoulder at a make-shift desk, helping him glue leaves onto a piece of art paper.

"See, the leaf looks just like a whole tree, doesn't it?"

Little Wallis held a leaf up to his eye, and then measured it through the window against a tree on the street. His face filled with delight.

Merri brought him here often, and he had the run of the place. Vicar watched the little boy's moment of insight with great interest and remembered similar epiphanies he had had through the years.

He recalled as a very young boy being struck by the thought that rivers were like arteries that circulated water, the lifeblood of the planet; that people were like little critters that lived on its hide. And much more recently, by the thought that, with eight billion people on this earth, there had to be at least eight billion versions of the universe. And who knows how many others, far, far away — every one of them with their own broadcast channel in the great multiverse. Some of them sensed others, but most lived in lonely solitude — like a radio picking up only static, forever tuned to the wrong frequency. He called out to the little boy.

"Hello there, Walrus!"

"Hi, Uncle Tony! Look, a tree!"

Merri looked on and remembered meeting Vicar and Jacquie when she first began looking for a home for Hot Thoth, with little Wallis along for the day — a bit of an adventure for grandma and grandson. Seconds after introduction, Vicar had turned his attention to Wallis and let Jacquie discuss the business. As the two women struck a deal, Vicar placed her grandson up on a high bar stool and spun him around while making sound effects. He was rewarded with squeals of delight.

He's great with kids, Merri thought. *Maybe they'll have a couple someday.*

Vicar got down on one knee and appreciated the construction paper masterpiece being created before him, far more attentive to the little boy than he was to anything else at that moment. Vicar briefly glanced up at Merri and smiled. *Goddamn, I love this.*

Eleven / A Match Made in Heaven

I t was a 1950 Chevy pickup truck — Poutine could tell from the vent windows. Slightly jacked up in the rear, barn red, sporting whitewalls on chrome reverse with baby moons. Poutine sized it up in an instant. He ran to the door and cocked an ear. *That weren't no straight six! Thassa V8*. He closed his eyes and listened like a submarine sonar tech. Small block ... Chevy, of course. A 350? *Nope, wrong music*. A 283? *No, wrong pitch. She was runnin' bad but then the driver revved to keep 'er goin'*. He guessed it was a 327; he'd bet a round of beers on it.

It seemed suddenly to die there and then, and the driver emerged from the cab swearing like a sailor. It was a woman!

She angrily opened the rattling hood and climbed up on the bumper, bending deeply over to see inside the engine compartment. Her capacious rear end was displayed proudly. Poutine's eyes widened and he felt a tingle in his fingers and toes.

Trancelike, he ambled toward the woman who was jiggling things under the hood and he asked, "D'ya need some help dere, missy?"

"Eh? This fuckin' fucked fucker has fucked up for the last fucking time, fer fuck's sakes."

Ross Poutine just stared at her, feeling a sense of arousal he couldn't remember having experienced since he was a teenager. This chick was HOT.

He guided her into Liquor and gave her a glass of hooch while he jiggered around under the hood. It looked like the spark plug wires had been chewed up by mice. *She's gonna need a new set, dere.*

Ross shouldered the heavy old truck into a safe parking spot in front of his store and went in to break the bad news. He came up with as much chit-chat as he could muster, which took the form of the goddamn weather, the goddamn taxes, and the goddamn noise, and then asked her if she needed a ride home.

"If you want I can git some new wires, dere, and install 'em tomorrow …"

She looked at him with surprise. "Really? You'd do that?"

"Why sure, little missy … I know cars."

"Well, if you fix my truck, I'll fix you dinner."

And that, as they say, was all it took.

■ ■ ■

Anna-Maria Theresa Lombardo's name had contracted through the years. When quizzed at a family dinner at the age of four what it was, she proudly recited it to her cut-up of an uncle, who replied with delight, "Dazza lotta macaroni!" It was indeed, and so through the years she became Anne-Marie, then Annie, and eventually just Ann, Ann Lombardo. That seemed easy enough.

Then she got married to a man named Joe Tenna, and so became, improbably, Ann Tenna.

When Ross Poutine had discovered that such a hottie was back on the market, he could barely believe his luck. He couldn't wait to introduce her to Vicar and Jacquie O. What were the chances that he'd find such a catch?

He awkwardly put forward to Vicar the idea of his new lady friend working at the Knickers, half thinking he could merely suggest it and Vicar would seize the idea because it made so much sense. But Vicar didn't think Jacquie was going to like the idea of hiring Ann Tenna one bit, even though he felt that he could not refuse.

Jacquie's welcoming personality had set the tone for the whole place and she was working very hard to keep things at a certain high level. Ann, bless her heart, could not have been less like Jacquie. But, like Vicar, Jacquie also found it impossible to say no, or even show a lack of enthusiasm.

She and Tony owed Poutine big time. He had saved Tony's life in what she believed was an act of great heroism. When she had been kidnapped by that despicable

Serena and her gang, Vicar had surrendered himself to them in order to buy her freedom, and then Ross Poutine and Farley had ended up saving Vicar as he stood at knifepoint, an instant from certain death. This counted for so much in Jacquie's estimation of him. He was so very rough around the edges, but he was a damn good man, plus he was an old softy, a fact not easily noticed on first appraisal.

Vicar euphemistically summed up Ann Tenna as having "unfiltered speech" when he described her to Jacquie. Ann swore and cursed more than anyone he had ever heard, using fantastically salty words delivered with a cheerful coarseness that occasionally left bystanders stunned. Less important but noteworthy, she sported a hairdo that was so comprehensively out of step with the times that people often stopped in their tracks at the sight of it.

She was blond … ish. "My people are from the North," she explained.

Port Hardy? Vicar wondered, unable to connect the town to a specific hair colour. After a disjointed clarification he realized she meant Italy; northern Italians were blond, she proclaimed. Vicar squinted with confusion, trying to recall a factoid about any country on earth that geographically segregated its population into hair-colour zones.

Her "northern blond" bangs were a flat facade, cemented in place straight up — the rest of her hair was meant to be poofy but never quite managed to stay that way. It made her look like a damp haystack with a spoiler.

When Jacquie met Ann, she had to force herself not to gawk at her 'do. She had never seen anything remotely like it, except in old yearbook photos from the 1980s. For a moment she thought it was a gag. But, no, it was genuine, worn with a totally straight face. As they departed that first meeting, normally non-judgmental, warmly inclusive Jacquie O muttered to Vicar, "Jesus, Mary, and Joseph … She's a makeover looking for a place to happen …"

Ann's employment at the Knickers felt more like an invasion. She waltzed in and took over after a few minutes of training, her unvarnished speech and brash manner completely altering the happy but dignified tone that had been set. Vicar had no idea how to communicate fine points or subtleties to her as she seemed impervious to advice, and so he gritted his teeth and let it ride for the time being. By the end of the first week, she had established her very own style.

"Don' like yer soup, huh?"

"I don't care for it …"

"HE DOESN'T CARE FOR HIS SOUP," she bellowed, pointing at the top of a customer's head. Everyone in the pub turned to see what the ruckus was about. Beaner, who had recently gotten the job as head cook at the Knickers, squinted out from the kitchen to see what all the fuss was about.

The customer shrank down into his chair.

"BEANER, RAISE MARTHA STEWART ON THE BLOWER!" Guffaws from all quarters, the soup complainer now red-faced but laughing.

She turned toward the kitchen and now fully yelled, "BEANER, DO WE GOT ANY O' THAT FUNERAL SOUP LEFT OVER FROM EARTH DAY?"

From the kitchen the echoing voice of Beaner called out, "*Wedding* soup ..."

Twelve / She Wouldn't Have a Willy or a Sam

They were on to something, Vicar could tell. He had begun mounting brass plaques on tables, inscribed with the names of his most dedicated supporters and customers — the ones who had advised or listened to him ramble on when the Knickers was but a dream, and most importantly, the ones who came to the pub regularly now that it was open. He was creating an old guard in a new joint, and his plan was working. The semi-formal presentation of the nameplates had been an instant hit. It was Vicar's way of saying thank you. The look on the faces of Poutine and his most faithful regular, Hank Wheat, assured him that he had hit the bull's eye — they were lifers, just like that.

He still wasn't ready to draw customers from far and wide before the hotel was ready to keep them for the night. All the rousing success was merely word of mouth so far, although the internet was alive with "Vicar Updates" and the Knickers's email overflowing with fan letters from all points of the globe. But everyone in town and the surrounding area came in to check it out first. Curiosity had immediately risen to fever pitch. As well, the appeal seemed to be all ages, with one couple even bringing in a babe in arms, which Vicar delightedly held and swayed as they tucked into their lunch.

"I might not give him back!" enthused Vicar as he snuggled the babe.

"Jus' take him with our compliments," joked the mother, a little fatigue showing around her eyes. "We'll pick him up after graduation."

He felt pangs as he cuddled the little boy — pangs of wanting kids. It had become more important to him in the last while. Jacquie seemed amenable to having children someday, but he seldom brought it up. She was still young and had lots of life to experience, he thought, before her focus had to shift to raising a family. *We're so busy as it is.* Vicar wasn't sure he could deliver the goods anyway. Just another situation from his misspent youth that he wished would go away.

Of course, there was a chance that things might have improved, but he never took any steps to find out one way or the other; he avoided even discussing it. He refused to let strangers monkey around down there. It made him uncomfortable and brought up awful memories. Plus, you had to supply a sample. Ugh.

"You've brought me up short, Vicar." He always called him Vicar, as if it were an honorific, not a surname. "Chief" Hank Wheat visited the Vicar's Knickers almost every day; he loved it there. Head bowed a little and staring at the table, he couldn't believe he was looking at a plaque with his name on it. He looked over at Ross Poutine's brass plate, and then back to Vicar. Wheat realized that he was now part of a tradition, which tickled him.

Hank Wheat was a retired chief petty officer, his entire career spent in the navy. He was built like a chunky tool shed — short, squat, and possessing of remarkable physical power. Though he had a paunch now, his arms still bulged through his clothes. When he grabbed Vicar's hand in gratitude, his grip, powered by Popeye forearms, was terrifying.

Vicar liked a man with a proper handshake — a guy like that won't fuck you around. Also, a guy like that doesn't like being fucked around. Solid and reliable. Keep it simple, stupid — a philosophy that Vicar endorsed heartily but had difficulty following.

Ross Poutine, too, was feeling emotional. The brass plaque before him read, *Permanently Reserved for Ross Poutine, Hero of the Siege*. Poutine thought back to that stressful day when everything had gone sideways. When him 'n' Farley took on Serena's gang. Everybody got in the paper that day, not just Vicar.

Wheat's nameplate displayed only *Chief Hank Wheat*, but it was screwed to the tabletop at his favourite spot past the far end of the bar, in a corner, from where he could survey the whole place in a glance.

A group of rowdy guys were feeling their oats on a Friday night, occupying the far corner of the Knickers, a few too many glasses of beer into a payday tear that was beginning to unravel dangerously.

Loud and unruly enough to set everyone on edge, they called Jacquie over and tried to make some time with her. They were four oafish numbskulls, and she had no trouble fending off their pathetic displays of virility. If skillful flirting was an elegant epicurean delicacy served with a flourish, these guys were turnips tumbling out of a wheelbarrow.

Chief Wheat watched the action and thought about the men who he had served with in years past. His boys wouldn't have made a peep had they known he was nearby, but these idiots didn't know where the line was, or where danger lurked. Plus, they were sitting at *his* table over in the corner. He had not asked them to move from the reserved spot — he really didn't see the upside in starting a scene with youngsters who were all lip and testosterone. One of them would surely turn it into a confrontation and Hank wasn't interested in disturbing the peace in his beloved local. He'd slide over to his spot if they departed.

Jacquie delivered their order and ignored their horseplay. As she put their money into the pocket of her apron, one of them slapped her hard on the ass. She spun around in shock.

Not twenty feet away on a bar stool, the Chief immediately stood up, about five foot eight and equally wide. He purposefully strode over to the one who had put his hands upon Jacquie.

"Laddie, it's time for you and your friends to depart." He was calm but his balding pate began to redden.

They loudly laughed it off and pretended to make light of the whole situation, with Jacquie standing nearby, her face flushed with anger.

Chief Wheat's viselike hand grabbed the shoulder of the arse slapper and squeezed with such agonizing strength that the man twisted downward and ended up on the floor.

The others leaped up, one of them unwisely putting up his dukes in a witless challenge. The Chief simply grabbed hold of his hand and held it immobile, like a father cupping the fist of his child. He glanced at the rest of them and asked calmly, "Any questions, gentlemen?"

Wheat's words dripped with irony. Gentlemen, ha! They were wearing headdress in the mess; greasy old baseball caps, in fact. The gaggle of punks fell into the street and continued their drunken performance, barking cowardly threats from the safety of the sidewalk, with Chief Wheat barring the doorway like a small truck barricading a roadway, huge arms crossed high on his chest, totally silent, steely mask offering no quarter.

No one in the Knickers had noticed Beaner Weens peering through the pass, the window-like portal where cook passed food to server. He recognized some of the troublemakers, had seen them around for a few years. He did not like them at all — he could call the police from the kitchen phone, he thought, but Chief Wheat had things well in hand. Instead, he grabbed a couple of large potatoes from the bin and went out the back door into the parking area. All attention was on the screaming out front; Beaner went unnoticed.

It was easy to figure out which vehicle was theirs — it was obviously the pickup truck raised up so high they might need scaffolding to get into it. He stealthily pushed a spud into each exhaust pipe, plugging it invisibly but almost completely. Beaner snickered as he stole back into the kitchen. Once those fools finally shut up and tried to leave, they'd have to abandon their Bonehead Limo and walk.

No one was the wiser. Beaner Weens had managed to pull off sly shenanigans without anyone noticing — his specialty.

■ ■ ■

The next morning, after Vicar had heard the report from Jacquie, he unscrewed the Chief's nameplate from the table and went to Lagoon Hardware, where they had an engraving machine. Beneath Wheat's name he asked them to add *Sergeant-at-Arms.*

Thirteen / Opposable Thumbs

With summer in full swing, Beaner knew the supply of valuable golf balls would increase dramatically, so he got ready. He found an old discarded rug behind someone's garage, a tired and faded brownish thing with a fleur-de-lis pattern, and hacked it up into a roughly hewn overcoat. Armholes cut into a wrap, really, with one end chopped off and fashioned into sleeves. They were attached to the wrap by sloppy strips of heavy tape. It smelled like dog, and was splotchy from mysterious stains, one of which was huge and might have been a pool of blood from a slipshod home amputation.

Yet when Beaner put it on, cinched it at the waist with a come-along, and crowned himself with the moose's head, he cut a figure that he was sure would be the answer to his golf-ball-recycling trespass challenges.

Beaner had been wandering around the alley behind the hotel, looking for discarded bottles, shuffling about stiffly in his new moose disguise — challenged mightily by the rigidness of the carpet-cum-costume — bending at the waist with the greatest difficulty, and looking unlike any known member of the deer family.

One lady at the far end of the road rounded the corner of her building and leaned out to see the moose, one antler now tangled in a cable attached to a garage wall and struggling to get free. She shook her head in disbelief and laughed; he had bumbled around back there the day before, too, bonking into walls and tripping on potholes, as he, for all intents and purposes, tidied up the lane a bit. Good lord, it was weird, but she weighed the possible downside of speaking with him, or "it" — and risking some otherworldly altercation. Hell, it was probably just some Green Party publicity stunt, anyway.

She took a picture of this errant, bottle-picking moose with her phone and forwarded it to her friend with the caption "Shirley, I think he can pick up bottles with his hooves."

Vicar had a philosophy about the Vicar's Knickers, which he tried to keep brief but never could condense down into a simple phrase. But he knew that whatever happened, the place had to be a unifier, a leveler, a place of inclusion — it should be Tony, as in *Vicar*, not tony, as in an off-putting showplace that made people feel intimidated. He strongly believed that a pint was symbolic, something more than merely a glass full of beer, almost like a thirst-quenching equivalent to a few signature notes in a great rock anthem. The pub that served it should be for one and all. To charge twelve or fourteen dollars for a pint of beer, as if they were some shiny clip joint in the big city, was to him like charging admission to enter a church. Pure sacrilege.

He recalled an awful dive, in the outskirts of Vancouver, the most ludicrous place he'd ever had lunch. He should have known, though. It was a converted muffler shop, for Chrissakes. It claimed to be a combo gourmet sandwich restaurant and sports bar and sat in the parking lot of an obese suburban shopping mall. Inside, it was as loud as an aircraft hangar during a NORAD alert and all around him he saw a hellscape of TV screens. Vicar utterly fumed. The place was called Gastro-Turf. A perfectly shitty name for a rancid place.

Twelve dollars for a pint. He was already pissed just *looking* at the menu. The lass brought the "pint" and Vicar said, "Oh, I wanted a pint, not a glass."

She replied, "That's a pint."

"That eyedropper is a pint? Uhh …" Vicar collected his thoughts for a moment. "Do you know how many ounces are in a pint?"

"Fourteen."

"No, no, there are sixteen fluid ounces in a pint. And in fact, in this country a '*pint of beer*' is supposed to contain twenty ounces. By law. I presume this is a fourteen-ounce glass." She nodded yes. "It is not a pint," he said firmly.

"Well ... it's *our* pint, in *our* pint glass."

"Umm ... you realize a pint is a measurement, not a nickname, don't you? What if I sold you 'shoes' that were just laces? Would you be happy about that?"

After a pause she said, "If a pint is sixteen ounces but it's supposed to be twenty ounces at a bar, doesn't that just make it a nickname?" She flashed Vicar a lofty look and departed holding the unsatisfactory glass of beer. His face twitched. She returned with a large handled, faceted mug.

"Perhaps this will do the trick," she said.

"Did the bartender top it up?" Vicar asked politely.

"No, he just poured your beer into this pint mug."

Vicar yelped, "Oh, Jesus Christ sideways on a bike." He slapped his hand on the table. "Are you screwing with me?"

His anger became her tears. Vicar stormed out after acidic words with a young "manager," a kid, probably only twenty or twenty-one, with a bizarre hairdo that looked like a brush cut interrupted by a fire drill, his shirt buttoned up to the top like his granny had dressed him. Vicar at that moment considered this little shit to be an accessory to crimes against humanity and an architect of social collapse. The kid could simply not understand what all the kerfuffle was about. His nametag read *Kyle*. Oh, Mighty Kyle, All Knowing Master of Semantic Measurements. *Little prick should spell it "Chyle"* ...

No matter what Jacquie thought about putting prices at the Knickers beyond the reach of the "bad element," he would have none of it. He must welcome clientele, not fleece them. And he'd never hire someone with "Kyle's" kind of hairdo. Somehow Ann Tenna's coiffure didn't even cross his mind.

Fourteen / Irresistible Force with Bacon

After several weeks of seven-day-a-week toiling, the Knickers was beginning to feel very much like work. Vicar and Jacquie hadn't had a day off in over a month. The minutiae never ceased. The amount of time they spent simply ordering supplies was inexplicable.

"Tony, how hard should it be to predict how much sausage we need?" Jacquie was looking heavenward tiredly.

"I'm gonna say there's never too much sausage, and that will be my opinion until there is no room left for people in here." He had already given up worrying about nonsense like meat purchases and condiment supply strategies. That was, he felt, like David Bowie allowing himself to get distracted from his grand vision by a wrinkled shirt. As a result, everything boring began to fall to Jacquie.

With only a skeleton staff, the hours were long; eating dinner at the Knickers did not appeal on that night. Jacquie absolutely refused to have shepherd's pie ever again. Beaner put corn in it, corn dumped from a sack, which she thought was abominable. She wanted barbequed corn, cut lovingly off the cob, and she had mentioned it to Beaner.

"Hey, Jacquie ..." Beaner spoke cautiously. "Where are we gonna get corn on the cob come January or February? Shep's pie is the most popular seller. It's a winter food typa dish."

No one else seemed to give a damn about the issue, which surprised and irritated her, even though it made things cheaper and easier.

As Vicar and Jacquie slowly drove home, takeaway food seemed the only remaining option, but the idea of getting dinner at a drive-thru was not appealing to Vicar; he knew it would be a fraught process. But he was beat and just gave in. Not having to get out of the car was the clincher.

The early evening sun poured through Vicar's window, still hot enough to cook his left shoulder, and the Peugeot idled unevenly, leaving him detached from the conversation, mostly attuned to the rhythm of the old motor, diagnosing its slow, steady demise with only his ears. It was like predicting the death of a beloved dog by listening to its stomach growl. Jacquie leaned over almost into his lap to read the menu sign, while he monkeyed with the driver's side window that sometimes didn't open, or worse, wouldn't shut. Today it *sorta* worked, but in lieu of simply fixing it he had instead done an exhaustive study on ambient temperatures over the last three years, and realized if it got colder or hotter, something would go wrong. Getting it repaired would take at least a couple of days of his mechanically inept life and he couldn't bear thinking about the execrable music they'd play while he was on hold waiting for the parts counter to pick up.

He'd learned his lesson when he had called about a replacement fuel pump for the Peugeot, speaking with someone who had used the phrase "I'm sorry, sir, but we are efforting to get the part in from an importer in Montreal."

Vicar replied, after a confused pause, "You're efforting?"

"Yes, sir."

"You are *efforting*? Like, really, really *efforting*?"

"Oh yes, sir, we are *fully efforting* on this. We drilled down and reached out to many suppliers."

He was perched on the toilet, having now wasted half his morning on the phone, hoping to save the day through his "multi-tasking." He glanced at his unhappy expression in the bathroom mirror and said, "I'll tell ya ... I'm on the pot right now — so you go about your *efforting* and I'll continue my *shittering*." *Drill down on that, motherfucker.* Vicar loathed verbifying.

The call had ended there, with notable abruptness, and so Vicar had remained *sans auto* until he found someone less *efforting* to field his next call.

He inched the Peugeot up toward the menu.

Jacquie turned to him and said, "Why don't you just get that stupid window fixed?"

He sighed, then changed the subject, looking at the pile of envelopes Jacquie had brought along with her from the Knickers mailbox. "What's with all the mail?"

Still fully occupied with reading the wordiest fast-food menu in Christendom, Jacquie mumbled, "Uh, promo kits from bands that want to play at the Knickers."

"Really? Who are they?" he asked, both annoyed and curious. He had never once advertised the pub as a potential venue and yet the word had spread like wildfire to every musical dreamer. Vicar was having trouble even getting himself and Farley set up in there, so the thought of others pushing their way into his precious space raised his hackles.

"Mmm, here." She shoved them into his hand, then pushed on his sternum to get good height to see the last few menu items.

"Ouch. Take it easy, will you? My God, look at this ..."

The menu sign seemed to emanate a guttural squawk that Jacquie recognized as a form of language. She pursed her lips and then chirped, "I think I'll have a Chicken Bacon Ranch Chipotle Siesta Topanga Canyon Avocado Fiesta Combo Supremo Burrito, with ..." She took a deep breath and continued, "Umm ... Spirulina Sweet Potato 'Wise Fries' and Imported Lite Organic Belgian Mayo, but I don't want regular salsa, I want All-Natural Pico de Gallo ... But only on half of it — on an Organic Tuscan Tomato Whole Wheat Tortilla ... and make it slightly crispy. But don't burn it. Oh yeah, hold the bacon."

At that, Vicar's shoulders went up as if recoiling from being struck. Hold the bacon? *What kind of god-damn world are we living in?* Jacquie gesticulated with hands and arms and head motions, like she was signing to a hockey rink full of people listening to a speech — yeah, like the kid could see her through the speaker.

Vicar closed his eyes and shook his head back and forth.

"Something wrong with that?" she asked in challenge.

"Four syllables, max. Three is preferred."

"What?"

"CHEEZ-BRR-GRR. Three syllables. You get the fourth if you want bacon. BAY-CUN BRR-GRR. Four."

"You really are a caveman, aren't you?" she retorted, now aggravated. She was sweaty, hungry, and getting snippy, but at any rate, she thought, he always ate like a wolf gorging on an overturned caribou.

"You are ordering from the torn seat of a jalopy parked right next to three large trash bins, NOT *Tour d'Argent* in *Gay Paree*." He paused, enjoying the moment, then continued in a TV announcer's cadence, "Your exquis-itely prepared *cuisine gastronomique* will be enjoyed in a moving vehicle and ordered through an antique Tannoy."

Though she didn't have the first clue what a Tannoy was, Jacquie glared and dug in her heels, spending an additional two minutes yelling across Vicar, going over her order in agonizing detail with a laconic kid who didn't give a rat's arse.

Her order was so complex that they had to leave the lineup and park for ten minutes. Vicar used the time to peruse the unsolicited promotional kits they'd received.

He slid out the contents of an envelope and examined it. "Ai yai yai ... Tragic: 'Pusy Galore.'" He began shaking his head and grimacing in a mix of discomfort and amusement. "Spell-check is your friend," he muttered. Jacquie glanced over with a look of disbelief.

Getting into it, he reached into another envelope. "Oh my ... What the hell is *cybergoth*?" The promo photo showed one guy with a bunch of laptops and a tiny keyboard. He had short, pasted down hair and was made up in whiteface with blackened eyes, looking like the cadaver of an unloved accountant, not missed by anyone until tax time. Vicar bared his teeth in disgust and said, "Calls himself Lord of the Files."

Jacquie smirked despite her rotten mood. Vicar opened another.

"Hatchback of Notre Dame! Says here they are a combination of two former groups, Carnival of Dennis and the Land Mimes." With that he started belly laughing, tears coming to his eyes. He looked at the pathetic eight-by-ten glossy of a group of fat old guys with hellish hair, most with arms crossed. They might as well have put bags over their heads given how obscured their faces were by beards. There was even a guy with a fedora, shades, a huge grey facial muff, and a black T-shirt accessorized with a Harley neckerchief. It seemed possible that he was a trained bear in sweatpants. Vicar imagined his show-stopping trick, drinking beer out of a wooden pail. To his delight, the guy lurked in the back of the shot as if he had accidentally stumbled into the frame. *He must be the bass player. Jesus.*

Jacquie was laughing out loud now, but for a different reason. She knew many of Vicar's bands' names — a too-long list with no purpose. They were every bit as awful as the ones from the promo kits he held; Gecko Chamber Orkestra was near the top of that list, delightful to Tony but not worth the unpacking. There was the absurdly named Hams Across the Water, British Invasion schtick featuring tired, stolen comedy and disastrous vocals that had made her eyes water; a repulsive grunge effort dubbed Girl with the Draggin' Patoot — she had been unable to disguise her horror at that one. The Pentland Squires ... She gave Vicar points for cleverness until he revealed that he thought it sounded "classic," like Paul Revere & the Raiders ... you know, ruffled shirts and tricorns. The air came out of his tires when she explained that it was a type of potato.

The wackiest name, she thought, was his folk group featuring Pete Giesbrecht, the appliance repairman who liked to make a punishing racket on his banjo, and often expected to be remunerated for his tinny assaults. They called the trio Fridge Over Troubled Water.

A knock came at the window, and when Vicar turned the crank, the whole pane of glass fell loudly into the door, causing Vicar to bark, "Oh, for fuck's sake! No, not you. Sorry. The window."

The girl delivering the food smiled uneasily.

Jacquie rolled her eyes, grabbed the bag, and unceremoniously rooted through it.

Vicar pulled onto the road and gathered speed for the ride home. A few moments later Jacquie squeaked, "No napkins!"

He yelled over the road noise now pouring into his absent window, "Do you think they had time to worry about napkins when they assembled that science project?" He pointed at the takeaway bag.

She glared at him. Sometimes he was such an ass. Rather than retort, she took an animalistic chomp out of her hemorrhaging burrito, grimaced, and exploded, "This is TERRIBLE!"

Vicar turned toward her and said dryly, "You seem ... surprised."

Back at the house a little while later, Vicar was on his knees and in a total funk, holding a magnifying glass and wearing a Cyclops-like headlamp, his upper body jammed partway inside the malfunctioning dishwasher. This was the very last goddamn thing he wanted to deal with right now. It wouldn't drain and a half hour on the internet showed him how to fix it. *POSSIBLY fix it*, he fumed. He imagined repairing it in "four easy steps" as the vid demonstrated — and then shook his head. *As if* ... He was furious before he even began the task.

Banging his head on the upper rack, swearing poisonously, he used an old yogurt container to scoop all the standing water out of the bottom. *At least that god-awful gloop is useful for something* ...

He lost his grip on the container and it splashed on the cupboard door, on the floor, on the wall, on him. He cursed percussively, like a cannon shot. He reached behind him and grabbed a lacy tea towel from the drawer and began to sop up the lake of used dishwater, just as Jacquie dashed into the room to see what all the swearing was about.

She noticed Vicar cleaning up the spill. "Don't use my good tea towels on the floor, Tony. Good God!"

Vicar, already frustrated, turned halfway around and barked, "What's the big frickin' deal? Is it the Shroud of Turin, or something?"

Then, in a blink, he morphed from cranky old codger into wonder-filled boy, just like that. "What a *great* band name ... Shroud of Tourin'."

erri Crabtree put on a full-face shield and a white haz-mat suit and lumbered to her hot sauce prep kitchen, looking a lot more like an astronaut than a chef. She had a large container of Carolina Reaper peppers ready to go and so double-checked her surgical mask was on properly then donned latex gloves.

She was now ready to bake the peppers that would soon be the base of Ross Poutine's weaponized hot sauce, more deadly perhaps than military-grade defoliant.

Even through her mask and shield, her eyes began to water and her nose to run as the peppers began to roast. She had made the rookie error of opening the oven door to check on them, and the fumes roiled out. They were exactly like those from aerosol spray used to chase away angry grizzlies. She backed out of the room, cautiously turning on the little kitchen fan as she departed; she was worried about where it vented — if it was out at street level she might end up on charges.

This was a completely different animal, she thought. All her other sauces were spicy and delicious. But this, *my God*, she thought — this was like fiddling around with napalm.

There was no staying in there for too long; she would have to prep it all in one go, seal the container airtight, and keep it under lock and key. This stuff, well, boy howdy … *At what point will this become a poison?* Merri had never imagined that making boutique hot sauce would involve ethical concerns, but honestly, this stuff might liquefy internal organs.

▬ ▬ ▬

Beaner found out about Poutine's hot sauce from the man himself.

"I got Merri makin' me custom sauce, eh?" Poutine confided proudly.

"Special recipe?" Beaner asked.

"Yup. Thunk it up m'self, dere. Gonna be hotter than the hubs of hell when it's ready."

"Hotter than her other stuff?"

"Waaaaay hotter." Poutine winked hugely, his tongue bulging out of the corner of his mouth.

Beaner started laughing. "Like, how hot?"

"How hot? A million Scooby-Doos, dere. It'll melt the smell off a shithouse door."

Beaner's face puckered up in fright; he had to agree. That sounded purdy hot.

Sixteen / Enigma Code

Jacquie noticed that Vicar was quiet, far more pensive than usual. Something had been on his mind in the last while, she could tell. He had mood swings now and then, and might be sinking into one of his lows, less frequent than in times past, but worrisome and mysterious when they arose. She was never quite sure what triggered them.

"Tony, are you okay?"

"Umm ..." Long pause. His thoughts moved over his face.

"It's all right, you can tell me." She sounded gentle, understanding.

"Well ..." Silence. He stared at the floor.

"Tony, just tell me and we'll work on it together."

He croaked out a couple of false starts and sounded a little like a skipping record.

"Please, Tony, just say it … Stop hemming and hawing."

Vicar looked out the window, glanced at Jacquie uneasily, and then closed his eyes.

"Jacquie … Well, umm, I …"

"Tony!" she said urgently. "Just say it! You've got me worried now."

"I … I think I've been serving tofu weenies."

"Huh?" She looked blankly at him.

"I fear the old chap is bedridden."

She shook her head, uncomprehending.

"*Ich bin toten hosen,*" he said in pidgin German.

"I am not following. Speak English."

"A dead bird cannot fly."

"The Eagle has landed?" she replied as if answering a code phrase.

"I might be firing blanks."

"Is this some kinda haiku game? Oooohhhh … *Blanks*! You mean …" She gestured at his crotch with her outstretched arm, her wrist flapping up and down vaguely.

"Yes. I had an accident a few years ago."

"An accident?" She instantly braced; she knew that bizarreness was incoming.

"Yes, I was doing the Elvis thing — you know — and I jumped off the stage right down onto a microphone stand that I didn't see."

Jacquie's eyes were wide with disbelief. She imagined the scenario and squirmed. *Horrible.*

"The pain must have been awful!"

He looked down at the floor and replied, "It was terrible. Worse than Paris Hilton's singing."

She suppressed a laugh. *Only Tony.* "So, uhm, and then ...?"

"And then I speared my junk."

She could not hold back a snort; it was too much. She fell into his arms cackling, imagining fake Elvis Presley, a halberd impaled in his ballsack, perhaps a cartoon mouse nearby trying to turn his face into the shape of the skillet he's swinging. "Omigod. Did an anvil fall on your head, too?"

She wasn't mad, wasn't horrified, wasn't put off. She was laughing. Weird, but ... a relief?

"You ... You're ... You're okay with that?"

"Okay with it? What are you talking about? You poor guy. Sorry I'm laughing — but really. Good God." She continued chuckling.

"I don't know if we could ever have babies ..." He was clearly very concerned about it.

"Oh, sweetie ..." Her voice had a catch in it.

Jacquie pulled back from her embrace and looked at him closely in the eye. She smiled gently at her partner, who was at that moment a crazy-assed man-child. The same guy who was willing to trade his life for hers and who seemed naturally geared to protect those around him no matter the personal cost, now stood before her, completely vulnerable, wondering if he was in trouble for a catastrophic testicle injury.

The *Tyee Logger*, a local newspaper destined to be remembered as the favoured publication for starting fires in wood stoves, ran a story on page 3 asking the cryptic question, "Where Is the Mystery Moose?" They used a blurry camera phone image to accompany it, which did little more than add a layer of spookiness to the whole tale. The image could have been of anything, from a beaver, to a dog, to one of the handmade sock puppets from the remaindered stock of mercifully defunct Konnie's Kountry Kottage.

The story speculated wildly, made some misleading reference to Ogopogo, the legendary Okanagan Lake crypto-creature, and was written in such a way that it left the town confused but abuzz. No one could be completely sure if there was a rogue moose flitting about, or if there was a person in a costume skulking the alleyways. More than a few readers took away from it that the town now had a sea monster. The vaunted local paper of record made only one thing completely certain: Higginbotham & Son Draperies were blowing out venetian blinds at 40 percent off.

Seventeen / The Great Cosmic Circle

It was dusk and the orangey-gold sun was nearing the horizon of the scrub-covered New Mexico hill; already the temperature was dropping, although at midday it had been hot and dry, just like every day had been for weeks.

"Cosmic Ray" McCullough sat on a crudely woven blanket laid down at the periphery of a large stone circle that held within it small rock cairns, a couple of effigies woven from tall grasses, crosses, stars, moons, and other harder to identify ceremonial objects, as well as sticks of smouldering incense. Lying beside him was a Guatemalan or Ecuadorian satchel, purchased for a colossal price at a third-rate folk festival, which for years had carried a beaten-up sitar, a couple of roughly hewn flutes, and a battery of small drums and shaky bits.

Ray was deep in thought. His old friend Tony Vicar had come to him in a dream last night. He had not thought of Vicar for some time. He rebuked himself for having left the band and the Bachelor Pad without explanation or goodbye to Farley and Vicar. His hasty departure was a huge regret. He could only imagine what effect that had had — he just knew it would have hit Vicar hard. Always a joker, Vicar never seemed to joke about the band.

But at the time, Ray simply had to leave, to get out. Something had changed in the blink of an eye, after his Alien Abduction. It had truly happened, he was convinced of it, and it opened doors to the whole universe. But he had become almost a laughingstock — nearly everyone took to calling him Cosmic Ray at that point. The locals were merciless, but he had to admit it was an amusing name. He ended up simply going with it.

Tony Vicar had not been cruel about the abduction but didn't believe him. More than anything it made Vicar defensive; yet another silly tangent that would take focus away from the group's progress. He urgently steered away from the topic if it even *smelled* like Ray might start talking about flying saucers again, like he was chatting carefully with an unhinged, tinfoil-hatted relative at Christmas dinner. The growing unease had played into Ray's departure. He wanted to be around people who were open to new possibilities.

Ray, suddenly immersed in disjointed spiritual gambolling, only knew that he had wanted out of the band, the town, the whole scene. He had decided he'd wall off that part of his life, maybe return to it later; he had convinced himself that time would heal all. But while Ray meditated in the high desert, Vicar, assailed by wasted time and lack of direction, wandered in one of his own making.

Echoing in Ray's mind, too, were the escalating arguments he had had with Vicar that began soon after the abduction. He uncomfortably brushed the yellowish New Mexico dust off his brown skin and remembered how he had begun to use a new tack with him — talking it out, everyone letting everyone else really experience their feelings, express them, no matter how far-out they sounded. He was hungry to hear thoughts that meshed with his, spoken in tones of peace and understanding.

At one point he had confronted Vicar, warning him that he was too aggressive. "It's not *cool*, man." The statement was meant to be a rebuke, but he only sounded weak and whiny — Ray had been new to protesting, after all. Vicar, in that instance, impatient that it was taking over an hour to decide on a five-song set list, had barked back, "We're done, Ray. If you don't like it, too goddamn bad." Vicar had never been much for dialoguing.

Ray had sensed Vicar needed to work though some trauma and even offered to perform some "energy work" on him — Vicar, conversely, thought Ray needed to fuck off with the hippie shit.

When the changes within him had begun to occur, Ray had lain in his lumpy cot at the Bachelor Pad realizing he had to find the answer to new and important questions that had begun to echo in his head. If Earth was being visited by aliens, what purpose did his present life serve? What good was it being a rock musician with a drum kit that filled the back of a truck? He was certain it would not fit in the cargo hold of their craft when they returned to take him away again — the saucer had seemed smallish. He abandoned his musical equipment, and even left behind his kilt and sporran, a gift from his grandmother, which had been such a hit with the ladies. A tall, handsome brown man with dreadlocks dressed in a Clan McCullough kilt seemed to make them weak in the knees.

On that critical night, the inner noise had gotten so intense that he fled the next morning, stuffing a few things into a backpack, emptying his meagre bank account, and bolting due south for Washington State. Once in the USA, he had drifted for a couple of years — he couldn't quite remember how long — from state to state until he found what he believed he was looking for in the high desert of the Southwest.

Ray had eventually found himself assembling a galactic vision that to anyone else would be a grab bag of ill-assorted superstitions. Unlike his old pal Vicar, Cosmic Ray never worried that his elevator might not go all the way to the top floor. He questioned his purpose but never his sanity. *If life always made sense, you might not be living it right ...*

In Ray's recent dream, Vicar was in trouble, was fighting foes impossible to see clearly, against the wall,

all alone, flailing wildly as he tried to fend off attacks. Lances, swords, disembodied jaws bristling with deadly fangs circled him and wounded him with a thousand cuts. Cosmic Ray felt certain that his friend Vicar needed him and that by returning he could right the wrong he had caused — and possibly convince him to downsize his gear ... Ol' Vicar might be able to bring a small acoustic guitar along with him when *they* came back.

Eighteen / A Death So Fowl / Easter 1970

Bogdan Kaminski glanced up at the calendar and wondered if the package would get there in time for Easter. It was March 11, 1970. Yes, that ought to be just enough time.

It boggled him to think the '60s had slipped by, just like *that*. They had been so busy raising children, building the house. He took the lovingly packaged baked goods from the counter and walked out the front door, making sure Larry's name was boldly marked on it. Just to be extra sure, he added the nickname *Valentine*. Larry said that everyone called him that now. Bogdan didn't want the care package to go amiss.

"Did you take the cookies?" his wife called after him.

"Yes, yes, missus. Look." He held up the box for her to see.

"Okay. Hurry back."

Bogdan missed Larry a great deal, although he didn't like to discuss it too much. He was immensely proud of him, having moved so far away to Vancouver Island and gotten an excellent job as a logger. *He was good boy*, as Bogdan said to all their friends.

He gently drove his Studebaker down to the post office and passed the chicken place. The boy liked that chicken so much. He used to beg them for it on weekends, even mowed the lawn without complaint to earn it.

Bogdan felt a tug at his heart and impulsively pulled into the parking lot. Not just cookies. He would send Lorko chicken, too.

Valentine was dying. He had been violently ill for several days and was now unable to move around, unable to help himself. He ached beyond imagining and his innards felt like they had been expelled. At least his incessant, lurching trips to the toilet had ceased. Clearly there was nothing left in him to evacuate.

It was the third day of this, and he was now so weakened that he couldn't even rise from the bed to help himself. He had begun hallucinating that he had gotten up and sought help, but then reality would fade back in and he would see that he was still shipwrecked in bed. Awash with despair, he'd drift back into a dream state again.

At one point it had dawned on him that he had contracted food poisoning from that chicken, a damned unrefrigerated death snack. What had he been thinking? More importantly, what had his *parents* been thinking? You can't mail *meat*, for God's sake. He was awash with shame, embarrassment, fear. What a pathetic gesture, to mail a bucket of chicken! What an act of stupidity to eat it. The deeply ingrained rule of his prairie childhood, put in place by parents who both nearly starved to death during the war — to never, never, never waste food — had taken precedence over his very survival. The pitifulness of the situation undermined him, and he spiralled downward.

He felt a dreadful sense of doom, a certainty that his situation would not have a good outcome. He couldn't even crawl to summon help; except for a dry, hollow croak, he couldn't make a sound. He was completely alone inside a building with people coming and going day and night.

Had this been a regular week he would have been discovered in hours — there's no way they'd let him miss a shift without checking on him. But it was Easter weekend. He wasn't to report for work until Tuesday. He knew he wouldn't make it that long.

Valentine drifted for a few more hours in and out of consciousness, completely outraged that his life, one that was just gaining momentum, would end in such an abject manner. He would never buy a pickup truck; more importantly, *he would never give his mother grandchildren*, her biggest wish and the only solemn promise she had ever extracted from him. For all his youthful sense of adventure he was still tied firmly to his family in an old-fashioned way. What was left of his body and soul were agonized by the waste, the sheer profligate irresponsibility of it all. He ached at the thought of the opportunities he would never have, and especially what his end would do to his poor parents. This would kill them in a way that the war had failed to do.

Sometime late on Easter Sunday he died, shuffling off his mortal coil in the humble surroundings of room 222 in the old Agincourt Hotel.

Nineteen / The Great Dictator

Sorely down in the mouth, Vicar eased himself slowly into his aging Peugeot and slid into the seat like an anchor settling in silt.

He knew the chances had been slim, but he had hoped that some medical miracle might occur. After all, so-called miracles had been flying at him like spit-balls in language arts class for the last few years. But there was no increased motility. The old soldier still stood faithfully on guard, but his musket was only ceremonial.

He laughed ruefully. A daffy leap off a stage while dressed as Elvis, directly down onto the shaft of a microphone stand he did not see, had ended his chances at reproduction. The agony had been otherworldly, yet he insisted that the show go on. Ray and the shoeless chick he had been hanging out with started babbling something about applying a "comfrey poultice" to the wound. Vicar, in agony, had looked at Ray venomously and he backed off. He much preferred ineffectual Ray, not this version that preached herbal solutions for everything from fatigue to nuclear disarmament. No effing magic plant was going to fix his nutsack.

He stuffed his pants with cotton wool from the first aid kit in the kitchen of the Moose Lodge and continued the show, as if finishing the performance while severely injured would be the selfless act of a martyr. Of course, it was not. He did, however, disprove the fallacy that such a wound would make him a soprano, gurgling out the rest of the show in a strained baritone moan.

Yet he had been unwilling to go to the hospital, claiming he was *just fine*. His friends tried to drag him there, but he utterly refused. He wouldn't admit it, but under no circumstance was he going to be taken to the same hospital where his mother lay, ready to take her terminal breath at any moment. *As if cancer wasn't an undignified enough end — then your only child pulls off an idiotic stunt like that?* He could think of nothing more pitiable.

The story had ended in a predictable way. He got an infection — a very serious one — and could not tell the pain of the laceration from the throbbing ache of its septicity. For all the boyish fixation he lavished on his own crotch, he apparently couldn't discern much more than "on/off" in the region. By the time the urgency of the situation had convinced him to seek medical help, it was already too late. *You can't put off a trip to the doc when you get harpooned in the taint*, he mused. He had, and could no longer believe otherwise, rendered himself permanently infertile.

Vicar, peering through the fog that had rolled in from the Pacific, picked up his phone and tapped the text app, dictating gloomily while driving back to the house.

"Home in fifteen minutes," he mumbled as he steered through the weather.

The software wrote out, *Feel phone in the simplex.*

He muttered and tried again, but louder and more clearly this time. "Home in fifteen minutes." The phone jauntily wrote out, *Bone to the princess.*

Argh. Nothing was easy today.

"Home in fifteen minutes." This time he practically barked.

Oh bone in buttocks this is CBC Radio 2.

Turning red now, he shut off the radio with a sharp slap to the dashboard and yelled, "You piece of shit!"

The phone accurately captured that, helpfully including an eggplant emoji. When he tried to backspace it into oblivion, his fat thumb accidentally sent the message.

At the other end of the transmission, Jacquie blinked a couple of times and stared off into the distance, rather puzzled.

Vicar tried to come to terms with his upsetting medical diagnosis and found that it bothered him a great deal. He wouldn't allow himself to think about it too much. It always opened a can of worms. He had hoped his luck might have changed, mirroring his improved luck in every other matter, but this seemed to be a rare occasion where he needed a miracle and it *didn't* arrive.

He had to get out and clear his mind and suddenly felt the need to get Frankie Hall's ancient Cadillac, now his, out of the garage and go for a spin with Farley, who had wandered over without calling first and beelined straight for the kitchen with only a grunt for a greeting to Jacquie. He had a huge crush on her, but this was a snacking emergency.

She watched him graze from the fridge with the door hanging open. He pawed at a thick sheaf of processed cheese, awkwardly peeling the plastic wrap off each slice, folding the cheese into four with great precision, and then devouring it in one voracious gulp. She could not tell if he was hungry or engaging in some type of eccentric ritual — it was done with such elaborate care. He stuffed the used wrappers in his pants pocket.

She looked at Vicar, her jaw agape, and then back at Farley, clearly wanting to say something in protest. But, blinking a couple of times, she gave up and simply left the room, shaking her head in defeat.

"Farley, let's take the Caddy for a spin. I haven't driven it for months."

Farley piled into the front seat of the massive sedan, Vicar at the helm, and they floated away regally onto Sloop Road for a joyride.

"This is the biggest car I ever seen, Tony."

"It's, umm, one of the biggest cars ever made, Farley. A real Elvis-mobile. He had dozens of rigs like this."

Farley could not imagine needing more than one of them. It was so large he could leap over into the back seat without even bumping Tony, which he did while they were in motion.

Vicar laughed and said, "Oh, so now I'm the chauffeur, and you're in the back like a bigwig."

Farley gloried in the feeling for a few minutes and then noticed that their freewheeling pace had been slowed by someone ahead, creeping along below the speed limit.

"Don't they know who we think we are, Tone?"

"Touristas. Lookit 'em, gawking at the ocean and going two miles an hour ..."

Vicar didn't really mind. After all, the view was tremendous, a wide shot up and down the Strait of Georgia; mainland of British Columbia on the horizon, islands floating in the blue drink between. It was a view he took for granted and knew he shouldn't. People came from thousands of miles away just to see it and drive too slowly for a few minutes. To his biased eye it was as beautiful as any topography on the planet, especially during a long, red-hued summer sunset.

Farley was quiet but annoyed with the slow pace and fished around in his shirt pocket for a doobie he'd stuffed in there.

"No smoking in the King's chariot, ya big dummy!" Vicar imagined blasting past the tourists ahead with pot smoke pouring out the windows, Farley grinning and waving like the Queen. Everything about Farley was slightly off-kilter but that's why, Vicar knew, he liked him so much. Vicar had struggled throughout his life to be a more patient person, but even when he lost it with Farley, his frustration had a special, indulgent tone.

Gliding through town as if steering an overstuffed couch through a tunnel of velvet, Vicar enjoyed his cruise in the gas-guzzling danger to nature. It was like time travelling. He swung past the Knickers and saw that prissy journalist out on the sidewalk with his grubby little cameraman, getting footage of the pub and hotel exterior.

As the massive Cadillac floated by, Richard Dick saw Vicar in the driver's seat and watched him pass, taking note of the blingy Caddy.

Twenty / The Compleat Dick

Glib Re-Post was a gossip rag and internet news site that specialized in sensational human-interest stories, clickbait crap, and teary-eyed rumour; exaggerated, unsubstantiated, irresponsible, but influential. One bad story in *GRP* could wreak havoc on Hollywood careers and had done so many times in the past. When photos of superstar Tom Kross emerged, showing him in a poolside tryst with his male assistant, his frantic and almost fantastical defence lost him credibility and box office draw, and so the end of one of the greatest reigns in cinema history came to a dribbling halt. All this due to two grainy photographs secured by a slimeball crawling around in the Carolina cherry.

When the first whispers of the "Vicar phenomenon" were sensed floating in the ether, a Burbank office filled with *GRP*'s editorial staff had looked at a thin dossier on this unknown Vicar person and unanimously the top, a perk, *inconvenience pay* for having to waste his valuable time in this backwater. If he were honest, his job was difficult, often hard to stomach, but he had clawed to the top, finally arriving where the money was good and the profile was high; rather than quit he treated himself as frequently as he could to delicious, pillaged booty. The more women he conquered, the more confident he felt. He lasciviously followed Jacquie with his eyes and glanced occasionally at Vicar, who was behind the bar drawing beer from the taps and chatting amiably with customers.

Jacquie came over to deliver Dick's order, conspicuous because it was the only drink in the last half hour that had not been beer or wine. Tony had to look up the recipe online in the backroom. What kind of tit wants a "bespoke Blood & Sand"? Tony had never heard of it before.

"Here you go ..." Jacquie said as pleasantly as she could to Dick and his oleaginous cameraman.

"Well, let's see if it passes," Dick replied coldly. This guy had a creepy vibe. She unfortunately knew his type well. Probably liked to screw in a mirrored room but only watched himself in the reflection.

"Well ..." He cleared his throat. "Close."

Jacquie simply smiled and departed, tray in hand, undulating with a naturalness that drove Dick to distraction; she reminded him of a girl he should have married, not that gold-digging witch who had ransacked his bank account and held his daughter hostage. Jacquie returned to the bar and spoke with Tony for a second.

Vicar said archly, "He really thinks he's the shit, doesn't he?"

"Oh yeah," she replied. "He is definitely the president of his own fan club."

■■ ■■ ■■

Vicar glanced over to Dick and rolled his eyes. Dick glared back coldly, attempting to portray power that instead was only bravado — he had difficulty telling the two apart.

One way or the other, Dick thought, he was going to get something out of this for himself, too, even if it was merely the tactical destruction of this Vicar idiot, who appeared to be stumbling from success to success without a care in the world. He would get the story and get the hell out of here. *Vicar's life is a bloody holiday ... What an asshole.*

Back at the motel where they had set up their base, Richard Dick put the phone into his pocket and looked out the window.

"Not happy. They want something bigger." He spoke to Handlanger, his cameraman, but stared straight ahead. His bosses in Hollywood were not satisfied with what they had received — puny little gossip stories of a ginned-up scandal, dark innuendo. They wanted drama, a full series of increasingly lurid reports that could really spark its own reality. Nice big, fat lies that, if repeated often enough, became the truth. They sensed they had something in Vicar that had legs, real staying power. They also made sure that Dick felt intense pressure to satisfy them.

Richard Dick's medical bills had been crippling before his daughter died of leukemia at the tender age of twelve and her long, painful demise had pushed him a hair's breadth from financial and emotional collapse. *Glib Re-Post* helped him with the expenses, and the funeral, too. Generally amoral, Dick was further compromised by the situation. He could no longer apply the brakes even if he had wanted to. But he seldom wanted to.

Handlanger, fiddling with a camera lens, paused for a moment and then said, "But he's like a Boy Scout. How do we take him down while he's collecting merit badges?"

"We're going to have to get creative …" Dick replied ominously.

Dick had just been tasked, in no uncertain terms, to produce material that would engage readers of *GRP*. It was just another story, and the sooner he got the ball rolling, the sooner he could get back to LA. He had already been stuck in this backwater far too long. Every second he spent here was an opportunity for someone back in Hollywood to get the drop on him. He had fought his way to prominence and wasn't about to let Tony Vicar screw him out of his primacy.

The viciously competitive part of him rose like a viper out of the mud. He suddenly didn't care what it was going to take to make this happen. He did not care; he did not care. Dick felt a sudden fury of impatience — the spectre of indebtedness wielded by his employers, who were little better than professional blackmailers, trumped any weak and toothless sense of fair play he might have had stuffed away in the back of his cranium. Dick pulled out his phone again and went to work.

Twenty-One / A Cache of Cash

The clutch of workmen all stopped and looked up at the ceiling. There it was again. Clunking and crashing and the sounds of someone thrashing around on the floor above.

One of them said, "Aren't we the only guys on shift this morning?"

Another looked around, counting quickly, and replied, "Yup. Four of us. Th' 'lectricians come at two o'clock."

"Well, who the hell is making all the racket up there?"

"I don't know and I'm not gonna find out!" They all smirked but were a little frightened. They had heard the stories. Everyone had.

■ ■ ■

Vicar wouldn't admit it, but he was completely unwilling to go back into room 222 without backup. He was too freaked out.

He enlisted one the construction crew to help him deconstruct the closet, that damned spooky closet.

"Okay, I'll just get in here and remove the inner wall; maybe you can take the wreckage and just stuff it in that thing." He pointed at a large plastic garbage can.

"Okay, Mr. Vicar. I'm just going to get my pry bar …" The young man turned to leave the room.

"No, no … Don't bother." Vicar was like a kid afraid of the dark. "I've got one right there in my tool box." He hoped he had covered up slickly enough to hide his fright in front of this burly young construction worker. He did not realize the guy was as spooked as he was.

"Okay, okay …" The young man was relieved.

Vicar went at the inner wall of the little closet, the aged wallboard coming off easily, snapping like peanut brittle into angular chunks.

"What's that?" he muttered. Looked like a dead rat. Ewww …

The worker leaned in and pointed his light down toward the place Vicar was peering. The little circle of light shone on a lump of something that looked like a sock, an argyle sock; old and discoloured, unearthed — as strange as it seemed — from behind a eighty-year-old wall.

Vicar gazed at it for an instant and then gingerly picked it up with his gloved hand. It had a bit of heft. He inspected it and found it to be stuffed with a roll of cash. Old money from back when the Queen was young, a few bills of a slightly newer vintage. There were singles, two-dollar bills, fives, tens, a couple of twenties.

Vicar didn't count it, but just at a glance he figured there were two or three hundred bucks in small denominations. He wondered who had stashed their loot here, in the bottom corner of a closet of a lonely hotel in the bush; and when that series of bills was in circulation, it really was the bush out here. What a strange find.

As he stuffed the money in his pants pocket the work light exploded in a shower of sparks, giving him a fright, blowing the circuit breaker, and leaving him in the dark.

"He really doesn't want to do an interview."

"Surely he wants his side of the story told?" Richard Dick was having no luck even speaking to Vicar and was trying to convince him to spill his guts via Jacquie, who was in fact even less amenable to the idea than Tony. She couldn't imagine that anyone could have so little instinct that they'd speak confidentially to this repellent *thing*.

"He will not do it. You're wasting your time and energy."

Changing his tack, he said, "Perhaps you should come visit us in Hollywood. I'm sure I could introduce you to a few producers who owe me a favour." He tried to tantalize her with greasy promises of stardom, but his words held an undercurrent of menace. His forced friendliness was a thin disguise, a Komodo dragon in a jaunty hat, reptilian stillness and dead eyes impossible to camouflage.

"Kind of you," she replied without enthusiasm, "but I am very happy here." She looked around the Knickers's interior.

Dick's eyes narrowed. There was no possible way that she could be happy out here in the sticks. He knew no one who wasn't vying for celebrity. *She's playing hard to get.*

Now he heard his inner voice begin bragging, competitively pumping him up for the challenge thrown in his path. *Why, her horizons have clearly never been expanded by someone with my connections.* The voice was scolding him to stay on it, stay on it, find the opening, keep pushing. It motivated him like a cattle prod.

Jacquie was now back at the bar and Dick watched her touch Tony's hand affectionately. He curled his lip in disgust, using the innocent gesture to fuel a perverse outrage. He turned to Handlanger and said, "What a nauseating display. I'd rather listen to old people chewing."

The cameraman looked at his boss and then at Vicar, and knew, without having to be told, that his task would be to gather footage that would tear Vicar down or push him until he lost it. He'd been through this before and knew the score. He was happy to assist.

Twenty-Two / Dewlaps and Dunlops

Beaner was awkwardly leaning over the water hazard near the ninth green. It was a green in name only, being November, with barren deciduous trees standing naked amongst the evergreens and the grass slightly worse for wear in patches. It was situated close to the road that ran past the golf course. The old farts around here would play in a tsunami, so even the bleakness of the season couldn't prevent them from strolling about, dressed like colour-blind kids who had slipped past Mom that morning.

He scaled down to the ditch with the greatest difficulty; the feat was near-impossible while wrapped in a carpet and wearing a moose's head. He was trying to fish out a golf ball lodged in the mud with a long-handled ball retriever.

A rent-a-cop on a preposterous scooter pootled up behind him. Beaner couldn't hear the little rig approach with his head inside the moose, and nearly shrieked when the guy tapped him on the shoulder.

"Sir, you have to leave. This is private property. You are, in essence, stealing those golf balls. You are committing a serious crime, and I must ask you to depart post-haste." His stupid ball cap said *Security* across it, in case he needed a reminder now and then.

Beaner listened to the incredibly nerdish admonition, right down to its overmodulated delivery — the guy sounded like the president of the Young Scientists' Club reading their mission statement to the school assembly. Beaner stood there for a minute, his moosie eyes unblinking. For reasons unknown they were blue and had whites surrounding them. This added intensity to a somewhat psychotic stare.

"Sir, if you don't leave, I will be forced to summon the authorities …"

Beaner looked at the sparkly red scooter. This dweeb apparently didn't even warrant a *golf cart*. He grabbed the end of the wire threaded down through his sleeve that controlled his moose-mouth. His head shook back and forth as if perplexed and suddenly the majestic moose spoke.

"Are you actually gonna arrest a moose?"

"Sir, you are not a moose. You are disguised as a moose."

Flapping the spring-loaded mouth in a highly agitated fashion, he protested, "No, you fool, I am a talking moose. I'm endangered, man."

The security guard tried to grab the moose's carpet-encased arm and the moose drew back, bellowing, "Unhand me!" He played up his mock outrage heavily.

"Sir, I must ask you to leave. And I shall arrest you if you don't depart on your own." The guard put his hands up as if he was going to touch him again.

The disgruntled moose erupted in a terrifying call at the best volume he could output. The security guard drew back, not knowing what to do. It sounded as if this antlered wacko was saying, "Oww, oww, oww." The guard thought he might have hurt the errant moose and became deeply confused. Mr. Moose shuffled toward him, refilled his lungs, and moose called again, this time louder, raspier, opening wide the mechanical mouth in a fairly good representation of how it would look if a genuine moose in situ had a turf battle with a part-time security guard in a navy-blue nylon windbreaker.

A car drove by and slowed down to watch the bizarre sight. The driver yelled out her window, "Do you need help?"

Moosie couldn't see her but just for good measure howled out a terrifying call toward the car, flapping the mouth a few extra times for added visual effect. The driver felt a vertiginous dissonance overtake her. Gasping, she feared that the end times might well be nigh and whooshed away as quickly as she could.

Her panic seemed to leap to the security guard, who was badly thrown off as he watched her escape at top speed — feeling the extreme weirdness of the situation flood over him like the flush of a gigantic toilet bowl. His nerve abandoned him, and the intimidating throw-rug-slash-ruminant instinctively pressed the advantage.

Howling madly, he took tiny little tippy-tippy-tay steps from within his broadloom overcoat, a balletic bourrée — stylish, yes, but technically challenging. The nerdy guard recoiled inch by inch. Finally, the moose lost his footing and teetered near the edge of the pond, his antlers coming perilously close to whacking the terror-stricken guard, who ducked away. He was spooked beyond logic now and ran away as quickly as his blubbery butt could take him — to his red Esteem Independence 1500 electrical scooting conveyance — and whizzed away in ignominy-moose retreat.

Twenty-Three / Dreams

icar lay in bed, vividly experiencing a REM cycle convincing enough to make him believe he was wide awake. There was a familiar sensation that came over him when these dreams visited. They were different every time, but there was something about the mood, the tone, that was familiar, like he was returning to the source, his inner wellspring. They floated along, combining the past, the present, and the future in a signature style. He could usually untangle their meaning, but not always. Sometimes it took him months to figure out what they were telling him. They had to be coming from his own mind, but why would he disguise from himself their meaning with symbolic, easily misinterpreted metaphors? *So irritating.*

This time he was wandering through a forest, a lovely, familiar West Coast rainforest, very concerned, for some reason, about his footing. He leaned on a tree to steady himself and found that it was not a tree at all; he was propped against the leg of a gently swaying elephant, which turned to him and gazed probingly. Vicar was not afraid, but rather fascinated. She was a mother. She did not speak, yet somehow made him aware of it. He could feel her rough skin, he could sense her power and protectiveness. He knew he was safe, but she wanted him to come along with her. She had something in mind.

He felt her pushing him gently with her trunk toward a destination farther into the forest. After a short walk with the mother elephant, the forest stopped abruptly; it just ended, and he found himself looking at a large sandy desert. The elephant had departed or vanished and before him were a maned lion and a huge mama bear. Between them stood his friend and former patron Frankie Hall, tiny in comparison to the two huge animals and serenely floating off the sand just a little. She had one hand resting on the head of the lion, and the other on the massive head of the great bear, both of which appeared to have accompanied her there and were silent but watchful of him.

Vicar knew it meant something, could hear his own inner voice saying, "Remember this ... remember this ..."

Frankie's mouth moved; she was speaking but the words were delayed, like a video clip with bad synchronization.

"Be brave, my boy. Protect them. You must protect them." Frankie peered at him in warning, an indigo glow emanating from her forehead, radiating more intensely until it blotted out everything.

And then Vicar woke with a start, the bedsheets soaking wet from his sweat.

Still feeling a little muzzy from his fitful sleep, Vicar thought about his dream and attempted to tease out details, if he could. His car was making a buzzing, rattling noise when he revved it up and he was certain it was going to explode and possibly collapse into a pile of rubble at any second. It was old, but he still liked it. It had character; he thought it gave him the mien of a man who might wear a Basque beret occasionally. There was just something a bit dashing about having a French car, even though it was one of the cheapest models Peugeot made.

If it stopped working, getting it fixed required a long tow to the only place up here that fixed "exotic" imports — the squares here even thought German cars were exotic. But French? Might as well be from Betelgeuse. So, he accepted the risk, patted the ol' girl occasionally while whispering, "Good Peugeot," and changed the oil like clockwork. So far, so good, but if all went south, he vowed to give it a good, respectful burial, and possibly the Croix de Guerre.

Jacquie had suggested he buy the Honda Fit that had been the delivery vehicle for Konnie's Kountry Kottage, its logo still emblazoned on the doors. He dismissed the idea without any thought, saying, "Jack, I'm not buying a car that's named after a conniption." He shuddered at the thought of being seen in that car … or "kar." Yet he savoured the idea of a vehicle that had once been tasked with urgent, hand-knitted sock-puppet deliveries — Scramble the Fit!

He asked Poutine, knowledgeable in auto mechanics, to just look over the Peugeot, to give it to him straight: Was it going to up and die any day now? Poutine absolutely refused to check it out. It was one of those sissy-assed IM-ports. If it weren't DEE-troit steel, he weren't in'rested, dere. Vicar, not surprised at his stubborn refusal, was still amused that a man like Poutine didn't realize his prize Chevelle, the car by which he measured all others, was probably manufactured in Oshawa, Ontario, not "DEE-troit." He decided to keep that little nugget to himself. It might ruin Poutine's life.

Vicar kept the revs low and slowed down for a pedestrian, letting his gaze drift around as he glided to a rolling stop. *What the hell?* To his right, in the alley, was a moose. No, a person dressed as a moose. It was the mystery moose! It was staring right at him. He tightly closed his eyes twice to make sure he wasn't seeing something else. His eyesight was going for shite, after all. But it was the infamous moose, and in fact, it was carrying a sack. Vicar's head twisted around hard-right as he glided past the pedestrian who was now nearly on the other side of the street — and gunned his noisy car, making a quick right turn, and then another, hoping to head off the mysterious creature. He nipped quickly into the far mouth of the alleyway and zipped up the lane, certain the creature, or person, would still be there, but could see nothing, no one, nary a man nor moose. But it had only been twenty seconds …

It was just past closing time at the Knickers, and Beaner was loudly cleaning the kitchen, producing a racket with dirty pots and pans. In the front end, only Ann Tenna and Vicar remained, doing the last of the cleanup, all the patrons now departed.

Vicar saw it inside the pub for the first time. He was wiping the bar and had a direct line of sight to the huge fireplace across the room. There, apparently sitting upon, or hovering over, one of the chairs was the black oblong void, the same terrifying *thing* that had so spooked him upstairs. There were lights glowing pleasantly on the little alcove-like snug but at that moment the dark blackness of the void absorbed all the light. It was as jet black as anything Vicar had ever seen, its darkness making the wall behind it look as if it was producing an animated hole. He stiffened as Ann brought a tray of freshly washed mugs to the stack beside him.

She saw the expression on Vicar's face and glanced where he was staring. She saw nothing out of the ordinary — just the snug, which was, by the way, a pain in the arse to clean up because you hafta crawl 'round the booth on your knees to get at the back corner.

Vicar pointed to the black void, which undulated against the wall in unmistakably clear view, and whispered hollowly, "There it is, Annie."

Ann looked toward the area he was pointing, and then back at Vicar. She looked once again, but she could see nothing out of the ordinary. At that moment Vicar saw the void move slowly toward the front door.

"Oh my God, it's walking around!" Vicar felt shivers go up and down his spine as he instinctively backed up against the wall behind him, grabbing Ann and dragging her back with him. He told himself to really pay attention to the otherworldly sight before his eyes.

"What're yuz lookin' at?" she asked, oblivious to the sight and annoyed to be manhandled.

"Huh? Look! A black blob. The ghost …" He jabbed his finger directly toward it to show her its location.

"I don' see nuthin'."

"It's right THERE! Can't you see it? It's moving toward the door!" He was whispering hoarsely, his finger jabbing, his arm moving rapidly. Ann scrunched her face up in confusion and disbelief.

"Tony, uhhhhh … there's nuthin' there. Are you okay?"

The black blob suddenly winked out and disappeared. Vicar blinked rapidly several times, grateful that the blob hadn't been moose shaped, as Ann turned toward the kitchen pass through which Beaner now peered, having overheard the exchange. He was trying to put it all together, but his only hint came from Ann, who was giving Tony the side-eye and

spinning her index finger around the side of her head.
Kuh–RAY-zee …

━━ ━━ ━━

Cosmic Ray found himself standing on the sidewalk
of downtown Tyee Lagoon well after midnight, having hitchhiked his way up from the ferry terminal in
Victoria after an interminable bus trip from Santa Fe to
Port Angeles, Washington.

Surveying the streets of his old stomping grounds,
he didn't even know what day it was; all he was sure of
was that it was "fool's spring" — a deceptively warm
spasm of weather in late winter, warm enough for shirt
sleeves but liable to change without warning. He had
been away from Tyee Lagoon so long that all the changes left him a bit disoriented.

The cigar shop was gone. In its place was now a
walk-in clinic, which seemed smart. Farther down, he
saw the old Agincourt Hotel, huge metal trash bins
beside it, clearly being renovated, and walked past the
little grassy square bordering the tracks. Moths swirled
around buzzing street lights in the unseasonably warm
night, and there was no one in sight, not even a wandering cat. This was probably for the best as he was
dressed in a getup that would likely result in a call to
the police if he'd been seen. He knew he looked grubby,
hadn't shaved in days, and his dreadlocks needed a
thorough shampoo. Luckily, he had kind eyes, but they
peered out from a gnarly overgrowth of facial hair that

made him appear, as his dad would have said, "utterly unemployable."

His poncho disgorged dust as he walked, and on his feet, he wore a type of moccasin-like boot that went up to the knee. Over his shoulder he had the purplish bag that contained his life: the sitar and his other instruments, a modest bedroll, his few clothes, a pair of binoculars for stargazing, and a small pile of notebooks filled with musings and doodles.

Ray looked up at the sky and told the time by the position of the Big Dipper. Too late to go anywhere. He found a nice little area under a pair of bushy trees in the square, shielded from the street lights and pretty cozy compared to some of the digs he'd slept in over the last while. He pulled out his bedroll and arranged it on the flattest spot he could find, gambling that the sky would not fill with clouds and unleash rain upon him while he slept. Sleeping rough in the cold rain was the worst. He hoped Vicar was still around; he would start looking for him in the morning.

■ ■ ■

Beaner was huffing and puffing in the kitchen, doing his best to keep up with the orders. His hairnetted underlings raced around to keep up to his desired speed and efficiency. He was such an easygoing guy, but as "Chef" he ran a tight ship. Every once and a while he'd yell out a response to Ann Tenna, who had taken to calling out to him frequently and making him a staple of her big show.

"HEY, BEANER, FIRE WHOEVER WROTE THE MENU. THIS GUY CAN'T READ IT." She pointed at the handwritten chalkboard hung near the bar.

Beaner's voice echoed from the kitchen, "You wrote it!"

"GOTTA FIRE M'SELF. BUH-BYE." And she marched right out the front door, all the clientele laughing at her strange behaviour.

Her act had already become standard operating procedure, and for inexplicable reasons had had no negative effect on business. Quite the contrary. It had taken Vicar a few weeks to fully understand it, but people came here just to experience her bawdy schtick. Anyone too picky or too slow to order got the gears at the highest volume. He hoped she didn't catch on to how much of a draw she had become because he couldn't possibly afford to pay her what she was worth. She was no server; she had become an entertainment attraction.

From behind the bar, he watched as she pretended to panhandle in the street, her customers chuckling, now able to confirm reports about "that crazy barmaid."

She accosted an approaching man, and then dropped the act as he spoke with her. She pointed over her shoulder with her thumb toward the Knickers, and the man walked to the door.

Vicar recognized the silhouette of the stranger instantly. *Oh my God*, he thought. *It's Ray.*

When Cosmic Ray walked through the door, he was thrown off. He had remembered the old beer parlour — who didn't? — but the changes wrought here were astonishing. And then he noticed Tony Vicar, standing behind the bar with his jaw agape, mouthing, "*Ray?*"

Vicar had a little bit of grey at his temples and had gained a few pounds. Not too many, but he bulged a bit more now — visual evidence of regular feedings. Tony must be getting something other than ketchup chips and jerky from the Turbo station in his diet.

Ray smiled and moved toward Vicar with his arms spread wide. Vicar shuffled hesitantly toward him, confused about the apparition before his eyes. For just an instant he wondered if there might be a selfish motivation for Ray's reappearance, prompted by all the press hoopla, and then shoved the thought aside. Ray had gone weird, but he had never once been calculating.

"I'm sorry, my brother. I'm so sorry I disappeared."

"Ray, Ray. For God's sake, where did you go? I was worried for months." He found himself hugging Cosmic Ray, who smelled full-on hippie, ponging of exotic oils, emollients, and dust.

"I know. My world changed. I had to get away."

Vicar pulled out a chair from the nearest table and motioned to Ray that he should sit down. And so, for the next two hours, Vicar listened as Ray unfurled his tale.

▬ ▬ ▬

Cosmic Ray's odyssey was recounted with meandering but familiar delivery that seemed to have gotten worse with time. Vicar was sure that if anyone else had had several years to rehearse an explanation, or whatever the hell *this* was, they'd be more composed than ol' Ray was at that moment. When he got nervous, he had an editing problem — he wandered so much that Vicar found himself rocking back and forth slightly, repeating in his head, *The point, the point, get to the point.*

Ray muttered, voice too low to be heard clearly, leaving Vicar to fill in huge tranches of missing audio. He scratched his arm impatiently in response to the inchoate tale; he decided to forgive Ray almost immediately, just so he'd stop rambling. He had always considered him a great guy, but now he remembered how effing annoying he could be — Ray too often left Vicar weary and baffled.

He gently put his hand on Ray's leg, as if pressing an imaginary pause button, and sifted through his jumble about chakras, spirit animals, and a dog that could talk (Ray swore he'd witnessed the phenomenon himself). *Sounds like peyote*, Vicar mused. As near as he could tell, Ray felt he had been selected as a special emissary who would act as liaison for "the human species" when the extraterrestrials revealed themselves to earthlings. He gave no date for this imminent event.

"You'll see, Tony. They're coming back. They put us here in the first place …" He conversationally ambled toward the ancient Sumerians for a few minutes.

Vicar kept a straight face but was positive that the last bong hoot administered by Farley and his Douche Bassoon, just before Ray stumbled away on that fateful night, had pushed Ray permanently over the edge. Clearly, he had had a powerful hallucination, an awakening sufficiently illuminating to knock him unconscious. Now that was a tidy little irony.

While Ray wistfully described his intricate interstellar impressions, Vicar found himself drifting off, disengaging from Ray's tortuous style, wondering if the next miracle in his life might be the rebirth of their band, a mighty power triangle.

Vicar became unmoored with remarkable speed, disregarding the all too obvious pitfalls, the biggest of which sat before him, meandering through a bizarre story. Immediately conjuring exciting, sunny scenarios, he heard himself saying, *It's right there before you, plopped into your lap.* He was enticed and anxious at the thought.

The old worries about Ray's tenuous connection to reality were tossed aside without a second thought; the seductive, majestic vision had coalesced and the madness they call "being in a band" took hold. *By God, a rebirth of the group was the reason for Ray's sudden re-appearance,* thought Vicar. Emotions swirled; with Ray back, would Hospital Fish be truly reborn, remounted, and triumphant?

Yes, it was more than possible! Thoroughly un-warranted musical confidence came winging back, blotting out any flaws in the plan, jetting off into the sky like a flock of excited rooks.

PART II

Twenty-Five / A Babe in the Woods

The forest sucked up all ambient light and left a blanket of black upon the houses of Sloop Road. A young woman drove slowly, shakily, toward her destination on that cloudy moonless night, her headlights barely piercing the wintry gloom. At the crest of the hill, she pulled over and turned off the engine of her little car.

Beside her was a newborn infant, wrapped in a couple of ragged blankets and placed inside a cardboard beer box. With unsteady hands she picked up the box and quietly shut the door with her hip. She limped painfully down the driveway almost as if shuffling to the gallows. Huge snowflakes fell gently, resting on her hair.

Her emotions were in a cyclone of conflict, whirling her around, dashing her against rocks, and making her feel momentarily nauseated. Finally, she took hold of herself, set the box containing the baby down at the landing of the old Tudor house, and rang the doorbell repeatedly while screaming at the top of her lungs.

When she saw a light click on through the frosted glass, she hobbled as fast as she could up the pathway toward her car, started it, and fled at high speed through the blanket of snow.

Tony Vicar, hair askew and wearing only tighty-whities, clicked on the front light and cracked the door cautiously. He saw tail lights receding through the trees, heard the roar of an over-revving engine, and discovered, right at his feet, being slowly bedazzled in snowflakes nearly the size of his palm, a softly crying baby.

■ ■ ■

Jacquie, jarred awake by the ruckus, thought at first that she was having a nightmare and found herself suddenly holding an infant, snuggling it closely. She was in shock, flooding with tears and feeling a crazy mixture of anger, outrage, sympathy, and protectiveness.

"Who? Who …?" She couldn't even speak.

She didn't need to. Tony Vicar had the same question. Who would abandon a newborn on their doorstep in the middle of a frigid winter night? Who had even dreamed of such a cold-hearted act? Leaving a baby in a basket on the church steps was an old trope, based on truth, but ghastly. And now, before their eyes was a real-life baby, suddenly left in their care. *Why them?* Vicar didn't have the first idea what to do. He didn't even know how to hold a newborn. What a bizarre Valentine's Day gift.

Jacquie struggled to find her mental footing.

The snow, which had been rather pretty when they'd gone to bed, was now falling heavily and there was already a thick blanket on the lawn and walkway.

Vicar looked at her, confused, and asked, "Who do we call? It's three in the morning!"

Jacquie glanced out the window at the worsening weather, her eyes rimmed with concern, and said, "Maybe we should call Con-Con."

"Call the police?" Vicar asked.

"No, call Con-Con at home and ask her what we should do."

She meant Hayley Constanz, member of the small local Mountie detachment, and known by most of the longtime residents of Tyee Lagoon as Con-Con. Yes. She would know what to do.

Vicar aimlessly looked around for his phone, slightly shell-shocked and unable to organize his thoughts. Jacquie was staring at the infant in her arms, cooing at it and rocking it. Was this babe a boy or a girl? They hadn't even figured that much out yet.

Finally finding his phone under a blanket on the couch he scrolled to find the correct number. At that moment the power went out, an all too familiar event when it snowed, and plunged them into darkness.

It was going to be a long, cold night.

"Hullo?" Con-Con asked groggily. *What time is it?*

Scratchy connection, then a voice. "Con-Con? It's Tony. We don't know what to do with this baby ..."

Baby? She squinted her eyes a few times, unable to see clearly. "Did you guys have a baby?" she asked with some alarm. Had they kept the pregnancy a secret? Was it a preemie? Were they in medical trouble? Con-Con laid out a comprehensive list of possible emergencies at lightning speed, even in her half-awake state, as well as a concise list of responses to nearly every one of them.

"No, no ... Sorry. I'm in a flap ..."

"Calm down, Tony. Just tell me what happened."

Con-Con's partner, Nancy, was awake now, squinting from the light of the bedside lamp, which had dragged her out of a perfectly satisfactory dream. Listening quietly, she tried to figure out the nature of the emergency. Late-night police calls out here in the country were few and far between, but when they came, Con-Con was out the door like a shot. They usually involved gory car crashes.

"Someone left a newborn baby at our doorstep, Con-Con."

"Couldn't this prank wait till morning?"

"I wish it were a prank."

At that moment, the baby erupted in a soft but hungry cry and Con-Con snapped fully awake.

"Oh my lord, Tony. You're not kidding!"

"No. I ... I mean we don't know what to do. I mean. Uhh ... It's ... a ... real baby. Y'know. Baby ... *stuff.*"

He could do no better than to stammer, the present situation being so strange and intense.

"Nancy and I will come up right away to help you guys."

"Thanks so much. Uh, bring a couple of flashlights. The power went out a few minutes ago."

Con-Con instinctively looked at the time on the clock radio: 3:22 a.m. She heard Jacquie in the background, clearly amped up, her voice sounding a bit panicky. "I think the baby's hungry. Tony, find food. Milk. Ack, what do you feed these things?"

"Tony!" Con-Con yelled to get his attention and gain some control over the rising panic over there. "Does the baby have any diapers or formula? Maybe a bottle? Was it left with anything?"

"No, no … The little one was in a cardboard box, wrapped in blankets."

She could hear Vicar stumbling around, swearing as he accidentally kicked a piece of furniture, the sounds of drawers opened and slammed shut clattering in her ear. Jacquie's voice rose into a state of alarm and was stuttering, on the verge of panic in the background, urging him to simply *do something*.

He took the phone from his ear and barked at her, "Whaddya want me to do, Jack? Rip up sheets and boil some goddamn water?" Jacquie went silent but her eyes continued broadcasting a red alert.

Water … Right … "Con-Con, if you can bring some water, too … No power — the pump for the well won't work either."

"Oh, man, the plot thickens," she replied.

With that, Con-Con's cordless phone went dead — the power had suddenly gone off at her house, too, plunging the bedroom into darkness.

Vicar's mobile phone had dropped the connection with Con-Con and he glanced out the window into the yard. Snow was coming down heavily now, obscuring the view, and the road was coated thickly with a blanket of slippery white flakes.

"Jacquie, I've *gotta* get help." He looked around the darkened living room as if assistance might be hiding over in the shadows.

Jacquie rocked the crying infant and looked at Vicar, her eyes rimmed with extreme urgency. *Yes. Do something, anything.* Vicar stared at her for just a second and thought, *We couldn't have been less prepared for this if we'd made it our life's goal.*

Jacquie carefully laid the baby on the couch while Vicar held the one flashlight he could find in the cupboard, which only came to life after he whacked it with the flat of his hand a couple of times. She gently took off the blankets to find the baby, a girl, it turned out, naked with a long umbilical cord flapping around, having been cut or bitten off a few inches down its length. For some reason Vicar was so angry at the sight that he nearly screamed. How *dare* anyone do this to a baby?

Snapping himself out of his state, he felt his way to the kitchen and rummaged through a drawer, finding a snap clip for potato chip bags. He came back and gingerly clipped it onto the umbilical cord at its base, and then stood back, feeling his head jerking back and forth, almost as if he was trying to sift better ideas through a screen in his skull.

"Well, she's a little girl. And that's pretty well *all* we know."

"Am I going to have to take her to gymnastics classes?" said Vicar, completely dazed.

Jacquie looked up at him as if he were from Mars. "Huh?" she blurted.

He was already grappling with the thought of this child abandoned forever. "Nothing. Nothing. I'm just babbling." Suddenly, Vicar blurted, "Merri!"

Jacquie knew precisely what he meant. Merri Crabtree lived close by. Maybe she still had power? Maybe she would know what to do?

"Yes. Go. Go now!"

Vicar flapped around the house. He found a heavy coat in the hall closet, and mercifully a hat and some gloves were on the shelf above. *What were the chances of that?* he mused.

"Okay," Vicar yelled. "I'm going."

Jacquie felt her anxiety rise when she realized she'd be alone with this crying, hungry baby, for how long she didn't know. She peered at Vicar, who was pacing in the entryway. Something wasn't right.

Then it dawned on her. "Pants! Pants!" she yelled with urgency. He had put on a winter coat but was so flapped that he had forgotten to don trousers.

"Aarrgh," Vicar moaned, in a muddle. He kicked off his shoes and stumbled to the bedroom to fetch some jeans.

Con-Con gunned the engine and the car swerved shakily out of the driveway and onto the road. She couldn't believe how bad the conditions had become since they'd gone to bed.

As a cop her driving skills were superior to most, but she cursed herself for not having bought an SUV. This stupid sedan was almost certain to leave them in the lurch. The wheels grabbed and threw them to the right, and she swore. Nancy tensed but stayed quiet; Con-Con corrected and rumbled onward.

Near the junction where she'd need to turn right and up the now treacherous hill to Sloop Road, she had to stop short. There, before her, were two, perhaps three — she couldn't tell in the poor light — huge trees lying across the road. It was blocked from the north and the south, neatly boxing off the intersection. Until crews arrived the next morning the whole area on the hill would be isolated. Shining a flashlight, she saw another tree across the rise, this one blocking the high roadway down to the junction. There were electrical power lines down everywhere, and this was a rotten mess. Barring a four-kilometre trudge through shin-deep snow, past downed power lines, up a steep hill, in the dark of night, Jacquie, Vicar, and the little baby were stuck.

━ ━ ━

Vicar's Peugeot with the balding all-season tires couldn't even make it up the driveway. He slid and went partially sideways and eventually gave up, rolling back downhill to the flat area below.

He then tried Jacquie's Jetta, sturdy and sure-footed, yet had no luck at all. Neither of their cars had the tires to deal with this freakish snowfall, a barely frozen slush. Thank heavens it hadn't come in the middle of the day, he thought. The normal pattern of the local drivers was to spend a half-hour trying to back the Buick out of the grocery store parking stall without death or dismemberment. If they saw snow, they'd utterly panic and drive home at warp speed for the first time in a quarter century, trying to "beat the storm," resulting in all the ditches filled with senior citizens, cold, confused, and worried sick about their cats.

Vicar kicked himself for his lack of preparedness. He never seemed to have a snow shovel handy, or good tires. After all, winters here generally took the form of incessant rain — but when it did snow, things became a shit show almost immediately. He rebuked himself for the countless times he'd laughed at news reports about people freezing in Florida or Texas during an unseasonable cold snap. "Put on a coat!" he'd jeer at the TV. But here he was, an embarrassingly ill-equipped Canadian standing in a blizzard without even a pair of proper boots.

Given the urgency of the situation, Vicar set out on foot in his running shoes, struggling to keep his balance on the grade, sliding and nearly falling. The snow had obscured everything, and he was unable to tell where the road ended and the ditch began until he was nearly falling into it. He hadn't taken their one rather pathetic flashlight, having left it for Jacquie and the little baby. All he had was the light on his phone, which at any rate was best served as a torch now as there appeared to be no signal anymore. Vicar thought cell towers had back-up power, but if so, it hadn't kicked in tonight.

Feeling his way down Brigantine Crescent, he saw Merri's house at its very end. Plodding through the thickening snow, he thudded up the steps onto the front deck and pounded on the door with his gloved fist.

After a time, he saw a flashlight moving down a hallway, and then Merri's face appeared in the kitchen window, which looked onto the deck.

"Merri! It's me, Tony! Help. Jacquie and I have an emergency. We need help!"

That's all Merri needed to hear. She hustled around the corner to the front door and unlocked it.

"Goodness gracious. What's the trouble, dear?" How the hell could she be so chirpy at four in the morning?

"Merri, someone has abandoned a baby at our doorstep. We have no power; we have no phone. We don't know what to do ... Can you help?"

"A baby? A human baby?"

"Yes," he clipped, momentarily exasperated. As if he'd come up here in the middle of the worst storm in twenty-five years to wake her over a basket of puppies. "A little girl, it appears. We don't know who did it or why ... Nothing. We're panicking. Jacquie's all alone with her and hasn't the first clue what to do."

Merri Crabtree could clearly see that Vicar's emergency was real.

"Now take off those wet shoes and help me gather some stuff. We have work to do ..."

"... Tea kettle ... This little chaise to lay the baby on ... A couple of soft blankies. Mmm ... Do you have a fire going?"

"Yes, I stoked it up before I left. Jacquie and the baby are plenty warm. There's lots of firewood." *That was about all I was able to do*, he said to himself.

Merri was well stocked because her grandson had just turned four years old and had recently needed these items.

"Here's an old bottle and some plastic liners ..." Merri kept muttering as she collected this and that.

Vicar stopped listening and just let her dump every-thing into the bag over his shoulder or the laundry bas-ket in his arms.

"How old do you think the little darling is?" Merri asked.

"Uhh … Well … She still has part of her umbilical cord attached."

Even she, the imperturbably upbeat optimist, felt all her indicators leap up to "critical" with that. "Oh my lord! We have to get there immediately!"

Racing now, yet careful to ensure she had plenty of tea bags, honey, milk, her favourite mug, and a little folding crib, not to mention a tin of baby formula, a large Thermos bottle filled with hot water boiled quickly on her gas stove, and even a couple of plush toys, she exited the house via a door directly into the double garage. There, next to her little electric runabout, was a big, chunky Land Rover, a vehicle clearly up to the weather challenges they faced.

With Vicar's help she raised the garage door to re-veal well over a foot of wet, slimy snow with the heavy blizzard incessantly depositing more. Making a sour face, she turned to Vicar and put the fob in his palm with both of her hands.

"You drive, dear. I'm just the pits in this kind of weather."

"Oh no, you aren't, Merri," he said gratefully. "You're in your element."

Serena had barely made it back to the motel before the snowfall had gotten too heavy to drive, and she stumbled into its cold, drab confines in a mental state that was near collapse. She looked back blankly at the snow she'd tracked onto the carpet and fell apart in wracking sobs and gushing tears, crumpling onto the hard and uncomfortable bed.

Of all the things she'd done in her life this one was the worst. But she didn't know where to turn. She was as alone as she had ever been, and the only lifeline she knew was Vicar, as pathetic as that was. She had really fucked up this time. Serena's anxiety rose inch by inch until she passed out from hyperventilation.

When Vicar returned with Merri in tow, he found Jacquie leaping madly around the house with a crying baby in her arms, up to highest dough over a wasp that had been hibernating in the firewood. It had come to and was flying around drunkenly. Jacquie was certain it was delivered there specifically to attack her and the newborn infant. She made little squeaking sounds as she swerved about, ducking and double stepping like a boxer in training.

"Jack! It's only a wasp. Just shoo it out the door." Vicar looked at the strange pantomime happening and realized he had to get Jacquie back to earth before they could do anything for the baby. In his present prickly state of crisis management, it irked him to see her flailing about. Her trademark had always been her level head.

That was Merri's cue — she strode in and occupied the kitchen like an invading field marshal, immediately giving orders and fixing up some formula as the first order of business.

"Calm down, child!" she said sharply to Jacquie. "How can you take care of a human life when you're afraid of a bug?" She was very serious but immediately followed her rebuke with her signature, all-forgiving laugh.

Jacquie went silent and sat down, embarrassed.

Con-Con and Nancy had never shown up and the phones were dead. Vicar couldn't even find out if they were okay. But now the baby had been fed and dressed in a diaper far too large for her, then swaddled tightly in a receiving blanket. Merri rocked her as she spoke in low tones.

"This baby is hours old. She needs someone around the clock. I don't think anyone can get through to help in this weather, so I'd better stay here with you for a while. You need a crash course in parenting, you two."

Jacquie looked at her with gratitude and relief. Vicar, completely dazed, looked off into the middle distance, feeling like he might barf.

No one had been able to get through the incessant blizzard. The snow came down hour after endless hour. They had been stuck indoors, no electricity for seventy hours by Vicar's count, their only supply of water melted snow warmed up on the constantly burning wood stove. Going without power was quite a hassle, yet doable, but having no running water … Well, it threw them back to the Stone Age.

They got almost no rest as they tried to learn how to care for a newborn while stumbling around in the dark, putting the contents of fridge and freezer out into snowbanks, digging through every hutch and drawer for candles. Despite this, Vicar was delighted to discover how many things he could cook on a gas BBQ — but then just as quickly began to worry about wasting propane. Whatever was left of his bachelor-esque "who gives a shit" vibe was quickly squelched down to almost nothing. Now he gave a very big shit, indeed.

The phones finally began to function, and Vicar spent a long time speaking with Child Services, trying to explain the situation — attempting to figure out what the next steps would be. Surely, there was a family responsible for this little child, somewhere. Babies don't just drop out of the sky onto your doorstep.

✖ ✖ ✖

Merri was back home now that the lights and water were functional again; Vicar and Jacquie were able to sit down and take stock for the first time in days. Jacquie spoke. "Well, we're not going to just call her 'baby.' We hafta give her a name. Even a nickname. Something to give her an identity."

She was quite insistent, though Vicar thought this was like a kid naming someone else's puppy that she'd found in the alley.

Smartassed, and desperate to change the mood, Vicar chirped, "Sure, let's name her after your mother!"

The look of disgust on Jacquie's face was one for the ages. Vicar couldn't help but burst out in laughter.

"Beulah? You want us to name this precious little thing *Beulah*?"

"Sure. Lovely lady — a little loony, I grant you, but she has a tried-and-true name."

Vicar knew that Jacquie's mother drove her around the bend. She was not the first woman he'd known who felt this way; he'd met other women who seemed to feel similarly about their own moms. It wasn't a deep loathing, just knee-jerk revulsion. Beulah was, after all, a *huge* character, which he loved, but Jacquie seemed embarrassed about — he could not understand it. He would have been very happy to still have a mom at all, no matter how outrageous. He presumed Jacquie's patience with him stemmed from years of close-up experience with dear, wacky Beulah.

Jacquie took a sharp breath and suddenly said, "Tony … we should call her *Frankie*."

Vicar's jaw dropped. That was *exactly* what they should call her.

Damn, first the pub, now the baby … Jacquie is really good at naming stuff.

Unlike any feeling he had ever experienced before, Vicar felt the cozy warmth of an infant. With the baby only in a diaper and snuggling against his shirtless chest, they lay skin to skin — his hand cupping her diapered bum and fingers of his other hand lightly touching her shoulder. Frankie's wandering eyes looked up at him as she made sweet sounds, grabbing his chest hair as if she wanted to pull it out by the clump. He felt a contentment that he had never known before, almost a completeness. Jacquie sat on the edge of the bed and just watched the two of them.

"A bit of a distance from living with Farley and Ray, huh?"

He just looked up at her and raised his eyebrows. It was as if someone had picked him up and gently moved him into a completely different dimension that had been unobservable from the Bachelor Pad, back on Earth.

"Jack, don't take it too hard, but I think I might be falling in love with another girl."

"I have been sharing you with other women since day one. Frankie Hall practically adopted you."

"Yeah. But you know, she lost her husband and her only son. Maybe I was a surrogate."

"Yes, yes. You're a perfect stand-in for dead guys ... and yet so lifelike." He rolled his eyes.

She continued, "I've watched your 'fans.' They want a little piece of TVic. You, my good man, are prime rib on sale. Good thing I'm not the jealous type." She winked.

Vicar was all too aware that Jacquie didn't need to waste time on petty jealousies, yet remembered how bad a licking she had laid on Serena when she had perpetrated her bizarre nude home invasion when they first began dating. *No, not the jealous type at all ...*

▬ ▬ ▬

Tyee Lagoon had been utterly electrified when the news leaked out that Vicar and Jacquie had discovered little Frankie on their doorstep. Calls came in, one on top of the other; texts lit up the blowers; the internet was abuzz; neighbours and friends popped in, desperate to confirm the truth of the unlikely tale. Vicar was surprised at the fuss exploding from mere acquaintances and near strangers. *Yes, a little girl. No, we don't have a clue who the parents are. Yes, yes, it's very sad. Well, thanks for saying that, but we're just doing what anyone would have ...*

Vicar, in charge of a newborn for less than a week, knowing they would have to give her back, suddenly found himself sick at the thought of it.

━━ ━━ ━━

Vicar hung up the phone and looked disconsolately out the window. Finally, he turned toward Jacquie.

"They said that they have to come take Frankie and have doctors look her over — and try to find her mother, or any family."

Jacquie looked stricken. "I ... I don't know if I like that ..."

"Well, Jack, she's not ours. We have to give her back."

Jacquie looked at the cooing babe in her lap and her eyes got misty.

"Tony, where is she going to live? In a facility? An infant prison? What has she ever done to deserve that kind of treatment?" She looked at Vicar, who had tried to suppress his parental feelings but suddenly felt them surge forth in an upwelling of extreme emotion. Breathing deeply a few times, he finally spoke.

"No, Jack, they place babies with foster families, people who have experience doing it, I guess."

"We have experience," she protested.

"Five days of it." He looked at her sadly. *Not enough, not enough.*

✗ ✗ ✗

They arrived to take baby Frankie away. The two social workers, not jail guards but professionals, were sensitive to the stormy sea of conflict that their arrival brought. Jacquie was in such a state when she handed over little Frankie that the woman from the ministry had to wrap her arm around her shoulder and take her into the other room, whispering in her ear.

Vicar wasn't weeping, but he was shaking like sand in an earth tremor. He was sick at heart, so keyed up he thought he might pass out.

"Look, I know this is difficult. It's not only the law, but the right thing to do, to find her blood family, if we can. Surely, you can appreciate that, Mr. Vicar."

"Yeah, I understand but I don't have to like it. Who knows what she'll face? A woman that abandons her child can't possibly be a reliable mother to her." Vicar felt sure of it.

"Well, that's not necessarily the case … There are so many factors involved in a decision like the one that brought you Frankie — is that what you've called her?"

"Yes, Frankie. Named after a … a … grandmother." He said it to save reciting a long, complicated story.

"Right. Also, we might discover that, even if the mother doesn't want her, the father might. Or aunties, or grandparents."

"Yes, but we can care for her perfectly well, right here. We're all set up. We don't even miss the sleep …" He was pleading now.

"Mr. Vicar, I give you my word that if required you will be considered for foster care. We have families in the area, but they can't always help. So, there's a chance."

Vicar brightened at the glimmer of hope.

"But of course, we still have to find her real family."

Vicar looked down at the floor and nodded in resignation. Voluntarily handing over that little girl was like agreeing to have a limb hacked off.

▬ ▬ ▬

Serena's thoughts had slowed down enough that she could think it through now. The baby was safe. She didn't know how to care for it; she could barely care for herself. Vicar was the only person she knew who had the tools to give her baby a home. Every other person she had ever known had disappointed, or hurt, or used her. Or died. If she had any worries about the tremendous upset the sudden appearance of an infant might cause in his life, she glossed over it — just like you don't worry about the mess you're making when you put out a fire. You just deal with it and clean up afterward.

Twenty-Eight / Starry, Starry Night

Vicar couldn't sleep so he put on slippers and padded through the living room, past the old piano with the photographs on it. He glanced at the image of Frankie Hall and her husband and saw that the carnation in the vase beside the shot of Billy Jr., her soldier son killed in battle so long ago, needed replacing.

He walked out onto the deck that looked over the ocean and gazed up at the sky. He knew he should be freezing, but somehow, he felt perfectly comfortable. All the snow had vanished, almost as quickly as it had arrived; all that was left were huge pond-like puddles, filling every low piece of ground.

Through the tall Douglas firs, he looked at the moon, low in the southwest and due to set soon, its soft glow washing out most of the stars. Behind him he could still see the Big Dipper, Cassiopeia, and, ahead,

Sirius wending its way down to the horizon. It wouldn't be too long before Orion, which Sirius followed like the loyal Dog Star it was, would set for the season and the warmer weather would arrive.

The night sky always spoke to him in a soothing way. It was black but he imagined it in the deepest indigo. The icy-white pinpoints of light he interpreted in rich colour. He loved to look at the stars, knowing that the light hitting his eyes might have left them longer ago than he'd been alive, sometimes longer than civilization had existed, and occasionally, longer than primates had swung from the trees. But there it was, tonight, above his mortal and worried head, as if all purely for his personal pleasure, like an unimaginably lavish gift. No one had yet found a way to charge a fee for a glimpse. *Give them time, give them time ...* He knew they eventually would.

The stars glittered brightly, unperturbed by his earthly worries, and reminded him that some things do go on practically forever, profoundly, quietly, endlessly, although no human could ever experience a similar infinity; few could even manage to grapple with the concept. He was at that moment grateful to even be aware of his own puniness. He knew that baby Frankie would come back to them, that they would become a family. It wasn't a hope, or a wish, or a negotiation with an invisible power. It was just a calm certainty that she would return. There was a more profound connection between him and the infant than merely a newly awakened nurturing instinct. No, this was deeper, older. He could not find the words, or nail down the emotion, although it seemed to combine responsibility with exultation. His mind's eye saw the starry sky being distorted, briefly allowing a glimpse of metaphorical buttresses that held it aloft, like the ribs of a cosmic tent. The vision wavered like a liquid and then returned to its familiar self.

As Vicar did in these meditative moments, rare and getting rarer, he visualized his energy, golden electricity coursing downward through his feet. At the same time energy escaped his head and raised hands, shooting upward toward the distant stars. He diverted some of it to encompass Frankie and, of course, Jacquie, who lay deeply asleep in the bedroom. *Just visualization, no big deal*, he told himself. But it made him feel grounded, balanced just a little bit — perhaps wishfully in control, and seated in his correct place on the fulcrum between earth and sky.

━ ▬ ▬

Ray, like Farley or Ross Poutine, had free rein to wander around the hotel and observe the renovation. Farley was offhand about it, mostly concerned about the Jacuzzi tub that was gonna be in the third-floor suite. *Classy!*

But Ray felt something. There was a vibe here, in the pub, in the hotel; something that he hadn't felt very often back here at home but had sensed a lot when he'd been in the desert. A presence, an essence, maybe a personality. There was something alive in this building that wasn't fully human, he felt sure of it. He slowly wandered the poorly lit hallways, touching walls and rattling doorknobs, just sensing the environment. It was just like when he talked to *the others* who orbited high above, always with one eye upon him. He didn't use words, but he knew they understood.

One phone call can change everything. Farley was so moved he had tears in his eyes. Vicar had sorta mentioned to him that it might be possible to get the band back together now that Ray was back, but he didn't want to rush things. Leave it a few weeks. *The hell with THAT!* Farley climbed on the blower the very next day.

He had somehow worked up the gumption and simply blurted out the question, "Ray, d'ya wanna git th' band back together?"

Ray had known the question would be coming soon and replied hesitantly, "I, I, uh, think so ... I always felt bad leaving you guys hanging ..." He found himself saying, perhaps a little reluctantly, the words that he knew Farley — and especially Tony — would want to hear. He felt like a mother agreeing to take her twelve-year-old son to a demolition derby. His enjoyment would have to come from their enjoyment.

Farley hung up and then immediately called Vicar, repeating the news. Vicar made him reconfirm it twice.

"Yeah, no, yeah … He feels bad 'bout breaking up the band. He wants to give 'er a go again."

He could hear furniture getting bumped as Vicar pranced around in delight. "Goddamn it, Farley, I *do* have mystical powers, after all!" For what might be the first time in his life, Farley had taken the reins, yet Vicar was convinced that he had, somehow, created this "miracle." The subtle dominance he had over his music-al sidekick had reared its unkind head for just a moment as Vicar swerved briefly into believing his own hype. He began to sing some hellish melody beyond his highest notes, sounding like an over-cranked power-steering pump.

Farley, all alone in his little basement suite, so accustomed to being overshadowed that he barely took notice, threw down his phone and started rocking his ill-coiffed melon like a headbanger, his toque flying off. A second chance! He felt his excitement rising and heard his inner voice say, *Farley, youze gotta keep 'er steady.*

Vicar was pacing around the house. *So awesome.* For the moment, he completely forgot the funk he was in about baby Frankie, the grief about his malfunctioning junk, the constant pressure to be the Liquor Vicar. Getting the band back together! He could push it all aside for a while if they could pick up the threads of Hospital Fish again.

"Showcase at the Knickers … We'll just do the 'riginals," Vicar said excitedly to an empty room. Hyperactively he began to paw through drawers and boxes for set lists and old rehearsal tapes.

Yes, they'd do their best tunes, the batch of songs he had written all that time ago with a heavily theatrical stage show in mind. He had even kept a couple of the costumes but was sure Farley wouldn't have kept track of his — and Ray, well, he'd abandoned almost all his belongings years ago.

He found cassette tapes in a drawer, and peered at them wistfully as he fancied how very close they surely must have been to a huge breakout. One tape read, *The Battle of the Undersea Forest: Radio Edit*. A showstopper; it would have been the climax to their big concert set. They'd had to cut it down from 12:20 to eight minutes. Farley had been bummed that they hacked out the bass solo. It was less a solo than just the same old part, a little louder and with guitar laying out. Vicar remembered getting bored partway through and peppering it with porno-style jigga-jigga-bow flourishes.

He glossed over the fact that they'd never even played an "A" room in Vancouver, not once, not even as an opening act. They hadn't been able to get a gig at even a stinky old dive in Victoria, not even for free. No audience outside of Tyee Lagoon had ever seen them except at that one "outdoor show," which had in fact been a picnic put on by the Regional Hospital Foundation, who had accidentally hired them, mistakenly thinking their name was Hospital *Wish*.

As soon as they began their set, almost everyone was motioning to turn it down. One lady sent up a note stating that "although melodious, you need to turn it down a few amplitudes." A postscript went on to request that they play the "Macarena" accompanied by a little happy face. Vicar was aghast. *These fools*, he thought. *We're giving them an audiovisual feast and they're acting like someone just took a crap in the middle of their stupid corn roast.* And the "Macarena"? Why not get Barney the purple dinosaur to sit in on vocals, too?

One woman from the entertainment committee scurried over to reason with Vicar, who was in high dudgeon about the appalling rudeness of the crowd.

"Do you think we're a jukebox? Ma'am, we are ARTISTS. This is Hospital Fish, a power triangle of art, folklore, and metal."

The woman, utterly out of her depth speaking with such an *artiste*, couldn't find the words. She was afraid that this effing weirdo in his mauve sushi jammies of satin-like polyester would eject his Pop Tarts and maybe even start spewing medieval incantations.

Her brow had creased as she pointed to a long line of audience members, some in wheelchairs, who, almost to a person, had their fingers stuck in their ears. One old fart was giving them a thumbs-down like an unsympathetic Caesar Imperator; Vicar bared his teeth but stifled a growl. The woman turned to Vicar and put her hands out, palms up, and made a silent plea.

Vicar, indignant, looked at the horrified audience and reluctantly turned down his amp.

■ ■ ■

As he leaned against the bar, Vicar explained to Jacquie that he wanted to present their old band as the first group to perform at the Knickers. Ray was back and raring to go, he proclaimed. He dreamily told her about the vibe of the group, using a few descriptors that had her feeling increasingly uneasy. When he said, "experimental progressive metal and orchestral music," she juddered.

"Oh God, Tony. This is a pub. Can't you just play 'Knees Up Mother Brown'?"

"Jacquie, this is *serious music*, electric symphonic explorations with multiple movements."

Jacquie was mocking now. "There'll be multiple *movements* all right." She jutted out her bum as she delivered the line.

"Haw-haw, Jacquie," Vicar said, irked. "You just don't have any feel for the arts. Don't trample on my dream." He paused and then lowered his voice. "I've been wanting to get this band back together for *years*."

Yes, you've been wanting to since this stuff was out of style the first time around. She took a deep breath, calling on invisible forces for patience and understanding, and asked, "What do you call this artsy agglomeration?" She braced for the bad news.

"*Hospital Fish.*" He said it with a lofty flourish of the fingers, like a cornball illusionist.

Her eyes bulged in disbelief. This was really going to be a shit show.

Jacquie had, with great difficulty, persuaded Vicar to admit that a permanent stage in the Knickers was simply not going to work. But, added to the high strangeness about the origins of his newly diagnosed infertility and how wrung out they both were over baby Frankie, she felt guilty about not supporting his band, however ghastly it might be.

Certain that it was the worst band name yet — out of a field of dozens of true stinkers — she was somehow convinced by a nearly pleading Vicar to let them give it a try. Jacquie insisted they limit their appearance to *one time only* and forevermore forget the idea of building a stage in the beautiful interior of the Knickers. She knew she'd have to be cagey.

"Oh, Tony, you'll be far too big to play the Knickers after the first show. You'll be at the hockey rink the next time." She kept a straight face.

Vicar was predisposed to believe her tactical lie, yet he did not. But he understood then how badly she wanted him to not clutter up the interior with some kludgy two-by-four-constructed, shag-carpeted riser. So, after a little time thinking about it, he came up with the "genius solution" — his words — to plunk the band in the middle of everything and they could play, as he grandly described it, "in the round." They'd just give the people a "taste" at the Knickers. He had been as excited as a little boy and temporarily forgot his woes.

After a week of frantic, disjointed rehearsals at the house featuring mediocre attempts by Ray to remember how to play drums, causing Jacquie to decamp, *stat*, the big day arrived.

This would be the embodiment of the dream, a huge relaunch with the group they'd started all those years ago and that had never quite gotten going. Sure, Cosmic Ray had gone AWOL, but perhaps this was meant to be. Maybe they had simply needed to mature.

Jacquie came into the Knickers and saw the huge area cleared for the band and the stadium-sized rental PA system. She felt herself tense up.

"This is going to be really noisy, isn't it?"

"It's not noise," Vicar said, taking umbrage, "it's a progressive orchestral conceptual trio."

Jacquie ballooned her cheeks like she was going to upchuck while Vicar responded with an arched eyebrow. He was awfully confident, but she had heard the material; glancing around the interior of the pub, she checked to see where they'd hidden the little elvish men with crumhorns.

Ray began to drag in his drum kit. He had sold it years before and borrowed it back from the new owner, who was thoroughly delighted to be rid of it from his garage. With the march of time, it had become colossally impractical.

And then Ray kept unloading and unloading and unloading from a borrowed cube van that also disgorged a small village of loaders, volunteers from band class at Queen E. High School. The kids had never seen anything remotely like the Brobdingnagian drum kit; they fussed around like they were transporting King Tut's treasures. Vicar was impressed, too — there it was, in its full and overwhelming glory, and by some miracle one of the bass drums still had the Hospital Fish logo on its front head: a salmon wearing a medical mask playing a lute.

Vicar brought in equipment he hadn't used in years, too. Stacks of big boxes that said *Marshall* on them. He also made sure to get a smoke machine. Well, not a smoke machine like the big guys used ... It was a garden fogger. Every bit as effective but cheap. It could cover an entire acre.

The drums just kept coming and coming. *And coming.* At one point Vicar looked back and counted ten tom-toms, two bass drums, three snare drums, ten cymbals, tubular bells, a medium-sized gong, temple blocks painted like human skulls, a table filled with hand percussion, a bell tree, and one triangle, cantilevered down into this percussion cockpit like a pinata on a string. *Awesome, man.* Once ensconced in his fortress of noise,

Ray would not be visible and likely would need his volunteer ground crew to extricate him. Vicar could not imagine where all that shit had been stored all these years. Farley brought in boxes, too. Black coffins so large that it took all three of them to budge their bulk.

The pub found itself filled by three men and a fever dream. All that was missing was *Australopithecus*, throwing a bone in the air.

Word had gotten out like lightning and so the Knickers, or at least the circle of tables and chairs pushed against its periphery, was full. Vicar was really hyped and quite nervous.

"Farley, we need you solid, man. No doobies tonight."

"Oh, man ... I'm cool." His eyes were suspiciously red and squinty; he was crowned by a new toque that was sent in the mail by someone who'd read about him on a website. For a change, he was wearing a piece of clothing that didn't advertise meat or lumber.

"You ready, Ray?"

Ray did a pseudo namaste-ish hand gesture and muttered, "I am prepared; rocking and/or rolling may commence."

They'd even hired a sound engineer to mix the audio, a young keener who looked like a teenager. Tony got the kid's attention and spun his index finger in the air, indicating he should roll the intro tape that he'd had recorded ages before and kept in an old whisky box in which his mother had once stashed photos. It had lived in the back of his sock drawer, almost always hidden from civilian eyes, only brought out on nights when Vicar needed to commune with the intense power triangle vibe, like one of the faithful might fondle a holy relic. For the first time in his career, the young sound tech, who had been presented the tape as if it were a sliver of the true cross, pressed *play* on a cassette deck.

The tape fluttered a bit and then began a menacing, low drone.

The house went dark, the smoke machine fired up, billowing vast clouds of smoke and obscuring the whole venue. It looked like a navy destroyer had just laid a smokescreen during a tactical withdrawal. Then, the boys tried to sneak from the "dressing room" — the vestibule outside Vicar's little office — to the "stage" in the centre of the room.

Ray led the trio, lurching confidently through the darkness, and nearly made it all the way without mishap but then piled into a table, knocking all the drinks into a lady's lap. There was a screech and the sound of breaking glass.

This was followed by Vicar, whose serious look would have been obvious had there been any light to see it. Peering through the darkness, he was startled by Ray's pileup and made accidental contact with the backrest of a bar stool; that is to say, he whanged into it, bashing up his Gibson Les Paul like it was the bumper on a tow truck, rendering it miserably out of tune.

Farley, who had lied about not being stoned, was so fiercely blunted up that he felt as if he might be flung off the Earth's surface if he let go of the door jamb. He instantly became lost in the pitch black and was wandering aimlessly near the ladies' can, feeling his way along the corridor. He started moaning in panic, "Tony ... Tony!"

The Voice of God recording began its introduction as they tried to locate their positions. With a regal, Shakespearean flair, it spoke.

"Here, men from the planet Earth first touched our watery world ..." The voice sounded like Darth Vader confessing paternity. *"These three adventurers, swimming in our sea, visiting our planetary ocean, learning our ways, came with knowledge and healing ... They came in peace but were shunned! THEY WERE THE ILL-FATED MUSICAL HEALERS OF HOSPITAL FISH!"* Vicar mouthed along with the words that he had memorized years ago.

Jacquie, leaning against the bar, shrugged dubiously at Ann Tenna, who was gawking openly. She turned to Jacquie and said with total disbelief, "They're fuckin' with us, right?" Her eyes were opened wide, her lips pursed into a tight, disbelieving circle.

Jacquie had a look of regret as she confided, "Oh, no ... This is what they've been practising all week."

Ann shook her head like a child fending off bitter medicine. Then she started giggling. Jacquie dipped her head downward so no one could tell that she, too, had begun to snicker.

She wanted to support Tony, but, well, *good God* ... At least when he did the Elvis thing, it was a piss-take, and his butt looked good in the jumpsuit.

An ominous string arrangement of the *Jaws* theme began to play, thrumming its tension throughout the venue.

Ray couldn't locate his drum kit. The soundman, up on the balcony and quite amused by the whole thing, pulled out his puny, dollar-store flashlight and shone it down on the disoriented duo. Now Ray could see only a cloud of smoke billowing from the garden fogger. It did not help.

Vicar felt his way to his position, and by some miracle had left his guitar cable flopped over the mic stand, so he plugged it in and made a deafening *zzzz-ka-thunk* sound.

Farley had now ended up back in the storage area, calling pathetically for Tony, not able to orient himself, having flashbacks of once being pantsed in gym class in front of the girls' volleyball team. He wanted to curl up in the fetal position.

The *Jaws* theme continued, Tony trying vainly to tune his guitar as it pulsed along. Ray groped around trying to find his sticks in the dense cloud and nervously reached out to locate all the drums with his hands; there were too many, so he gave up. His accuracy was already a tad off and things were going to sound hideous if this fog bank didn't dissipate soon. As he attempted to mentally prepare himself through a wave of nerves, the garden fogger lost its smouldering pilot light and the mosquito repellent oil it had been burning now streamed out in a high-pressure spray of slippery, greasy fluid. It covered Ray's back and his drums and his hands and his sticks. Desperately he tried to wipe his hands off on his pantlegs but they, too, were oily.

At last, the cue arrived and they plunged into their prog rock adaptation of the *Jaws* theme, ready or not, with Ray playing both bass drums like a thundering herd of bison, holding on to slippery drumsticks with a death grip. They would have to do this without Farley. Vicar answered Ray with a weak imitation of the French horn part, sounding more like a befuddled elephant. Ray had not played for years, and his left leg gave up the ghost about ten seconds in and lagged far behind, the thundering bison now sounding geriatric and hobbled. Farley was supposed to be holding down the *dun-dun-dun-dun* bass notes, but he was on his hands and knees near the loading door, flailing around blindly like a marooned spacewalker, while his bass guitar dragged on the doormat.

The lights flashed rapidly, an epileptic's nightmare, and smoke had smudged the entire building. The emergency exit signs were obscured, the bassist missing in action, the audience transfixed and temporarily undecided about this unfathomable, hazy tableau. Had squid people suddenly emerged from a starship in the Dairy Queen parking lot, they could not have been more mystified.

At that very moment, *Jaws* ceased abruptly, memories of killer sharks now cut adrift. Vicar began softly plucking at his guitar, playing harmonics, and he said into the microphone, with a ridiculous put-on accent, "Pahht One: The Splashdown ..."

He strummed gently and began moaning out a high spooky motif interspersed with curious yelps, slathered in reverb and echo, that sounded very much like labour and childbirth as heard through a hydrophone.

"The Splashdown" over, Vicar launched into "Swim" and "Ocean Child," the double movement with the call-and-answer guitar and snare drum, which came before the climactic "Battle of the Undersea Forest" — Vicar's proudest compositional achievement, featuring some tricky 7 over 4 action that none of the three had managed to play correctly even once during rehearsals. Farley, especially, was out of his depth given that he always counted beat seven as "sev-ven" — two beats, not one. It was meant to be sheer musical combat, to peak in an explosion of pick slides and a loud, majestic stroke of the gong — the clangorous gong's sole rationale for being part of the drum kit. The audience would be awed.

Vicar stomped around in the predetermined manner, trying to remember all his guitar parts as he stiffly moved through the blocking of the preposterous dance-like stage routine. He moved rigidly, Tyee Lagoon's own Ötzi the Iceman — a Neolithic corpse frogmarched down the Alps and placed on a stage. Jacquie watched his creaky moves with incredulity.

Vicar was desperate for Farley to show up and get him out of this mess; he kept his eyes on the vestibule area, the last place he knew him to be. *Damn you,*

Farley ... Not again! Vicar wore the look of someone who had tripped on the carpet and knocked the *Mona Lisa* off the wall. Jacquie now had her hand over her mouth.

At that moment Farley came crawling toward the light on his hands and knees, a man who appeared to be sliding down the birth canal of rock and roll, presenting headfirst as is only proper, crowning from within the circle of audience seating. Some of the crowd craned around to witness his halting entrance. Within a moment or two, the whole place was gawking at Farley, focused mostly on his panicky, lemur-like eyes. Vicar's complexion turned ashen when he sized up the emergency they faced. Ray just kept slapping the kit like he was beating laundry on a rock.

In desperation, Vicar bailed out of the densely arranged math-rock epic and pointed at Ray without any warning, yelling into the mic, "Drum solo!" The dread that crawled over Ray's face could be read from every corner of the Knickers and he almost froze, breaking it down for a few moments, just pumping on the kick drum.

The audience was transfixed as Vicar threw off his guitar and ran toward Farley to help him to his feet. One audience member, giggling uncontrollably, rose from his seat and helped Vicar guide him toward his position onstage.

Ray, his hands oiled up, barely able to keep a grip on the sticks, attempted to play a surprise solo for the first time in years. He had no chops, no strength, no stamina, in fact no ability whatsoever, and simply started whacking this and that in a random manner, sounding like a frightened animal rampaging through an orchestra pit.

Farley kept tipping over, but he finally maintained his balance after stooping, his back rounded, looking like he might ralph at any second.

Vicar gingerly backed away from Farley while Ray's arrhythmic drum solo thundered; he wore an apologetic mask as he scuttled back to his guitar, his retreat finally prompting the audience into open mirth. They began to hoot and whistle, encouraging Farley to remain upright, congratulating Vicar on his efforts to keep him vertical, clapping heartily for the inexplicable sight before their eyes.

With Farley temporarily stabilized, Vicar put his guitar back on and chopped its neck downward at Ray, indicating he should cease with the frantic delaying action. He ended with an unceremonious wash of cymbals — he was too weak to do more.

The audience rose to its feet, cheering like the home team had just won the Stanley Cup in overtime. There were people sitting in front of Vicar who had laughed so hard that they were wiping away tears. A couple of chairs were knocked over. It was Tyee Lagoon's version of sheer pandemonium.

Vicar stared out at the crowd, completely perplexed. He felt like a pair of brown shoes at a state dinner, but the cheers were authentic. An awkward mixture of embarrassment and satisfaction surged through him. They were all loving it. He turned to Ray at the drum kit and saw him rubbing his oily hands briskly on his butt, the only part of him not already slathered in scented lubricant, and then looked at Farley, quivering like a newborn calf, hunched over as if suddenly stricken by severe osteoporosis.

Jacquie and Ann Tenna stood at the bar, watching the look of confusion on Vicar's face, and began howling with laughter.

"This is fantastic!" Jacquie yelled delightedly to Ann above the ovation.

"They're so goddamn bad they're good," Ann replied, as she bent over laughing, replaying the look of sheer unadulterated panic on Farley's face. She slapped the bar repeatedly. "Vicar's got horseshoes up his arse!"

Vicar regrouped as the ovation settled, realizing that the rest of their big Art Rock Review of Epic Triangular Metal Majesty was going to have to get turfed. Farley had to concentrate on breathing, for God's sake, so playing in 7/4 time was out of the question.

He mumbled quietly to Ray, "Let's just give 'em some Clarence Clotheswasher Rinse Cycle." He went to Farley, whispered for a while in his ear, making sure not to tip him over again. Ray was perplexed about the set change, shell-shocked at the events of the last five minutes, but mostly grateful not to be soloing anymore. Farley, trying hard to adjust to his surroundings, felt as if he had just been kidnapped by one of Ray's space aliens. On Vicar's count, they began chugging through a rusty old rock standard.

Almost immediately, the audience got up and started dancing and gyrating around with extreme joy, laughing and yee-hawing, with Vicar relieved, baffled, and barely able to keep his wits about him.

Jacquie could see Richard Dick, clearly still skulking around, sitting on a stool off to the left of Vicar, his jaw agape, in total disbelief, blinking deliberately as if he was hoping to erase the image before his eyes. Her laughter escalated at the sight of him.

Farley couldn't possibly manage to sing, and his buggy, frightened eyes made him look hyperthyroid. A dancing patron grabbed his microphone and began to sing along with her local hero Vicar, who crooned a warning that a bad moon was on the rise. He heard her harmonize, "There's a bathroom on the right ..."

Thirty / Wishes Granted
by the Gross

A week and a half later, at dusk, Richard Dick and the lickspittle cameraman Handlanger were driving slowly around Tyee Lagoon's nearly lifeless downtown, checking out the scene before they once again went into the pub to observe — and cause discomfort if possible.

There. Over in the alleyway.

"Whazzat?" Dick jabbed his finger toward the mouth of the back lane. "Is that a reindeer or something?"

Handlanger yanked the wheel in the direction of Dick's pointed finger and his headlights caught the reflection of antlers.

"Boss, I think that's the mystery moose."

"A moose ... or a walking carpet. How rustic."

When the "rustic" moose realized he'd been lit up by a turning vehicle, he scurried into the Agincourt

Hotel's loading door and disappeared, Dick and his minion pursuing him in their rental van as far as the parking lot.

Now alarmed, Beaner, unable at first to doff the moose's head for fear his identity would be revealed, dashed into a storage room, quietly clicking the door behind him and removing his costume. He placed the head on the top shelf and rearranged some boxes to hide it, rolled up his carpet, put it behind the door where it'd be harder to spot, and then quietly snuck out, hoping not to get busted as he strolled into the pub, acting perhaps just a little too nonchalant. He was a decidedly peculiar guy, so no one would even be able to measure if his cool-as-Fonzie saunter was the *real Beaner* or just an act. Fact was, no one even cared.

Dick sat in the van, which idled in front of the loading door, and shook his head. "Well, well, well … Mr. Vicar seems to have a secret life as a moose. A moose that gets babies delivered to his doorstep. How bizarre. What kind of freak is he?"

Dick felt he now had material that could paint Vicar as thoroughly bonkers, a snake oil salesman with a *ghastly* band, a love child, and a furry fetish, just making a quick layover at planet Earth until his Cadillac-shaped flying saucer got repairs.

■ ■ ■

"It seems you might get your wish." The social worker looked at Jacquie and Vicar pleasantly. "We presently have no available long-term foster families in this area. The ministry will temporarily allow you to act as foster parents. That is, if you want to …"

Jacquie was slack jawed but nodded a rapid yes, yes, yes; Vicar was stunned. He thought his crazy life couldn't surprise him anymore, yet there seemed to be solid footing under him no matter where he stepped. He looked at Jacquie and then back to the social worker, trying not to say something stupid.

What had seemed an inflexible barrier, an impenetrable wall of bureaucratic impedimenta, had suddenly melted away. They could keep baby Frankie, keep her for at least a little while longer. *Oh, please, yes …*

"Could we adopt her at some point, like … maybe?" Vicar hadn't even broached the subject with Jacquie, it had seemed too big a mouthful, but it slipped out, from where, he wasn't sure. Jacquie showed surprise but no displeasure.

"Yes, potentially, but I have to forewarn you. We make every effort to find her family, her mother and father. We turn over every possible rock. And, the application process for adoption is long and difficult. It is extremely strict. It's possible, but I warn you not to put the cart before the horse. There is no guarantee."

Jacquie clearly understood the obstacles before them. But for Vicar it was just another miracle in what was becoming a miracle-heavy patch in his life — but this one, he thought, well … *It changes everything.* As if all the previous ones hadn't.

Thirty-One / Sweet Freedom

For the first time in weeks, Vicar and Jacquie went
out for dinner. They hadn't really wanted to but
Con-Con and Nancy could not wait to get their
hands on Frankie and begged to babysit. They had
felt so badly about failing the baby during the blizzard on the night of her birth, having had no other
choice but to turn around and go back home when
they found the roads impassable. It had been beyond
their control, yet they felt they'd let all of them down
in their hour of need. At any rate, being entrusted
with baby Frankie made it clear that there were no
hard feelings.

Vicar was so new to organizing things like sitters
that he didn't even know how to do it.

"Okay, well, we'll have to bring down a bunch of
stuff. We're sorta like a travelling flea market, to tell
you the truth."

"Why don't we just come up there, Tony?" Con-Con was amused by his slight flap.

Well, duh. "Oh yeah," he grunted with dawning awareness.

The pair of overqualified babysitters came up far too early, when Jacquie was still putting on makeup and Vicar was attempting, without success, to find a suit jacket. He strode about, purposeful but aimless, instructing them overconfidently on how to take care of a real live baby, delving into his deep, weeks-long experience.

Nancy was such a gentle soul, but clearly, she had had enough of his yammering and disorganization. "Tony, go find your jacket. And put on some dark socks, will you? You look like a twelve-year-old." Vicar's eyebrows went up to his hairline. Nancy was so retiring, she seldom said anything at all. Man, his socks must really blow.

Jacquie was careful to choose a restaurant not too "highfalutin." She was all too aware that Vicar reacted badly to trendy places that charged a fortune for minuscule servings of pretentiousness.

Vicar, on the other hand, was aware that Jacquie was so much more sophisticated than he, in some ways at least. The thing that bugged him was that she never called bullshit on places where people in crappy old blue jeans flogged through the most expensive wine on the list just to show off, and practically yelled conversation after a bottle or two of it. *Reserve that behaviour for a campsite.*

Jacquie had always accused him of having a selective memory; no matter the facts, he was confident that he was always extremely polite in a restaurant, so much more polite than he was anywhere else. Any previous outbursts, he was certain, were simply his attempt to remedy grievous wrongs. He could not comprehend why the very rude always thought he was the rude one when he pointed out their rudeness.

Jacquie was feeling cocky now, having found a place Vicar liked, so she began manoeuvring hard to get *him* to order what *she* wanted to try — she'd just have a bite or two of his … She'd get a couple of appies of the other things that looked good.

"Jacquie, I do not want the Prawn Okra." He looked at her pleadingly.

"But everyone says it's so *great!*"

"It is okra. *O-K-R-A*. You are fully aware of how I feel about that nasty stuff. I would rather be plunged into a pool of live eels than eat it."

"I want to try it but I don't want a whole order. And I want *you* to try it. You'll love it. You always say it's disgraceful to be fussy."

"Jacquie, that does not count with okra. You might as well eat a slimy loofah."

"I heard loofah is delicious …"

He grimaced. "If you want to munch on an exfoliating sponge, be my guest, but we need to cease discussing this now. You're going to make me hurl."

Vicar began fishing around for his reading glasses, realizing they were on the nightstand at home.

Trombone-like, he moved the menu to and fro in the candlelight, badly deciphering the elegant but obscure font, feeling aged.

While he squinted, he was interrupted by a man from a nearby table. "Are you the Liquor Vicar?" He had a slightly stupid grin on his face, half awkward about intruding, half trying to turn his intrusion into a charming little performance.

Vicar, now used to this, held out his hand and said, confidently, "Tony. Nice to meet you." Vicar dragged him through the normal checklist, hitting every mark like a pro, and then agreed to pose for pictures, a couple with the guy, then one with Jacquie. And then, *Oh, oh, oh, can we do just one more with my wife?*

Vicar just went with it, even though it was clearly disruptive to all the other diners. Just get it over with, *quick.*

Jacquie, as she always managed to, had a smile pasted on her face, but Vicar could tell from her eyes that by the guy's third or fourth photo she was beginning to feel like a lab animal. Mercifully, the guy finally departed.

A few minutes later, she muttered, "Oh Christ, Tony ... Now they're watching us eat."

A tiny part of Vicar was happy that she was feeling slightly uncomfortable — it was a small taste of his day-to-day life, but she had been trying for a couple of years to convince him to just be more easygoing about it. This guy's amped-up enthusiasm was small potatoes, surely, but it was an event he'd be able to use as a reference point with her when he started feeling smothered, surveilled, or swarmed. *Remember how you felt, Jack?*

Their orders taken, they chatted with no immediate worries, no crying Frankie, fully formed sentences in big-people talk, not one utterance to do with diapers. It wasn't much by the standards of a while ago, but on this night, they felt they'd been sprung from the clink.

When they had just finished dinner, another person came up and touched Vicar on the shoulder. She had sad, apprehensive eyes.

"Mr. Vicar, you don't know me, but my mother once wrote to you asking for help."

"Oh, is that so?" Vicar could feel this one came with a story and braced.

"You might not even see your mail. I'm sure your secretaries do it all for you."

Secretaries? Mr. Vicar has a skyscraper full of Kelly Girls on standby, madame.

"What help did she need?"

"My father was very sick, and she needed you to write to her, perhaps call, to send some kind of blessing … There was nothing further they could do, and they were so far away from you — in Halifax."

Vicar jolted. He remembered that letter. They had even sent money in it. It had been at that moment that he realized how out of hand his fame had gotten, how ridiculous the propaganda about his "powers" had become. It had knocked him for a loop.

His throat suddenly dry, Vicar played dumb. This was too much, delivered in the wrong place and time.

"I don't recall receiving the letter, ma'am," he lied, wanting the conversation to cease, right away.

"That is too bad, Mr. Vicar. My father died shortly afterward and was in great pain. Mom still thinks you could have helped. She's quite haunted by it. If only you'd received the letter …"

Vicar's vision went dark and he stood up abruptly, pulling Jacquie out of her chair, throwing balled-up cash on the table, and rushing toward the exit. He had to get the hell out of there.

▬ ▬ ▬

Jacquie lay in bed and replayed Tony's panicked retreat from the restaurant again and again. He was stricken, looking as if he just been falsely accused of murder and dragged off to a cell.

He had not said very much except for the cryptic statement, "I didn't help Mom, either." He had just gotten into bed and curled up like a child. She stroked his back gently as he eventually drifted off to sleep. *So much pressure, so many expectations.* She felt as if she knew him so well yet understood him so little. She snuggled a little closer and drifted off to sleep.

▬ ▬ ▬

Richard Dick, hanging around the pub again after another day of pestering the locals, watched Vicar interacting with the room, autographing merchandise that they sold over in the corner that took the form of cotton briefs emblazoned with the logo *The Vicar's Knickers*. Very popular item, often worn on the head.

He overheard the whispers, the unchecked admiration. There were people now visiting the pub from distant places: Germany, France, Brazil; he knew that there had been one older couple from Russia. It was as if Vicar had cleverly set up his net and dredged the internet to capture all the fishes in the sea; nearly all of them wanted some kind of recognition from him, wanted to *kiss hands*, wanted what amounted to a blessing. At this point even just a hello with Vicar was claimed to have special significance, and it was rumored that there were tour companies specializing in West Coast Canada trips with the Vicar's Knickers now listed as one of their feature stops. They touted it like a pilgrimage to the Vatican. It seemed completely absurd.

Dick refused to take it at face value. Town character, sure, but spiritualist in blue jeans? A bartending Buddha? Six-pack Chopra? *Bullshit!*

The moose costume, though … This guy was surely off his rocker; his solar panels were facing the Great White North. He turned it all over in his mind again and again. The pressure from head office was getting almost vindictive, so he found himself defaulting to the company line: two dimensions. White hats versus black hats, with Vicar eventually revealed as a complete fabrication, a homespun con artist who needed to be outed by *Glib Re-Post*, the upright guardians of truth. For a price, they'd later spearhead his "comeback."

Richard Dick hadn't the time to be more nuanced, could not easily envision any other angle that would work for *GRP*, and anyways, his readers hadn't the patience for abstract rambling. Most of them had come to their conclusion after the picture and the headline.

Dick narrowed his eyes at Vicar, who was at that moment attempting to repeat a phrase in Japanese that a fan, visiting all the way from Tokyo, was teaching him, and muttered, "Don't worry ... I'll sweat you down to size."

Thirty-Two / The Chicken and Mr. Ghost

Poutine had come up to Vicar's place on Sloop Road to borrow folding chairs but sat at the kitchen table for a few minutes, sipping a coffee. Vicar had something on his mind.

"Ross, please don't tell anybody … I'm afraid I'm losing it. I keep having weird, uh, 'experiences' at the hotel."

"Experiences, ya say? What kinda experiences you talkin' 'bout, dere?"

Vicar looked Poutine in the eye and then looked away, uncomfortable with the confessional line of their conversation, and taken aback by the strong goaty odour exuding from Poutine.

"I, uhh …" He hesitated.

"Spit it out, fer Chrissakes. I'm so old I musta heard everythin' by now."

Poutine was as rough-hewn as they came so Vicar was a little hesitant to unload his esoteric worries on him. Yet Poutine had proven again and again that underneath the coarse exterior lay a person who could cut to the heart.

"Okay, but it's weird ..." Poutine was glaring at Vicar now, clearly losing his patience over all the pussy-footing. Vicar launched into his story.

"I, uh, have seen this *thing*. Like a black blob, maybe what you'd call an entity or a ghost."

"Where?"

"At the hotel. I've also heard strange sounds, maybe voices?" It was half question, half statement. "It's scaring the shit outta me."

"D'ya think maybe yer under too much pressure?" An obvious place to start, but Poutine's tone indicated he already had a better theory.

Vicar replied, "I, uh, don't think so, although I did see a moosie kind of creature walking on its hind legs in the alley behind Arbutus Street a while ago, so ..."

"Okay. So, you seen a ghost? Or a moose?"

"Well, both. But not at the same time."

Poutine scrunched up his face in doubt and bafflement.

Realizing he was losing Poutine, Vicar rushed to clarify. "I saw a ghost at the *hotel*, but I saw a moose in the alley."

"Oh, totally git it, now," Poutine said dryly.

Vicar slumped. There was a long pause while a series of funny looks crossed Poutine's face. Finally, he regrouped.

"Okay. Ghost. Didja see it up on the second floor?" Poutine asked.

"Yes, usually on the second floor. But not always." Vicar looked at him hopefully, thinking he might offer something helpful now.

"Y'ever have one o' them 'experiences' up in 222, dere?" Poutine had one eye scrunched shut.

"Oh, God, yes. How did you know?"

"You musta heard that there was a ghost dere ..." Poutine replied.

"Well, sure, but every old hotel claims to have a ghost. It's good marketing."

"Well, I never seen it but there's supposably one of 'em at the Agincourt, eh." Oddly, he spoke the hotel's name with its more elegant French pronunciation.

Vicar had heard versions of the legend since he was a kid. Everyone had heard some wild account, but it was just local colour, nothing more, passed by word of mouth and exaggerated until it sounded as if the joint was filled to capacity by phantasms. Campfire-story fun, but Vicar was interested to hear more.

"You mean there's something to that ghost tale? Some kind of backstory?"

"Oh, shit yeah," Poutine replied, now enthusiastic. "Happened so long ago nobody remembers, 'cept maybe me ... Just b'fore I move out here there's this kid who dies up in room 222 from some kinda food pois-nin'. He was sick fer days — dies in his bed, dere. When they find him he's stiff as a board, all black 'n' blue. All the boys sez he's still up dere, hauntin' the place." Poutine gave him a hilarious look, one eye bulging out like a cartoon monster.

Vicar turned over all this new information. He was positive he'd seen *something*, a blob or an outline or a thingamajig. And he was sure he'd seen it in room 222.

"Do you know anyone else besides me who's had a sighting?" Vicar asked, hoping to find someone, anyone, with whom he could compare notes.

Ross Poutine was not given to lying or flights of fantasy. He stood, engineer boots firmly planted in the here and now. He replied honestly, "Some guys said they saw it, but I think they were fulla shit. Just tellin' scary stories to purdy girls, dere."

Vicar looked down, slightly disappointed.

"The kid's name wuz Valentine. He was prolly eighteen, nineteen. Too young to die, fer sure. And food pois-nin' … He puked hisself to death, dere!"

An awful way to go, thought Vicar.

Poutine paused for a minute and then concluded, "But like ya sez, a ghost is good plub-licity …"

few days later, Vicar found himself glued to a TV show featuring two sisters who presented themselves as cable television psychics. They had made their name by helping to solve cold-case murders. The detectives involved were all convinced, on-camera at least, that they were the real thing. The endorsements had been enough to get them their own show.

The episode found them crashing around in a darkened laundry room, chatting to the undead around them. They had an unerring way of turning their impressions into full-on, highly detailed historical scenarios, complete with dialogue — far-fetched in the extreme, but always ending in a smash cut to a close-up of a fabulous dessert. They were awfully fond of sweets.

The Rubenesque psychic siblings would hover over a treat, preparing to pounce as they made one last prediction along the lines of: "We can sense we're gonna love this pie!" It was all totally preposterous, in remarkably bad taste, and a big hit.

Vicar called over to the kitchen, "Maybe I should call these gals for a read on the hotel, Jack. I bet they could make sense of it all ..." He chuckled but was clearly fascinated by the program; it was somehow compelling yet absurd. It reminded him of his own life.

Jacquie had no patience for the show and wanted to make a wisecrack but instead replied, "I know enough about psychology to know that you need to talk to somebody."

Psychology, not psychics? "You think I'm nuts?" Vicar asked, not totally joking.

"That's not a word a psychologist would use. Honey, you have to look deep inside yourself to find out what is propelling all this stuff." She had studied to be a psychologist all right but struggled to apply her knowledge to her fascinating but strange life with Vicar.

"But I don't think it's imaginary ... And, by the way, why can't I just talk to you?" She would naturally conclude it was a psychological issue; Vicar was not fully convinced but he waffled back and forth.

"Umm, well, you can talk to me — to a point. But I can't be totally neutral. You need to speak with someone who hasn't co-signed a line of credit with you." She looked at him impassively.

Ugh. Money. *Foul shit.* It always stuck its ugly head above the parapet. Vicar had struggled with the concept of money and wealth his whole life. Jacquie was trying to remind him that they couldn't afford any abstruse spiritual journeys, wasn't she?

She saw his face and quickly added, "Don't take that the wrong way, Tony. I just mean that we have entanglements that go too deep for me to be neutral. Our lives are linked."

The comment was meant to be a comfort to him, a reassurance. But to Vicar it sounded more like a veiled reminder of black-and-white, brick-and-mortar, here-and-now responsibilities. They had a baby they should be worrying about now, not some hotel-haunting spectre. *Shut it down, Vicar, stay on target!*

Jacquie was correct to not be his counsellor, he realized this; but Vicar didn't think she fully appreciated the delicateness of his state.

Jacquie was holding it together in impressive style, imperturbable, except for the wasp; graceful … mostly; clear-headed, except for choosing him — but undoubtedly feeling slightly abandoned, too. That added even more pressure.

He made no excuses. But no swordsman on any battlefield, he felt, had ever been assailed in such a far-out, three-dimensional attack. Awake or asleep; now, yesterday, and tomorrow all working in cahoots — every blessing he could count seemed wrapped around a curse that had another blessing beneath it. How far does a guy hafta dig before the pattern becomes crystal clear? Should he simply stop digging? If the answer was yes, how could he stop when he didn't even understand how it all started?

Richard Dick turned to Handlanger and said, "Be ready with the camera. He always comes in through the front door and I have them ready to pounce." He pointed at a small gaggle of women, dressed as if it were Carnivale and happy to get international exposure and a nice paycheque. They sat at a table and giggled nervously. Every eye in the place was on them — it was as if the Solid Gold Dancers themselves had suddenly plopped into downtown Tyee Lagoon for a quick wine spritzer.

Dick went to the table and instructed, "Remember, ladies, when he comes in, I want you on him like he's a piece of meat." They all nodded, and he disappeared.

Sometime later Vicar entered through the front door, precisely as predicted, followed at a distance by a sneaking Handlanger, camera in hand, slightly hunched over and ready to push through the door behind him when the action started.

On cue the women squealed and jumped up as a group as Vicar entered, like cheerleaders celebrating a touchdown, and ran the few steps toward him.

Vicar was taken aback and thought it was a prank. *Not a bad one, either.* But then the women surrounded him tightly, and one particularly gymnastic woman put her arms around his neck, pushed her lips onto his, and wrapped one leg around his waist. She clamped onto him like a remora and spun him around so that her back was against the wall, and Vicar appeared to be in control. She started grinding her pelvis on him as if he was giving her the business right then and there. The hilarity of the "prank" went sour at that point and Vicar's alarms started ringing. He tried to push her away as she moaned orgasmically, the rest of the girls voyeuristically encouraging him. The cameraman had manoeuvred himself into a good angle, but low and hard to locate in that crowd of jumpers, and got it all, right down to close-ups of their faces and egregious crotch shots.

Finally, Vicar dislodged the grinder, forcibly shoved the other women away from him, and tried to muscle all of them out the door. Confused, he worried that he was being unhospitable to customers, but then imagined Jacquie looking on. With that he ejected them. He did not notice Handlanger backing out, video still rolling.

He turned to look around the pub only to see every patron silent, eyes wide.

"What the hell was that?" Vicar asked out loud.

No one responded except Ann Tenna, who called out, "YOU WEARIN' PANTHER PISS?"

Vicar stormed back into his little office, dazed and baffled, locking the door behind him. Dick, sitting outside in his rental van, just smiled. Maybe this would get things moving.

× × ×

"Liquor Vicar Unfaithful — Jacquie O Forced to Care for Another Woman's Love Child."

The headline was lurid, the story awful, and the fall-out sure to be disastrous. Vicar's face was in his hands and Jacquie looked highly distressed.

"This is disgusting. It says you're the father of baby Frankie and you're using me to care for her ... while you go off womanizing." A still photo showed him appearing to neck with a woman up against the pub wall.

He looked at her, too upset to defend himself, a pained and powerless look on his face.

"It also claims that you are the one who's running around town dressed as a moose. Now that's weird shit ..."

"Jack, I have nothing, *literally nothing*, to do with a moose or mooses or *whatever the hell*. It's *so* out there."

He felt sick. It was yet another side-swipe that made peace and quiet impossible. Everyone was on about an effing costume moose and a love child, and he was twisting in the wind, unable to even find a through line that would allow him to mount a logical defence.

It was not his child, of course. It was not possible medically, nor emotionally. Once he had fallen for Jacquie, that was it. No one else could ever compare now. Falsely accused, he was hurt and defensive, unable to organize his thoughts. He was also deeply concerned about what she thought and couldn't just lamely stand there.

"Please, Jack, please believe me. You know they're just making all this up, don't you? *They're trying to ruin our lives.*"

She looked at him seriously; it was hard not to feel doubt at a moment like this. She tossed the whole thing around again. The story went against her gut instincts and it came from a wholly unreliable source. She also knew that no baby could result from any dalliance by Tony. She paused before speaking.

"I know, Tony." Another agonizing pause. Vicar just sat there, stricken, seemingly holding on for dear life. She finally finished her thought: "But now I understand how they make people believe all this horseshit."

Somewhat relieved, he asked, "Did you see the footage?" He pointed at the phone.

"No." She clicked play and watched the tightly edited piece multiple times.

After leaving Vicar to his own fears for several minutes, she spoke.

"I recognize two of them."

"You *KNOW* them?" he blurted, surprised.

"Yeah, from Beaver Fever in Victoria. One of them did a snake act ... 'Mistress Hiss' or some stupid thing. Kept her snake in a box and fed it mice from the pet shop. Disgusting. The other one did a gymnastic act. She's the one with her leg wrapped around you. I forget her name."

"So, they were hired by somebody ..."

"Well, duh, Tony. Look at 'em. That's reality TV if I ever saw it. Have you ever seen a random gaggle of hotties just attacking a guy? Ever?"

Well, uhh, why not? Vicar now found himself ashamed for believing they might be overzealous superfans, as if he were the world's most eligible bachelor-prince who had slipped his bodyguards for the day. What a strange set of circumstances, but of course, Jacquie was right. *As if a snake lady would come up here without getting paid!* Mice were expensive. He knew who had splashed out the cash for the blackmail cheerleaders.

"Okay, Walrus ... Let's go downstairs and find your Nana. I think it's closing time."

Wallis jumped up and down in the empty tub a few more times and then crawled over the edge, with Vicar lending a hand to ensure a safe landing.

They were on the third floor in the quickly developing "show suite," Vicar inspecting the workmanship of the recently installed tub. Baby Frankie was in a little backpack. Vicar looked around, estimating how much room would be taken up by a bed and deciding that the TV would go on the east wall. He was quietly delighted at how uptown it already looked even in its unfinished state. This was going to be their nicest room.

As they left, the heavy lock clicking behind them, Vicar was briefly aware that he oversaw two little kids and felt totally comfortable with it. Not too long ago, the very thought of minding either one of them would have terrified him. He took Wallis's hand and they walked down the stairs.

▬ ▬ ▬

Serena saw the footage on *GRP*'s feed, which she had been following closely, since it covered Vicar more than any other outlet. The wild accusation that he was the father of the child made her pause and regroup.

This was an angle that might give her a few more options down the road. She was surprised she hadn't thought of it herself.

Anyway, luck had been on her side to an extent. Serena had felt sure that she would give birth during her trial, and the baby would be taken away if she was locked up. But the charges against her had been dismissed; her lawyer had been watching the calendar like a hawk and pounced at the earliest moment. He had made a Jordan application to dismiss and the judge agreed; it had taken far too long for the Crown to get its ducks in a row.

She was off the hook, but she had been days from giving birth. She had no family to turn to. Who better to look after the baby than Vicar? Serena felt a twinge of satisfaction at her plan — a slapdash panic, in truth, but she was now reaching backward to retrofit it while she groped ahead to find her next moves.

Thirty-Four / Cosmic Ray Reads the Room

Sitting with Ray in one of the booths at the far side of the Knickers, Vicar explained, "The first time I wasn't sure that I had actually seen anything. It was kind of just something in the corner of my eye." He went on to recount his ghostly scare with the falling hangers and his terrified flight down the stairs. "I heard something that time, too, Ray. Growling. Like a dog. Or maybe a bear."

Ray looked impressed. "Will you show me where it happened?"

"Well, sure, of course. But it's happened other times, too."

Ray was unusually direct. "Tell me."

"I had a really clear look at a black blob, sort of an oblong shape, the blackest black you ever saw, right there." He pointed at the snug close by. "That's when I really started to question myself. Ann" — he gestured vaguely toward her as she clowned around loudly with customers — "was standing right beside me. I was pointing at it, but she couldn't see a thing. It was plain as day! Scared me half out of my wits but she was oblivious to it. Now she thinks I'm a couple o' tracks short of an album …"

Ann Tenna arrived at the table to tidy it and overheard the topic of conversation. She inappropriately piped up, "I dint see nuthin', Tony. I think you were havin' a hell-OOO-sinashun." She said it with a backward tilt of the head, as if baying at the moon.

Ray mumbled, "Tony … I've heard about this b'fore. A vision, not a sighting." Dishes clanked at the table nearby.

Ann snorted. "What're you, sum kinda puh-sykick?" She was unable to hide her doubt.

Vicar ignored her and replied, "Ray, there's no way that was some vision. It was as real as the furniture."

Ray hesitated and then said, "I dunno if it's true, but I have heard that things shake loose during renovations. I've heard that lotsa times." He had been told a thousand Fortean tales.

Ann Tenna departed, whistling an eerie *woo-woo-woo* melody.

Vicar, trying to hide his misgivings, waited until she was out of earshot and asked, "How?"

"Well, I think the spooks live in the walls and the floors — changing anything wakes 'em up."

Vicar looked at him dubiously. Ray could practically hear the voice in Vicar's head warning, "This is as goofy as the Alien Abduction story." Ray was not concerned. *Why exactly had Vicar even asked for advice, then?* He knew that Vicar, for all his doubts, could see that something deeper was going on and wanted another opinion — even if he ridiculed it at first. *Some people can't just believe — they hafta be arseholes about it for a while.*

"Really? So, I'm sorta bringing this on myself by renovating?" he asked with hesitation.

Ray, his lips scrunched up and eyebrows raised, said, "Well … kinda, yeah."

Vicar sat back and turned over Ray's comments. Revealing experiences of such high strangeness left him feeling vulnerable, especially since he'd turned to a guy who claimed to hang out with space aliens. What was weirder … the problem or the guy he was asking for an explanation?

Ray continued, now wandering off topic — muttering about dharma and entanglement theory and recurring hauntings, then conversationally lurching over toward organic beet chips — as the pub hummed with quiet activity. Vicar's thoughts were loudly interrupted by Ann Tenna, now over on the other side of the room yelling, "BEANER, DO WE HAVE GIRAFFES OF WINE?"

Beaner leaned out, barking back, "Carafes? Yeah. Look at the menu you wrote, fer Chrissakes."

━━ ━━ ━━

The phone rang and Jacquie answered.

"Yes, this is Jacqueline O'Neil …"

She listened quietly for a few moments, the colour draining from her face. A jumble of frightening memories flashed, and her emotions flared.

"So that's it, then? How long has it been? … All right, thank you." She hung up and began deep breathing to calm her nerves. Tony was not going to like this at all.

■ ■ ■

"Tony, I got a call about Serena."

Vicar stiffened. The trial. They'd have to attend and be witnesses, for sure, and he had been dreading the thought. There were plenty of other concerns without the pressure of criminal court proceedings. He didn't want to take his attention away from Frankie, and he definitely didn't want Dickedy Doofus hovering around the courthouse, gobbling up all the salacious details and rearranging them for maximum negative effect.

"When's the trial?" he asked quietly.

"There will be no trial."

"Huh?" Vicar didn't understand. "I was pretty sure it had to happen soon. What's going on?" *Had she died?*

"Sit down for a sec, Tony." Uh oh, really bad news. "The charges were vacated."

"Vacated? You mean, thrown out?"

"Yup. Dismissed."

"They just let her off?"

"Yup. Kinda. The Crown couldn't get its case together in good time, so a judge vacated all charges. Speedy trial and all that …"

"Oh my God!" The enormity of the news hit him. "Sure as shit she's going to come back, isn't she?"

"I hope not. I really hope not." Her sigh was like a full conversation. The tangles she'd had with Serena had left Jacquie with a few emotional scars, and as strong as she was, she recoiled from the memories. Serena was bad, bad news.

Vicar's gut tightened as he felt a dizzy numbness come over him. He had fancied himself a man of the world, but the chaos and destruction that Serena had visited upon him and Jacquie were beyond his experience — even beyond his imagining; but if nothing else she had opened his eyes to what was possible if all reason and good judgment were removed from human behaviour.

Now he would have to pick his way even more cautiously through the minefield before him, fighting not only psychological demons, but living ones, too.

He looked at Jacquie, who was visibly anxious, and wondered how much more would be piled upon them. Surely, he was at his limit. In the same breath, he shut down that line of internal dialogue. *Don't tempt the fates, Vicar.* Asking "how much more?" was like begging for a demonstration.

Thirty-Five / Trippin' Balls

andlanger the cameraman strolled off to the men's room at the Knickers, and when done, slipped quietly out the side door that led into the unfinished hotel lobby. No one really took notice as there was plenty of activity in the pub.

He softly quickstepped up the stairs to the second floor and moved to the fire door at the end of the hall, checking to ensure that the fire escape steps were solid and usable. From his coat pocket he took out gaff tape. He ripped a strip long enough to prevent the fire door from latching, stuck it over the mechanism, and then stepped onto the fire escape. He quietly let the door seat, now permanently unlocked, into place behind him. He had an easy way in now, providing no one discovered his jimmy. He calmly descended the stairs to street level, and ambled casually around the corner, re-entering the Knickers via the main door. No one had taken any notice at all.

As unbelievable as it seemed, he and Richard Dick still had enough nerve to enter the pub, even after all the havoc they'd caused. The "attack of the floozies" was now the talk of the town, but Dick evidently felt that no one in the backward burg could *possibly* be smart enough to connect him to it, even though he had been witnessed, plain as day, instructing the women before Vicar arrived. And where else, pray tell, could the footage have come from but Dick and Handlanger? In truth, everyone in town knew he was the culprit and wished he'd crawl back under the rock from whence he'd come.

Dick had engaged the supercharger in his mind that took him from standard-issue egomaniac to abhorrent narcissist. He did not ooze anymore, he now ejected slime in a high-pressure spray.

■ ■ ■

Cosmic Ray was hanging around the Knickers, which was normal routine since his return to town. He was sitting with Ross Poutine, who had ambled in, looking unusually smug. He was chatty and Ray tried his best to unravel the goat Latin he was speaking. Their conversation, led by Poutine in his grammatically impaired Sportuguese, countered by mystical ramblings from Cosmic Ray, would have left nearly anyone except their closest friends in the deepest dark.

Poutine had proudly brought along a bottle of his special new hot sauce custom made by Merri Crabtree at nearby Hot Thoth, and pulled it out of his pocket during dinner, showing it off to anyone willing to listen. He had named it "Dumpster Fire."

He splashed some on his bangers and mash and immediately got a response from Ray, as well as the surrounding tables. The terrifying, acidic aroma that came from it could make eyes water from several feet away. A cloud surrounded him, and the radioactive bangers gave him a wicked case of death breath, to boot. Anyone able to do so backed away from him, like bears repelled by mace. The general area around Poutine smelled like Satan's pet goat, but he was oblivious to it, as he was to so many things. He was jes mindin' his own bizznus.

Chief Wheat was at his table in the corner by the bar, surveying his little kingdom but unhappy about Dick's recent arrival. He kept watch on him.

Dick wandered around the pub as if he owned it, pretending to make small talk, conspicuously advertising his "untouchable" status, but mostly wanting to leave everyone tensed up and unhappy. He hoped that they would conflate their dislike of him and attach it to Vicar's stupid pub. Any tiny cut he could inflict would be delightful.

Vicar felt the rising urge to deal with the guy the old-fashioned way — give the twat a backhand and send him on his way. The sight of that sonofabitch prancing around a tiny coastal village wearing a poncy cravat and a too-tight suit was enough to make Vicar's slapping arm twitch. But he wasn't that guy anymore. He breathed deeply a couple of times to cool his rising anger.

There was some connection between serial killers and certain gossip columnists — Vicar was sure of it. *Serial killers never stop until somebody stops them, right?*

"Ahh, aren't you 'Cosmic Ray'? How charming. How is your return to civilization going?" Dick's comments dripped with venom and Poutine, across the table from Ray, looked at him warily.

"Fine, thank you," Ray mumbled, managing to speak from the back of his throat using only implied consonants. His read on the guy was ominous. He had an aura of darkness, of something verging on sick. His eyes alone gave Ray the shivers — so cold. Ray sensed in him a brand of suffering that had flipped and morphed into a terrible gift that keeps on giving. This was not a man who suffered pangs of conscience.

Unbidden, Dick pulled up a chair from the table behind him and sat down, Ray and Poutine both recoiling as if someone had just placed a snake on the table. He looked at Poutine like he was a raccoon carcass on the highway and turned back to Cosmic Ray.

"You're helping propagate Vicar's fraud if you don't out him — you realize that, don't you?" He looked through narrowed eyes.

Poutine had never heard the word *propagate*, but he knew what *fraud* was. The guy was even worse than everybody reported. He, too, thought Richard Dick had the presence of a snake. But *his* response to snakes was to grab the nearest hoe. He swivelled his head around and observed the general unease Dick had created. *This creep is rude and scarin' all the ladies. Needs a lesson in manners.*

Someone tried to muscle into a seat behind Dick, giving him a reason to turn around and communicate lordly displeasure. Poutine, now grossed out and feeling aggravated, looked at Ray and said, "A leper don't change his spots, dere, duz he?"

He uncorked his bottle of plutonium-like hot sauce. In the briefest moment, while Dick was turned the other direction, he gobbed several shakes of the noxious potion into Dick's reddish cocktail. It merely added to the frightful smell already wafting from Poutine's dinner.

Ray watched Poutine dispense the liquid death and his eyes flew open — in alarm mixed with barely hidden delight. Once Dick got that in his fetid yap, there was going to be a shitload of ki-yai-ing! Though Ray was a man of peace, this seemed karmic.

"I know you're his friend …" Dick purred as he turned back to them. "But I see it from a different angle. You might say we disagree upon the veracity of Vicar's story." Ray, aware of the turmoil Vicar was going through, felt himself get colder as his sympathy for Dick ebbed to nothing. Ray and Poutine sat there, tight-lipped, so Dick stood, pushing the chair back with a loud, careless scrape. He departed and dipped his head grandly, taking a long, showy pull on his cocktail as he walked away.

Ray watched carefully. Within two heartbeats Dick's face was purple, and he was spewing cocktail out of his mouth, choking and gasping. Poutine's lips turned up in a lopsided grin. He was thoroughly pleased with himself, gleeful as if watching the sudden eruption of a bench-clearing brawl. Ray, as well as a couple of people at the nearby table, though they knew it was in poor form, laughed out loud.

Chief Wheat had been watching intently from across the room and stood up at that moment, ambling slowly toward the front exit, rubbing his hands absently, innocently looking around.

Within a few seconds everyone in the place was aware that something was wrong. The ragged gagging and loud wheezing emanating from Dick were probably authentic but it seemed over the top. In Hollywood, an act like this would have had half the place racing around, wringing their hands or ringing their attorney. Here, everyone just snorted derisively. Dick was bent over, tears streaming down his cheeks, almost unable to breathe.

Too panicked to think clearly, he stumbled toward the exit. He needed air; he couldn't breathe. This was an emergency.

Chief Wheat leaned up against the wall and watched impassively. Someone was coming in and stood aside for a lurching, gagging Richard Dick. Chief Wheat smiled pleasantly at the man holding the door.

At that moment, Dick stumbled past, barely able to see, arms flailing around to find the opening. The

Chief's right boot jutted out, Dick tripped over it, and he fell headlong into the street. He tried to get onto his knees, choking and sputtering, his fancy suit now in need of extensive repair, as Chief Wheat muttered vaguely, "Oopsie, watch your step, lad."

— — —

"They tried to poison me!" Richard Dick was outraged and dramatically told his side of the tale with theatrics beyond anything that Con-Con had ever witnessed. His head was back, his hand on his chest; at that moment he looked like a soap opera actor, emoting like a mofo. She was forced to suppress a smirk and had to look away toward the empty desk beside her.

Dick and Handlanger had gone directly to the police station as soon as Dick could see and speak. He hectored Con-Con, in her uniform, standing behind the desk. He demanded justice. He was bent on pressing charges but wasn't sure who was to blame — so he blamed Vicar, and a vaguely described person he dismissively called "Rosco Teen, that stinky hobo," and threw in the entire clientele of the Knickers for good measure. *While you're at it, send that idiotic "Cosmic Ray" back to the desert, too! He smells like mothballs.* Aggrieved at the inaction of this Mountie before him — he seemed to expect her to pull out her side arm and randomly fire in the direction of the Knickers — he was livid that she couldn't understand the magnitude of this monstrous assault. Didn't they realize who they were dealing with?

As was her duty, Con-Con took all the details down, asked a few questions, and attempted to be totally neutral, suspecting she knew exactly what had happened. Hot-sauce attack while sitting at a table with "Rosco Teen"? You didn't have to be Columbo to unsnarl that one.

She assured him she'd launch "a thorough investigation" immediately and even gave him her card. He left somewhat mollified but still grumbling.

Con-Con looked at the report, walked to her desk, and then placed it at the very bottom of a pile of complaints four inches high. Then, in a leisurely fashion, she strolled over to the coffee pot and poured herself a fresh cup.

▬ ▬ ▬

Dick had little faith in the Mountie he had spoken with. Chances were she'd reveal herself to be a glorified Keystone Kop, walking into walls and falling out of police cars. A fine example of this place; backward, stupid, lazy hillbillies.

Back at the motel, he fumed. He had never been so disrespected. He had suffered a gang assault by a roomful of violent peasants. Good thing he had brought more suits; that one was ruined. He shuddered at the thought of yet another trip back here after returning to LA, tail between his legs — again without the big story. More flights, more pain-in-the-ass border crossings, more puddle jumping on planes the size of a go-kart, more camping in a shit motel with toilets "sanitized for his convenience." He was utterly sick of the whole thing.

He would wait no longer. What had been a battle of manoeuvres would now be full-on hand-to-hand combat. Dick was going to take the war right to his enemy, push things well beyond the tipping point. Vicar would watch his world begin to crumble and feel the wrath of Richard X. Dick. He and his whole Dogpatch gang could go to hell. Dick would get his story, and his pound of flesh, too. It was going to be glorious. *Fuck Vicar and his stupid pub.*

PART III

Thirty-Six / Burnin' Love

By the late summer, Frankie had grown from a little package that could be engulfed by one pair of large hands into a pumpkin of some weight. Merri Crabtree swung her gently in the crook of her arm and simply enjoyed the feeling of holding an infant. No one else in Jacquie and Vicar's circle could be so easily convinced to babysit, that was certain. The mere sight of a baby flipped a switch in her — she simply *had* to hold it. She knew it bordered on obsessive, but she couldn't help herself and honestly didn't want to. Babies were to her like shoes to Céline Dion — there were never too many in the house.

Merri had set up a little basket in the backroom of Hot Thoth, where baby Frankie could nap, and she could conduct business. The shop was doing well but it certainly didn't draw like the Knickers did, where Jacquie was often required. In return Jacquie and Vicar would mind little Wallis on those rare occasions Merri was busy or had to leave on an errand. It amounted to old-fashioned daycare. Merri felt the pain of her husband's death abating just a little as she saw her days through the eyes of the children.

■ ■ ■

September on Vancouver Island is usually beautiful and this one had been no exception so far. The crystal-blue, cloudless skies were the biggest feature of the hot afternoons, which gave way to early dusk and crisp, starlit nights. Dick and Handlanger, cruising around in their unseemly surveillance van, slowed down as they passed a slapdash-looking fireworks kiosk by the side of the road.

"Pull over here."

The cameraman pulled onto the gravel turnout. Dick jumped out of the van, walked over to the attendant, and said, "I'm looking for fireworks that sound like gunshots, you know, pistols being fired … Bang, bang, bang." He pretended to shoot in the air.

The attendant knew exactly what to sell him, and as he did, took note of the unlikely buyer who seemed so out of place. Who wears a suit to buy fireworks?

■ ■ ■

Jacquie had laid a drowsy Frankie down on the bed with a bottle as Merri put a blanket on Wallis. The two kids looked so sweet snoozing beside one another, and Jacquie felt a tug at her heart. She had built a fort of pillows around Frankie in case she rolled around in her sleep and then stood back to watch for a moment. They were snuggled up quietly — comfy-cozy, safe and sound.

Gathering their things, Jacquie and Merri walked down to the lobby where Vicar was chatting with Beaner, who needed to know whether Ann should have used *there*, *their*, or *they're* on the Sunday Special menu. Jacquie interrupted the barnyard erudition, saying, "Merri and I are going shopping. The kids are asleep now, so just check on them every few minutes. Back around five-ish."

Vicar answered easily, "Yeah, no prob. Ann's got the bar and I was going to putter around down here."

"Later, honey," Jacquie said. She and Merri departed the front door of the hotel and walked off to the car.

Vicar got on his hands and knees beneath the front desk of the hotel and organized some wires, running them along the floor and attaching them neatly with tidy little harnesses. Sundays were quiet and he was enjoying being alone, under a desk, with only a screwdriver and his phone — which was acting as both a jukebox and a flashlight.

He realized he hadn't checked on the kids and padded up the stairs to the newly finished show suite that would demonstrate to everyone how nice the rest of the hotel would look once the remodelling was complete. He quietly cracked the door, saw that both kids were still fast asleep, and crept in, the slightly acrid smell of brand-new carpet assailing his nose.

Vicar adjusted the blankets and, as quietly as he could, shut the curtain just a little more. The sun had moved, and a crack of its bright light was creeping toward Wallis. He had previously been instructed to not let babies sleep too long, but thought, *The hell with that*. There was nothing quite as delicious as an hour or two of uninterrupted quiet.

Enjoying the sensation of stillness, he left them to snooze, tensing up as the lock clicked loudly behind him. He stood there for a second, ear to the door, to hear if the noise had awoken them, but the room remained silent.

Vicar strolled lazily back down the three flights of stairs, remarking to himself that the elevator refurb better be finished soon or they'd never get older people up here; doing the stairs many times a day even beat the hell out of Jacquie, who was quite a jock.

Returning to the front desk he ducked back down to continue his job when the heavy door between pub and hotel creaked open loudly.

"Tony, Tony?" It was Ann Tenna, calling for him, unaware that he was under the desk right in front of her. "Where has that fucker gone, now?" she muttered coarsely.

Singsong, he called out mockingly, "He's under the desk, Annie ..."

"Eh? Oh. Some guy in here wants to meet you. Said he come from Ire-lund."

"Ireland, huh? He came *here* for a pint?" Vicar was impressed.

She laughed and said, "Yeah, he's here with a buncha people. They just wanna shake yer hand ..."

Vicar knew the drill. He stiffly climbed to his feet, hiked up his baggy pants, and followed Ann into the Knickers to do his public relations duty.

▬ ▬ ▬

Without one of his many cameras in hand for a change, Dick's photographic sidekick, Handlanger, was hunched in the dark corner of room 222 as he laid out a long stringlike fuse in a spiral on the wooden floor that led to a small pile of fireworks near the bare studs. He waited a moment until he was satisfied that it was lit and then left the room quickly. The jimmy he had installed had stayed in place and his entry had been as simple as pulling the door open; he could barely believe it. These people were as trusting as children. He passed back through the heavy door and climbed down the old fire escape as silently as he could. He bent over a little and ran along the hedge, down the fenceline, zipped to the van on the side street, and opened the door.

"It's lit," he said, slightly out of breath.

"Good work. Get your camera and let's get ready for action."

▬ ▬ ▬

Vicar bade his new Irish friends goodbye, apologizing for his work pants multiple times, delighted at their lilting delivery of hilarious byplay.

Ann had come along with him to fetch some more bar towels from the storage closet and they passed through the door together.

"Do you know how many pubs there are in Dublin? Over seven hundred! In one city! And they flew *here* for a pint."

Ann looked at him, disbelieving, and began to speak. "Are you serious …?"

At that moment they heard a muffled *pop, pop, pop.* Vicar bounded to the front door and cautiously opened it. It sounded like gunshots — not that he'd heard many before, but like on TV.

Cautiously he crept out to the sidewalk and rubbernecked up and down the street. Nothing. It was as quiet as a mouse out there. He came back and said to Ann, "Car backfire?"

Ann quizzically tilted her head.

▬ ▬ ▬

Jacquie spied the van that Dick and his cameraman had been using for the last while parked down the road from the hotel, muttering to Merri, "My God, those scavengers are still out there."

They had begun to irritate beyond her normal limits of patience. Under her breath she muttered, "They really chap my ass …"

Merri glanced over and could see someone leaning out the window, and she realized it was probably that guy with the camera, photographing them at that very moment.

"And to think you were worried about attracting those hairy apes from the *H-E-Double-Hockey-Sticks* Angels … Maybe they'll get what they want and be on their merry way. Think of it as free advertising." Her trademark giggle ended the statement.

Jacquie made a wry face. No matter the situation Merri laughed after almost every utterance. "My hometown has been wiped out by a giant flood," *giggle, giggle*. She was averse to the slightest hint of conflict, no matter how submissive it might make her look. Jacquie could not believe how far Merri would bend in order to maintain that everything was *just fine*.

Jacquie thought of Tony, of how annoyed he could get at blind cheerfulness, illustrated by his distaste for morning TV hosts — he had once grumbled that he was suspicious of anyone who was "too goddamn happy." *Cult members are always ecstatic as motherfuckers, too, Jack. Then they go off and gargle pesticide, or something.* Yet he seemed able to forgive Merri.

Jacquie rebuked herself; Merri was as solid and grounded as they came, she just acted like a jolly cherub. She had seen for herself how Merri had taken command when Frankie suddenly appeared in the middle of the blizzardy night. But no matter the situation there was always a sugar chaser. When Jacquie really looked at it, Merri's was quite the disguise.

But she also remembered Vicar's warnings about never settling for *just fine* when *excellent* was at their fingertips — and this gave her an insight. *Just fine* often means you are passively settling for less than you deserve, eating it; getting shat on and thanking the shitter. Tony could be way out there, rather weird, occasionally cantankerous, but man, he had taught her a lot about fighting the good fight.

Gaining speed, she turned her attention to the shopping they'd be doing and glanced in the wing mirror, where she saw the cameraman crawling out of the van and looking up at the hotel. She thought about calling Tony to tell him, and then said to herself, *You're getting paranoid — it'll all be fine.*

■ ■ ■

A console table on the little landing above the Agincourt lobby, halfway up the stairs to the second floor, tipped over. A tall vase that had perched upon it shot torpedo-like down the stairs and smashed on the antique chequered tile floor.

"What the hell?" Vicar yelped. He was thrown off, trying to correlate the gunshot sounds with the falling table and vase.

Ann Tenna looked at the broken vase on the floor, and then upward to the table on the landing. She snapped her head toward Vicar and croaked out, "Earthquake maybe?"

"Uhh ... I didn't feel anything. Did you?" More

popping sounds. *Maybe it's electrical transformers blowing?*

She immediately ran back to the heavy steel pub door and stuck her head in. "Everythin' calm in there." She came back and began picking up shards of pottery.

Thinking aloud, Vicar muttered, "I hope we don't have some structural failure happening ..." Ann overheard him and her face tightened in alarm. But Vicar was sure they were good. He and Jacquie had been careful, had paid an engineer a boatload of dough to make sure this reno was okay, and got the correct inspections. He was *pretty* sure. No, he was sure. Totally sure. Well, sure-ish.

Alarmed and confused he climbed the short stairway and felt the wall with the flat of his hand, pressing gently here and there. It all felt sturdy. No give, no cracks, no bulging protrusions, no Rice Krispies sounds. He looked back down at Ann and finally said, "I dunno ... I think you're right ... I'm gonna say earthquake."

He knew that little quakes happened here many times a day and were such a strange phenomenon that, sometimes, a person sitting in a living room would feel a tremor, while someone else over in the nearby bedroom wouldn't notice a thing.

Ann got up from her knees and said, "I gotta check on the customers ... I'll come back'n help ya in a bit ..."

As she said it, there was another jarring crash from above, this time accompanied by a rumble that shook the whole lobby. Vicar's eyes flew open as she drew back.

Instantly, he thought, *The kids ... the kids ...* "Annie, get everyone outta the Knickers. I think the hotel might be collapsing! Evacuate! Get 'em out on the street." He was yelling over his shoulder as he leaped up the stairs at top speed.

Ann Tenna stood rooted for one heartbeat, yelped out, "Fuck me!" in alarm, and then ran screaming into the pub.

Thirty-Seven / Two Frankies and One Valentine

Vicar rounded the top of the stairwell and came to the site of the latest crash, a huge bookshelf. It had fallen face first and partially blocked the last run of stairs up to the third floor, but as it went over, it had disgorged a mound of books, a few nautical knick-knacks, figurines, and one silly Troll doll that now lay face up on the floor, arms outstretched as if it had just fallen on its back from the top of a tall building. Vicar looked for signs of structural failure around him.

He needed to get the kids out of the hotel before something terrible happened. He manoeuvred awkwardly around the bookcase, holding on to the bannister to pull himself upward — and then he smelled it. *Oh God. Smoke.* The kind of smoke that indicates you are going to have an extremely bad day.

He looked up and saw the hallway filling with it. He was truly scared now. With every ounce of oomph he could muster, he dashed up the last run of steps.

— — —

"Baby, get over here quick — the hotel's falling down." Ann Tenna was practically screaming into her cellphone as she shooed patrons out into the street.

"Eh? Calm down, fer Chrissakes. What's goin' on?" Poutine was confused.

"The hotel is collapsing. It's falling down! I think we're gonna die. Hurry, hurry."

Ross Poutine had never heard Ann afraid, not even for a second. Cranky, yes, but this made his klaxons scream. He ran outside as fast as he could to his Chevelle, started it, and had the back tires lit up within a blink.

Dick and his cameraman had moved their van around to the front of the Knickers in order to get the best view of any chaos, which Dick had hoped would provide him with excellent footage of the event, showing Vicar powerless to stop fleeing customers, staggering around helplessly, out of his element, in no way magical, vividly illustrating the first chapter in the saga of a remorseless collapse, as written and directed by Richard X. Dick. Handlanger had his equipment set and ready and was already rolling when they had both heard the pop-pop-popping of the fireworks. Man, this was going to be a great show!

Con-Con was patrolling around somewhat aimlessly. The day had been very quiet so far — her only stop had been at the home of Mrs. Morrison, a tediously persistent phone-in complainant, who today was having a fit about her neighbour, who had parked his truck in front of her yard — in no way illegally. Dispatch had sent her out with a chuckle, and once there, she was forced to spend a half-hour listening to the town's tartan busybody as Mrs. Morrison railed righteously about the potential property devaluation caused by "workman's lorries" in front of her rigidly manicured, joy-free home, located, as she said twice, "in the highly desirable seaside subdivision of Sandringham Mews."

Standing on the front steps, Con-Con peered at Mrs. Morrison's plaid skirt with the big gold kilt pin and redundant sash, wondering if there was anyone else outside of Scotland who was as punctiliously Scottish as she. Con-Con had heard of virtue signalling before but this was more like "thistle signalling," right down to the bogus accent that randomly threaded its faux burr in and out of her intricate grievances.

Her previous complaint had to do with "shoddy, abstract rubbish bin placement." *This street is not a Picasso exhibit, Constable* ... Con-Con tried to predict her next call — perhaps she'd set her sights on tides that failed to obey the published chart. Con-Con listened until she finally ran out of hot air and then headed for a much-deserved cup of coffee.

Driving slowly, she spied a vehicle roaring toward her at a crazy speed. As it approached, she recognized it. It was Ross Poutine, hurtling down the road in his prized car at a deadly clip. She did a quick three-point turn, clicked on her wig-wags, and gave chase.

What is that crazy old goat up to? In her powerful cruiser, she caught up to him quickly. He glanced up at his rear-view mirror and then stuck his arm out the window. He was waving at her to follow him. He put his boot to the floor and the powerful Chevelle leaped ahead like a missile.

— — —

Vicar reached the top of the third-floor stairs and glanced around. There was a fire all right, but he couldn't be sure where it was located. He just knew he had to get the kids outta the newly completed suite. His heart was racing, his respiration ragged. He was inhaling smoke now and the state of emergency was getting more acute with every passing moment.

He ran down the hall through the quickly thickening cloud, one arm out in front of him, the other covering his nose and mouth. Hearing a fearsome crackling sound, he looked over his shoulder and saw the upper fire exit clouded in heavy smoke and flame. *Oh God ... no escape that way.* It'd be back down the main stairs or no way out at all.

— — —

Ann Tenna raced through the pub as fast as her short legs would take her. No one was in any of the bathrooms, no one in the lobby, no one under the desk, no one cowering in closets or storage rooms. It was empty except for her … *But what about Tony and the babies?* A sense of horror coursed through her. She smelled the bitter odour of a burning building. Was the place collapsing or was it on fire? Or both? As the lobby filled with tendrils of poisonous smoke, she stood trembling for a second and decided she had to get them out.

◼ ◼ ◼

Poutine had hit ninety miles an hour. At that speed it took only a minute to get all the way downtown, with Con-Con on his six like glue. She had her siren going now and was concentrating on her driving as best she could.

When they rounded the bend, she understood what was happening instantly. Flames were shooting out of the southwest corner of the Agincourt Hotel and smoke billowed heavily upward and to the east. She grabbed her radio and called it in as she four-wheel-drifted around the last corner that would lead her to the front of the hotel.

Poutine, just ahead of her, jammed on his binders short of the hotel, screeched sideways in a very Starsky and Hutch manner, and was already on foot for the main entrance before the Chevelle had even stopped rocking.

Richard Dick saw heavy smoke curling out of the side of the hotel and stiffened up. He hadn't thought a *real* fire would start. A little smoke and some fake gunshots would have been enough. But whatever. The hotel was just an empty hulk getting a reno, so he decided to see what might come of this newest wrinkle. They had burned him, now he was giving them a little payback. Repeat mantra: *Fuck Tony Vicar and his stupid pub.*

Vicar was on the edge of panic now. The fire was growing exponentially. The smoke was thick, his eyes were burning, he was trying to breathe through his T-shirt, hastily pulled up over his nose.

He fumbled with the key card for the door lock and couldn't make it open. He reversed the card, trying the other end, then flipped it over laterally. The anxiety was rising inside him like he was full of Pepsi and Mentos.

Finally, the damned thing clicked open, and he recklessly threw open the door. There before him was the most beautiful sight he'd ever seen. Two little angels, sound asleep in a hotel room yet untouched by the fire. He pushed the door shut behind him and barged into the bathroom, turning the shower on full blast.

Grabbing two large bath towels he soaked them with the cold rushing water and then slopped them over toward the kids.

Wallis, at four years old, could be communicated with, at least.

"Walrus, Walrus ... Wake up, buddy. We hafta get out of here. Wally?"

Vicar was now shaking him hard and he woke with a start, apple cheeks glowing, a sleepy look on his face.

"What's wrong?" Little Wallis could see the extreme alarm on Uncle Tony's face.

Vicar hesitated and then just explained the situation.

"Buddy, there is a fire and we have to get out. Be calm and brave and we'll all go together. Okay?"

Little Wallis II, named after Merri's deceased husband, just looked up at Vicar with big eyes and sat up.

"Good man." As he spoke, he picked up little Frankie in his arms. She didn't even awaken.

"We're going to hide under these wet towels for a minute. You have to keep it on your head. You hafta. Okay?"

Little Wallis just nodded, his saucer-like eyes trying to make some sense of this sudden scary scene.

Vicar stuffed little Frankie inside his shirt and grabbed Wallis with his other arm.

"Put your arms around my neck, buddy. Ride me like a sideways horsey." He draped a cold wet towel over Wallis's head and then a second one over his own that also covered little Frankie. He moved to the door, felt it, and then paused for a second.

"Stay under the towel, bud. Promise?"

"Yeth …"

Vicar cracked the door, peeked out, and then moved as quickly as he could toward the main stairwell. The hallway was now very hot and dangerously smoky, and he had to peek out of the towel to stay on course.

Vicar was hunched and trying to protect the kids with his encircling arms and could not manage to free his hands to guide him through the smoke and down the railing. He had to put his shoulders against the wall as a guide, his arms grasping the little ones desperately.

The wall was terribly hot, but he tried to ignore it and step as carefully as he could. He was trying not to panic, but the responsibility of keeping the kids alive was overwhelming. He knew if he stumbled and fell, they'd probably not make it. His vision darkened into a tunnel, as if he was gazing through a fish-eye lens.

Through the smoke and panic, a disembodied voice spoke. "Just a little farther now. Be careful. Slow and steady, slow and steady."

"Okay, okay, I'm okay. I'm okay, I'm okay …" Vicar babbled trancelike in response, recognizing it as the voice of Frankie Hall, a woman long dead, the very same Frankie Hall who once owned this place and had willed it to him. *No fucking time to hallucinate, Vicar,* he screamed to himself.

He slid downward to the second-floor landing, tripping over a large lion-shaped ceramic pot filled with elephant grass that sat against the hot bricks, and was confronted by an impenetrable, raging wall of flame, beyond which lay the collapsed bookshelf and his only route to safety. He and the children were going to die.

Ann Tenna climbed the stairs as quickly as she could. She knew Vicar had gone up to get the kids from the suite on the third floor, but she didn't know if she could survive in the smoke much longer. A thought flashed through her head: *Better dead than someone who let kids die in a fire*. She was going up until she perished if that's what it took.

Reduced now to feeling her way along the hot walls, she stayed low and managed to get to the stairwell that led to the third floor, her eyes burning, choking desperately, stars flashing in her eyes with every cough. She felt terrifying heat from the blaze that blocked her pathway to the third-floor stairway as she was confronted by the wall of flames causing it. There was an upended bookcase in front of her, the base of it now beginning to burn. She could go no farther and fell apart. She had to back away from the searing flames and began to scream in abject terror.

On the other side of this wall of flames, Vicar could hear her and moaned out, "Here, we're here ... Help us ... I have the kids, I have the *babies* ..." Short of breath, he wasn't sure he could be heard over the malevolent roar of the fire. Vicar was losing strength and felt his knees buckling, sensed his back sliding down the hot wall behind him.

Little Walrus peeked out from the towel, saw the flames, and was instantly terrified. He began to bawl in sheer fright. Vicar heard him and tried to straighten up, to get his feet under him. But he didn't have the strength to climb back up the stairs and felt certain they had no other way out. He weakly tried to calm Wallis and prepared himself for death, cradling his precious little Frankie as tightly as he dared.

■ ■ ■

Jacquie had been ignoring her phone for the last few minutes, letting it go to voice mail as she shopped for Egyptian cotton sheets with Merri.

Finally, after the fourth call came in, she grabbed the phone. It was Beaner, calling from the street, still in his dirty apron.

"Jacquie, y' better get back to the Knickers. The hotel is on fire."

"What?" For a second, she didn't believe him.

"The fire department is here but I don't see Tony … It's bad, Jacquie."

"Oh my God … *the babies*!" she shrieked, and Merri knew instantly that there was an emergency.

Jacquie quickly said to Merri, "The hotel is burning down, and they can't find Tony!"

"The babies!"

They both ran as fast as they could to Jacquie's car and fled back toward Tyee Lagoon at top speed.

— — —

Ross Poutine dashed into the hotel lobby and could barely see his hand in front of his face. He knew the layout of the place, though.

"Annie, Annie …" He bounded up the stairs, now thick with smoke, and began choking. Arm over his face, he continued as quickly as he could around the structure to the next staircase and then saw Annie, on her knees screaming and wailing. She had collapsed in front of a wall of flame.

He grabbed her arm and tried to pull her to her feet in the thickening, deadly smoke as she screamed, "Tony and the kids … They're on the other side of the fire, there … there …" She pointed urgently.

Poutine looked at the situation and his heart sank. He heard the frantic calls from his friend and the crying of a child but there was no going through that. He couldn't see fire extinguishers and didn't think they'd even been installed yet. He had to at least save Annie and himself. He tried to move her, but she would not budge. She just knelt there in the direst emotional agony he'd ever witnessed.

— — —

Everything had slowed down. *I guess this is how it is right before you check out*, Vicar thought.

With the fire directly ahead of him, the stairway to the third floor at his left elbow, and certain death on his doorstep, Vicar suddenly noticed a black shadow on the stairs. He thought it was some part of the building collapsing in on them and prepared himself for burial under this hideous conflagration; he would protect the two little children with his body to the last breath.

But it became a pair of legs. Two trouser legs now descended through the smoke. Whoever was coming toward him had an argyle sock on one foot and was barefooted on the other. He came swiftly but smoothly to Vicar. He was young, just a kid, in an old work shirt and with tousled, short hair. He leaned down to Vicar, pulled him to his feet, and shepherded him forward.

Vicar now concluded that he had died, and this was some kind of afterlifey shite, so he dazedly allowed himself to be led by this calm young man. They approached the wall of fire and Tony Vicar felt no heat, no searing, melting temperature that should have lit them ablaze in an instant. With the mysterious guide at his side, he and the two children shuffled through the blazing doorway.

▬ ▬ ▬

Con-Con threw her cruiser door open and plunged into the lobby not far behind Poutine, half chasing the reckless fool, and half wanting to rescue anyone inside who might be trapped. She had to feel her way up the stairs, and she feared she'd trip over a pile of dead bodies. Rounding the corner, she shone her flashlight around and saw movement and approached it with as much speed as she could manage through the smoky haze. It was Ross Poutine, trying to drag his Annie to her feet in this horrible death trap, desperate to save her life. She, on the other hand, was begging him to save the babies. Con-Con felt sick but needed to get the pair to safety.

At that moment, she saw before her, walking through a deadly wall of flame, Tony Vicar, two children in his arms, choking, exhausted, but alive.

Not quite believing her eyes, Con-Con nevertheless leaped toward them and grabbed little Wallis, who howled in terror, and practically threw him at Poutine.

"Get the hell out of here RIGHT NOW!" she screamed with incredible authority.

Poutine hesitated and his eyes flicked to Ann Tenna, still collapsed on the floor.

"I've got her; *get the kid to safety.*"

Poutine awoke to the priorities of the situation and fled, stumbling back down the route that brought him there, coughing, eyes pouring tears, Wallis and his wet towel locked in his arms.

"They're okay, Annie, they're safe, they're safe." Con-Con coughed. "Let's save ourselves ..." She had to get Ann up and onto her feet and moving under her own steam; she didn't think she could suck enough air to carry her to safety.

Ann, who had been staring petrified at Con-Con, glanced away from her momentarily; suddenly her eyes widened as if they might pop right out of her skull. Con-Con followed her gaze and saw only Vicar, haloed by tremendous high-temperature flames, his arms covering baby Frankie, whose head poked out from under his shirt; the tableau looked like the coat of arms of Hell itself. On the floor in front of him was a liquefying Troll doll, now nearly a puddle.

Ann, however, saw something Con-Con did not. There before her was a young man, wearing only one sock, who calmly looked directly at her and paused for a heartbeat. He held up his hand, palm facing her, as if acknowledging her there, collapsed on the floor. He gazed vividly at her, then turned around and passed back through the deadly wall of fire — serenely wading into the conflagration, toward certain doom.

For just a second, she sat there as if having been slugged in the jaw. She could not credit what her eyes had just shown her. He really ought to have burst into flames, but now, no matter what, she knew they could no longer help him; whoever he was, wherever he came from, he was beyond rescue. The whole stairwell was ablaze, the entire third floor soon to be, too. The young man was gone, he was gone. He had walked right into the worst of it and had vanished.

They only had moments to evacuate. Ann snapped to and lumbered to safety as Con-Con shoved them all, yelling and chivvying like a curling skip, delivering them to Fire-Rescue who were just arriving on the scene.

- - -

In a miracle of timing, the volunteer fire department had been doing a weekend training exercise, so when the call came in, they were quick to arrive. There was an ambulance already on-site and two more on the way.

Ross Poutine stumbled out of the main entrance of the Agincourt and fell into the arms of firefighters rushing to the entranceway, who took little Wallis from him and put oxygen masks on both.

Vicar lurched unsteadily down the stairs, Ann Tenna just ahead of him, Frankie still stuffed in his shirt, Con-Con with a death grip on his arm. As he wobbled outside, he looked back at his burning hotel. What a bloody mess.

There were patrons out in the street, wandering around in front of the blazing structure, some with their pint glasses still in hand, staring upward, aghast at the flames bursting out of the roof.

He saw that sonofabitch Dick Dick and his pond-scum cameraman running around from onlooker to onlooker, rudely shoving his microphone into their faces and asking things like, "Is Vicar to blame for this tragedy?" Vicar was disoriented and a little confused yet still wondered how they had managed to show up already, while the building was still in flames. Fucking vultures, he thought.

A Knickers evacuee, who had had a microphone pushed rudely into her face, looked over at Vicar, who was perched on the back bumper of an ambulance, face blackened by smoke, oxygen mask on, cradling a baby in his arms. She roughly pushed the mic away and growled, "Are you insane?" She stormed away disgusted. Dick simply moved along to the next person.

Vicar didn't have the strength to punch that asshole in the nose, but he wished he had. He simply sat there, rocking back and forth, thanking his lucky stars that he got the kids out. Against his chest he held, safe and sound, his little baby Frankie. He hadn't heard a peep from her. In fact, she was quiet in his arms and might well have slept through the whole thing. He had been far too busy to notice. He buried his sooty face in her shoulder and raggedly exhaled.

When Jacquie and Merri arrived at the hotel, the emergency had already passed. Tony sat in the ambulance, holding Frankie, while Ross Poutine snuggled with Wallis, who had been given a Glow Stick to play with and still breathed oxygen from a nearby tank.

Merri looked gratefully at Poutine and hugged Wallis, whispering to him urgently, horrified at the fire, even more horrified that she had not been there to protect him.

Jacquie had confirmed that everyone was safe with her own eyes and then dissolved in tears, her face in her hands, reduced to a wet dishrag of emotion. The vision of what might have happened passed before her eyes and she collapsed onto one knee, with a nearby EMT grabbing her as she went down.

Vicar scanned the scene, too weak to respond, still terrified and now angry. He tried to make some sense, any sense, of it.

The Tyee Lagoon Volunteer Fire Department was a ragtag bunch of locals, certainly not qualified to knock down a fire in a metropolitan high-rise, but plenty good enough to deal with the Agincourt blaze.

They had exactly one truck with a ladder and made excellent use of it, and if truth be told, they were slightly excited by the whole affair. People were snapping pictures on their phones and, once they were confident that everyone was out of the hotel and safe, they became slightly camera conscious, posing just a little now and then. This *never* happened in Tyee Lagoon. The last time they had to defeat a big fire at a commercial building must have been twenty years ago, or more.

The entire southwest corner of the hotel was burned to cinders. The damage resembled a big V, chewed out of a huge cube of charcoal. Merri's Hot Thoth had been consumed, the back end of Liquor was mostly gone, and the hotel rooms above 222, as well as much of the south corner of the third floor, were completely burned away. The Agincourt Hotel, for all intents and purposes, was in ruins.

To Vicar's deep surprise, though, was the state of the Knickers. It had suffered far less fire damage, and the heavy doors that they had installed had even kept out the worst of the violently roiling smoke. Man, he had bitched about the cost of upgrading at the time. Part of the south wall was badly scorched and would have to be replaced, but he was immensely grateful that the Knickers had been, for all intents and purposes, saved to serve another pint.

Poutine picked his way into the burned-out hulk of his formerly beautiful new shop and put his face in his hands. *Such a goddamn waste.* A few feet away Merri Crabtree could be seen gazing around, visible through the burned-out wall that had separated the two shops. She stood mutely, ashen and upset as she surveyed the damage to Hot Thoth. She was wounded by this cruel twist but put the feelings aside when she saw Poutine's grief.

"Oh, Ross, I am so sorry. You worked so hard on this." For once she didn't giggle after her statement.

"And you wuz doin' so good ..." Poutine trailed off.

"Well, at least you still have your old store. You can keep going until this one is fixed up again ... You are going to fix it up, aren't you?"

Poutine stared at the rubble for a couple seconds and muttered, "Yeah ... I'll start again ... Goddamn it all. What're you gonna do?"

"Umm, not sure. I don't know if I have the energy to start from scratch again." She looked at the hundreds of broken hot sauce bottles that littered the fire-blackened floor.

"Y'know, Merri ... I think you should open up yer shop over in the corner of my old shop until we get this place back up to snuff."

That was the famous Ross Poutine generosity, coming at the right time and place, she thought, her heart filling with warmth for this smelly but wonderful man.

━━ ━━ ━━

"It started in the last room of the second floor and spread in all directions from there. It moved very, very quickly and appears to have been started on purpose."

"On purpose? Like, arson?"

"Yes, Mr. Vicar. Arson. It was set deliberately. I can't be sure what caused the blaze, but someone started it in the corner of that room."

The fire investigator pointed toward the burned-out hulk of room 222.

"We also discovered the melted remains of heavy tape put over the door mechanism of the emergency exit, which was deliberately placed there to prevent the locks from engaging."

Vicar looked at him, startled. "Someone jiggered with the door lock?"

"Yes. Did you check to see that all the doors were locked before closing every night?"

"I may not have ..." He immediately felt he was to blame. "I checked but I might have missed a day or two. I just can't be sure ..." He trailed off, knowing that he had probably failed to do the rounds on at least that critical evening. *Damn.* He even left his keys in the ignition most of the time. Such a country mouse.

The fire investigator replied, "A lot of arsonists gain easy access due to someone's forgetfulness." Vicar was looking at his shoes. "I know, Mr. Vicar. It's a terrible lesson to learn."

Someone burned down my hotel and violated the peace of this little town. Vicar felt that his entire sense of place in the world, the safety and security it provided him and his circle of loved ones, was now under attack. He felt an inner rage coming to the boil.

Thirty-Nine / The Feels of Wheat

One thing about sitting at a kiosk by the side of the road, waiting for people to pull over and buy something, was that it was as boring as shit. Summer season was over, but October was just around the corner. The young man working there listened to tunes, had a couple of hot rod magazines to look at, and incessantly scrolled through his phone, looking at the same things again and again, impatiently waiting for any updates to help pass the time.

Today, it was going to be warm and he wanted some beer to drink. He had a magnetic wrapper that disguised beer as "Cola." He'd just rip through a few cold ones to help him through his day.

He stopped at Liquor and appreciated the '66 Chevelle parked in front of it. *Wow, a real beaut.*

"That your car?"

"Yup," grunted Ross Poutine grumpily. He was none too happy about being stuck back here at the old shop. His heart had been set on opening the new one.

The young man continued speaking over his shoulder as he wandered around looking for cans of his favourite beer.

"I need a little pop to pass the time … It's so quiet. It'll be crazy when Hallowe'en comes, but now it's super-slow."

"Slow here, too," agreed Poutine, deciding to try chattiness for a rare change, hoping it might force him into a better mood. He heard the echoes of Annie calling him an old "retrobate," or somethin' like that. What the hell did that mean? It sounded bad and he didn't like her mad at him.

He piped up, "The other week my buddy thought he heard guns shootin' in the street. That's a laugh. No excitement like that 'round here …"

That shook loose a memory in the young man's head. "Hmm … Some guy came by a couple weeks ago and asked me for fireworks that sounded like gunshots." Like the customer had done, he used his fingers to simulate a pistol shooting in the air. "Maybe your buddy heard his fireworks."

Poutine just nodded but then after a moment stiffened. "D'ya remember the guy? Fancy? All dressed up like he was goin' to a funeral?"

Merri Crabtree, organizing some sauce bottles and not fully tuned to the light banter, suddenly looked up with interest.

"Yup. That's him ... Freak was wearing one of those *ass-cots*. And another guy. They had a white van. I remember. It was one of those serial killer vans with no side windows."

━━ ━━ ━━

Vicar strolled into the old Liquor location to buy some wine and check on his newly homeless renters, Poutine and Merri Crabtree. He remained, weeks later, in a terrible state about the fire, and felt a continual nauseated knot in his stomach. His good friends had been burned out of business and it bothered him a great deal. Merri's shop was a hobby, so she'd be okay, but Poutine's business was his principal means of income. Thank God he still had the old shop to limp through.

Poutine piped up, "Hey, Tony, I think mebbe we figured somethin' out ... Y'know how you thought ya heard a gun shootin' out in the street when the fire started?"

"Yes ..." Vicar was immediately attentive. How often did Poutine offer any conversation of this variety?

"Well, umm ... The guy what sells fireworks up on the highway sez he sold some to that Dick Dick, dere."

Vicar's eyes opened wider, but he said nothing.

"Sez the fucker asked him fer firecrackers that sounded like guns shootin', dere, uhh ..." He shot finger pistols.

Vicar paused, then swallowed hard. He looked at Merri, emotion rising in his chest.

"I was there with Ross, Tony. The guy was telling the truth." She gave a nervous laugh, as if nervous to be sure of anything at all, that Vicar ignored. "Jacquie and I saw that pair of buzzards near the hotel when we left to go shopping."

His jaw jutted out and he began to hiss, "Oh my. Oh my … *Oh my* …"

"Now that you mention it, we did see those two skulking around when we left. I was going to warn you but I never for a second thought they might be up to something that awful." Jacquie was shocked.

"Well, Jack," Vicar replied, laundry-listing his growing suspicions, "someone jimmied the door, someone set a fire in room 222 — we know that for certain now. Someone set off firecrackers that sound like gunshots. I heard them myself. Annie heard them, too. Now we know that sonofabitch Dickcheese bought fireworks that sound like gunshots — and you and Merri saw those bastards outside the hotel just before the fire." He saw the colour drain from Jacquie's face.

Vicar's face, on the other hand had been red for some time and now became even redder; he could hear blood pumping in his ears and his hands were shaking. He chewed on the mounting evidence, getting angrier with every minute. He *knew* they had set the fire, those abominable monsters. He knew it. *They tried to murder us all!*

VINCE R. DITRICH

✕ ✕ ✕

Later that night as they sat at the dinner table, Vicar announced, "I have no idea if the cops can link it to him, but if I ever clap eyes on that sonofabitch again … Well, let's just say, no body, no crime."

It might have sounded like puffery, but Jacquie knew he was deadly serious and felt a sharp jab of fear. Everything had been so peaceful before those villains arrived.

But Farley, uninvited yet again and munching merrily, repeatedly making the cushion on the chair produce a farting sound, merely nodded in silent agreement and tucked into his slice of pizza. *It just isn't right … Maybe you can get away with that in Hollywood, but not Tyee Lagoon.* Then he leaned back on the noisy cushion and produced an awesome ripper.

▬ ▬ ▬

Chief Wheat stood respectfully outside the fire-damaged Agincourt and hung his head. Many of the townsfolk drove or walked past to see the damage, most tutting and clucking in dismay. The entire community had been proud of Tony Vicar's efforts. He was putting them on the map, for better or for worse.

Of course, there were a few old turds who were convinced that his fame would result in nothing but traffic headaches and the influx of a "bad element." But if asked, Vicar would no doubt have agreed with them. What worse element could there be than Dicky Dick?

Beaner had been inside the hotel, picking through the wreckage and trying to wash the smoke residue off the walls in the Knickers that had been untouched by fire. He took a break and saw his old friend Chief Wheat standing at the curb.

"Helluva thing, huh?"

"Yes, lad. A tragedy. But sometimes setbacks are put in your path to strengthen you. A horrible accident but at least no one was hurt."

"Umm ... This wasn't no accident ..."

Chief Wheat turned to him, a serious look on his face.

"What do you mean, lad?"

"Tony says that Dick Dick set the place on fire. Said he used fireworks. Musta snuck in."

"Does the Vicar have any proof of this?" Chief Wheat was thunderstruck by such a serious accusation. Like nearly everyone in town, he loathed Dick, but this kind of talk took matters to another, far more serious level.

"Yeah. Fire investigator says it was arson. Tony says he can prove it was Dick. I'm purdy sure he's gonna kill that prick if he ever sees him again."

Chief Wheat was suddenly sick to his stomach and wandered back toward his house, deep in thought.

Forty / Junk in the Trunk

"Beaner, can you help me out with a little shopping? I just don't wanna go anywhere right now. I know it's a pain, but can you help a brother out? You can use the Caddy if you'd like." Vicar felt weary and was fighting off a wave of depression.

Beaner's initial hesitancy was wiped away by the offer of the Cadillac. He had been hoping to take that thing for a rip for a long time.

"Sure, Tony. You mind if I do a couple things for myself, too?" He didn't mention going to the golf course to retrieve balls. That was top secret.

"No problem. Just don't ding it up. It's a lot older than you are."

"Oh, I'll drive it slow, like a little ol' lady ..."

▄ ▄ ▄

Handlanger had dropped Dick off near the golf course, far enough from the water hazard that he could quietly make his way there on foot unnoticed. Handlanger, in the white van, spun around and made his way up to Vicar and Jacquie's house to continue the harassment. Dick, mobile phone in hand, soon discovered the colossal 1974 Cadillac Sedan de Ville ahead of him in the parking area and gawped at it, hardly able to believe its size, capturing it on video for posterity as he approached it. He had once stayed in a microscopic hotel room that was about the same dimensions as this behemoth when on assignment in Hong Kong. He understood now how a fully racked moose could fit inside it.

Walking to the edge of the parking lot and looking toward the water hazard he could see the moose in question, holding a sack in one hand and a telescoping golf ball retriever in the other. *Finally!* He had caught the elusive Vicar in his strange disguise, collecting golf balls like some touched savant.

He got his phone ready and ran toward the moose in the near distance.

"TONY VICAR! Why are you dressed as a moose? Why are you collecting golf balls? Who is the mother of your love child?" He was yelling and approaching aggressively. He got up very close, so close that Moose was badly startled and tried to make a break for it. He was determined to keep his anonymity.

Moose ran, Dick trailing a mere step behind, pawing at him like a cougar trying to down its prey. He turned his head sharply and accidentally struck Dick in the face with the end of his antler.

Dick's pretty face was suddenly gushing blood, and he was knocked to his knees, his fancy mobile phone submerged in the water beneath the bulrushes, his expensive shirt now red with squirting blood. For a moment he thought his eye had been gouged out.

Moose didn't pause for one second; he did NOT want this asshole to learn his identity. He ruined lives for a living! Moose flew as fast as he could, yanking open the car door and forcing himself behind the wheel. Into reverse gear he went, trying to back out as quickly as possible without hitting the low guard rail that surrounded the whole area. He was unable to fully close the door because his massive antlers required a good deal of manoeuvring — or the assistance of a spotter — to thread through an open window.

Dick swung into view again, this time angry as a bull, his face flowing with blood, looking like some TV show bad guy and running pell-mell toward the car. He was soaking wet and covered in weeds and blood. For the first time, thought Moose, he looked scary.

He spun the Caddy's wheel hard to the right, making the reversing land yacht hook leftward sharply. He jammed the accelerator down and gravel sprayed like buckshot.

Dick, now running at full tilt, was unable to change his heading and got a terrible hip check from the fender of the quickly reversing two-and-a-half-ton behemoth. His body bowed, bending sharply over the hood of the car, and then twanged the other direction, lofting quite impressively over the gravel-strewn parking area. He smacked down and skidded like a bag of potatoes falling off the back of a moving truck and folded into a crumpled heap.

"Oh, shit ..." cursed Moose.

He untangled himself from behind the controls of the Caddy and surveyed the carnage. Dicky "the Dick" Dick was moaning but appeared operational. Moose popped the trunk, a boot so capacious that revealing it to modern-day appreciators of automobiles elicited hushed wonder.

Dragging Dick to his feet, wobbly, bleeding, and disoriented, he pushed him headfirst into the trunk, banging it shut with a thump.

With his camera beside him, Handlanger skulked around Vicar's house and hid in the bushes. From the untrimmed hedge he could see evidence of landscaping in progress and a stepladder lying against the house. Above the ladder, on a higher floor, was a window — not too large but big enough for his purposes.

If they wanted more footage, they'd have to get it here, at Vicar's house, because the Knickers was shut down and the hotel was a burned-out hulk.

He hunched over and rushed to the ladder, attempting to keep the clattery old thing from making too much noise as he hefted it to the vertical, his camera at his feet.

Gently, quietly, he climbed up, the camera now balanced on his shoulder. He tried to be silent as a mouse, but the ladder rattled and rubbed against the side of the building. It did not occur to him for even a second that scaling a ladder to spy inside someone's house might be indecent. Nope. In this business you can't worry too much about the feelings of your subjects, otherwise the whole industry would just go away. No, you looked at the state of play, found your angle, and did what it took — and did it before someone else could scoop you. There was a job to do, it was dangerous and outrageous, and that was just the way he liked his assignments.

There was no knowing what he would have done in life without this horrible occupation at his disposal. This guy, well, he might have done well as Torquemada's executive assistant. Heaven only knew what his family thought. What mother even for a fleeting second looks at her newborn son and whispers, "I think he'll grow up to be a henchman." He had all the conscience of a virus.

His boss, Richard Dick, encouraged heartlessness, a learned trait. "Don't *take* it on, *pass* it on" was something he frequently said. It seemed to be the way he kept his head above the mire. If he had felt bad about the *accidental* fire, he didn't show it. Dick had toughened himself to his role and Handlanger knew that if he wanted to stay in this league, he had to stay well away from pangs of conscience. *When they're on the run, keep chasing.*

As clever as he thought he was, he had not planned his mission well. For one thing, Jacquie and the baby were alone in the house. Even a dunce would realize that this made his surveillance seem all that much more threatening; he thought Vicar was out because he could not locate the big Cadillac in the garage. In fact, Vicar was in the backyard, fumbling around in the shed, extremely agitated about recent events and deep in thought, muttering angrily at the lawn mower.

He put the camera in position and began recording, hoping to get a glimpse of something through the window, under orders to keep up the incessant pressure on Vicar until he did *something*, gave some reaction they could use to hurt him.

He found himself peering into a bathroom. He twiddled with the focus and leaned away from the eyepiece, trying to stay still and silent. Suddenly it dawned on him that his target, Jacquie O, with her back to him, was literally sitting on the toilet, not more than two feet from him through the wall.

＿＿ ＿＿ ＿＿

Jacquie could see shadows moving on the wall in front of her and immediately thought that the trees must be swaying madly in the wind — yet she could hear no gusts. How odd.

She stood and did up her pants, the camera catching it all, and then looked out the window. There, to her deep shock, was a man looking at her. She shrieked loudly and fled protectively toward baby Frankie.

At that same moment, Vicar had exited the little shed, his splitting maul in hand, an axe-like tool that was half sledgehammer — he had intended to split a few pieces of wood for a cozy fire.

Vicar heard Jacquie's blood-curdling scream and looked up at the house. His heart almost stopped as he saw Handlanger, that evil reptile, up on the ladder with a camera on his shoulder. Jacquie's shrieks continued. He snapped, running headlong toward the house, his maul in hand. He was screaming like a banshee, "You fucker! You fucker!"

Handlanger knew there was serious hell to be paid and struggled to get down the ladder before Vicar could get to him. But it was too late. Vicar was speeding like an enraged locomotive.

He got down three rungs but no more. Vicar, on the fly, brought the splitting maul up to his shoulder like a baseball bat and swung at the base of the ladder with all his might. It had stood on a walkway with a little gravel on its surface, and so when it received the impact of the battering, it gave way instantly, the camera plummeting earthward first, followed an instant later by the cameraman. Both were now non-functional.

▬ ▬ ▬

"Shirley … I'll be damned … It's that moose again. It's driving a car, now!" The cackles of her friend on the other end of the call could have been heard from across the street.

"I swear to you … It's driving a limousine or something."

A couple of people farther down the same street also gawked at the massive black Cadillac whizzing by, operated, they would also attest, by a moose, one antler sticking way out the window, the other one clattering away inside. They also could hear the muffled sounds of someone yelling and kicking.

There was a reason for this: Richard Dick had regained his senses while still trapped in the apartment-sized trunk of the Caddy and had started screaming bloody murder.

Beaner didn't know what to do. Even he, almost totally oblivious to his own eccentricities, was aware that a moose driving a car with a bellowing hostage in the trunk was slightly irregular. Confused, his homing instincts kicked in. He turned the big car toward Vicar's house.

Once he got out of the main part of Tyee Lagoon and onto Sloop Road he relaxed a little. The kicking and screaming wouldn't abate, so, a bit annoyed, he jammed on the brakes a few times and put the right wheels into the roughest parts of the shoulder. The protests turned from outrage to the frightened squeals of a schoolgirl. At one moment the screaming was so satisfactory that Beaner pulled the mouth string of his moose head while he laughed, making the lower jaw flap up and down with mirth. Most enjoyable!

Approaching the hairpin turn he slowed the land yacht down and veered into Tony and Jacquie's driveway. The big radials crunched on the gravel as he caught sight of Jacquie O running toward him, her face as white as a ghost. She could clearly hear the kicking and screaming from the trunk.

"Wha ... What in the *HELL* is going on?" Her shriek was a mixture of anger and fear.

"Oh, I've got Dicky Dick in the trunk," the driving moose said, offhanded. "I just didn't know what to do with him." He seemed nonchalant — like he was trying to find a home for unwanted lawn furniture. *Mrs. Moose was so dreadfully tired of wicker ...*

Jacquie was bewildered and her eyes were rimmed with terror.

"Beaner? Is that you?"

"Yuppers. Howzit goin'?"

Dick was unquestionably in the trunk; she heard him in all his outrage. She did not know why or even care at that second. *This is all so bizarre; it must be true.* She began to quake. The muffled protests from the boot increased. For a brief flash she longed for the boredom of university.

"Turn around and get the hell out of here. As quick as you can. When Tony finds out that you have that sonofabitch, he'll haul him out and kill him. Go. Go." She frantically waved her arms, shooing him desperately. She had just seen a look in Tony's eye that no one, surely not even Tony himself, had ever witnessed before. Despair washed over her. He had worked so hard to become a kinder, gentler man ...

Beaner sat thinking for a second as Tony poked his head out from around the corner, eyes narrowing as he heard Dick pounding on the inside trunk lid of the

Caddy. Vicar heard the voice of his mortal enemy calling his name. *Transported here by justice itself to receive his due punishment!* He picked up the shovel that stood against the wall and briskly approached the car.

Jacquie began shrieking and implored him to leave immediately. "Go, Beaner ... This will be a catastrophe. *Please GO.*"

Making a rare good decision, Beaner jammed the Caddy in reverse and bounced backward recklessly into the middle of the roadway above, blindly backing up, having a hella bad time with the rear-view mirror. He shifted into D, turned the wheel, and peeled out, heading back into town, Tony Vicar now glaring murderously from the mouth of the driveway while a violently protesting Dicky Dick rolled around, log-like, in the trunk.

Sloop Road was too dangerous to drive at the speed he had been pushing it, so Beaner slowed down a little and tried to collect his thoughts. As he approached the little groceteria, he saw Farley Rea ambling along the street. Needing someone to talk to, he screeched to a stop and yelled, "Farley, get in!"

Farley, never one to pass up a ride, happily climbed into the moose-chauffeured Caddy, trying to find a safe place for his head near the clattering antler.

"Tony, why are ya driving in a moose costume?"

"It's me ... Beaner."

"Beaner?" Farley replied, surprised. "I thought Tony was the mystery moose."

"Nah, it was always me."

"Cool." Farley had little more than that to offer the conversation and was having some trouble understanding why Beaner the Moose was driving Frankie Hall's old car with … Well, he didn't want to be rude, but — with someone in the trunk?

Beaner nearly blew through the four-way stop sign. His moose vision was awful, and he could only see a tiny cone of his normal human visual field.

"Uhh, Beaner, d'ya mind if I ask ya a question?" Farley asked hesitantly, while bobbing and weaving his head to avoid the flailing antler.

"What is it, Farley?"

"Ummm … do you got someone in the trunk?"

Even Beaner thought this was a moronic question and tried to look at Farley, his left antler clacking loudly on the door frame as he turned.

"*What?* Of course. It's Dick Dick. He came after me at the golf course and I accidentally hit him with the car. I took him up to Tony's, and Jacquie was real scared. She chased me outta there like you wouldn't believe. Tony come after me with a shovel. He wanted to get his hands on Dickface."

"Hoooooo-eeeee. That's bad. Tony knows he burned the hotel down … I, uh, think this could get ugly. Like real bad."

"Yeah, I know." Beaner felt his heart quicken.

Except for the muffled bellowing coming from the trunk, there was silence in the car.

Richard Dick was being held hostage in the boot of Elvis's limo, being driven aimlessly by a moose; Farley

THE VICAR'S KNICKERS

was even more confused than usual; and there was no obvious plan in play.

Farley beseeched the antlered ungulate next to him for guidance. "Well, whadda we do now?"

Beaner paused for a good long moment and finally said, "Maybe we should go ask Chief Wheat."

▬ ▬ ▬

With Beaner having fled in a panic, Vicar went back to the fallen cameraman and looked at Handlanger, broken but alive, writhing around in pain on the ground, his leg bent at a nauseating angle.

"Jacquie!" Vicar bellowed her name and gripped the shovel.

His eyes now piercing like the Death Star's laser, Vicar began scooping the pile of gravel and dirt they had just recently removed from around the perimeter of the house. He was going to bury this sonofabitch alive.

Jacquie tore around the corner, baby Frankie now held protectively in her arms, and saw what Vicar was doing. "Tony, Tony. Stop! Stop! Don't do this! You're going to kill him. You're not a murderer ..." She knew he had finally been pushed too far.

His eyes made him look unhinged, and he glared insanely at the half-conscious man at his feet, yelling, "Are you sure? 'Cause I feel exactly like one right now." He kept shovelling.

Jacquie pushed herself and baby Frankie between Vicar and the injured cameraman and gently held him.

"Don't, honey, don't. Let's just call the cops." She deliberately held the child close as if to soothe him, but it only reminded him of how close these bastards had come to killing her.

He steamed and growled like a mad dog. She had never witnessed that depth of anger.

Handlanger, now in shock and in great pain, looked at his cockeyed leg and screamed at Vicar as if it were *his* rights that had been trampled upon.

Very gently, Vicar nudged Jacquie and Frankie aside and stood above the injured cameraman.

"Really? You're going to sue us for everything we're worth? That's what you're thinking about right now?" Vicar just stared daggers at Handlanger for a few moments. Then he sharply kicked him in the broken leg. The scream the awful cameraman emitted was the worst cry of pain Vicar had ever heard, and he found it most satisfactory. He turned to Jacquie and looked at Frankie. He said tersely, "Take her inside."

A realization dawned on Jacquie: this is what happens when you threaten the family of a good man. Handlanger faded in and out of consciousness and, awed, Jacquie left Vicar to do his duty.

As she departed, he kicked Handlanger again. And again. And again.

eaner and Farley had rolled up to Chief Wheat's
front gate and Farley came around to help extricate
Beaner from the car. Manoeuvring the antlers was
a bit of a job and so Farley suggested they remove the
whole moose costume.

After a long and complicated process, they had extracted Beaner from the getup, which now lay in a pile
beside the car. Lovingly, Beaner knelt, rolled the carpet,
and unscrewed the lifelike antlers, while Farley looked
on, confused yet engrossed. Beaner then gingerly placed
it all in the back seat of the Caddy, the trunk currently
being occupied by the most odious character ever in-
flicted upon Tyee Lagoon.

They banged loudly on Chief Wheat's front door.
He answered it quickly, a look of irritation on his
face.

"What's going on?" he demanded. Almost no one visited him, and all that pounding on the door … *There must be a tidal wave on the way.*

The door was barely cracked when Beaner started babbling, "Uh, Chief. You're not gonna believe it but I got that Dick Dick guy in the trunk of the car. I went up to Tony's place cuz I didn't know what to do and I was dressed up like a moose and Jacquie chased me away. Tony looked like he wanted to kill something."

Wheat, sick at heart about the hotel fire, and now aggrieved after having heard Vicar's strong suspicions of arson, sat down on the bench inside his front door and rubbed his chin.

"Bear with me, lad, while I untangle all this. You're saying he's here? In the trunk of your car? And you were disguised as a moose?" He listened to Beaner recount the story again, slower this time. Wheat had his hand over his mouth and gazed vaguely toward the flower box hanging just outside the door. He had once required morphine for an injury and wondered if he might be on it right now. Chief Wheat had heard a few old sailors tell some tall tales, but this sounded like the biggest whopper of all time.

When the epic had been laid out clearly enough that he could assemble it into something understandable, he reached for the mobile phone in his pocket and scrolled down to Vicar's number. As it rang, he looked at Beaner and asked, "You were the roving moose, huh?" Beaner just gave a little shrug.

Jacquie answered Vicar's phone. Farley and Beaner watched and listened while the Chief nodded and grunted. Finally, he spoke. "Tried to bury him, you say? Oh my. Pictures of you on the toilet? Well, that's not on. All right, dear, I'll take it from here …" He rang off and looked up.

"Lads, I'm going to discuss some options with Mr. Dick."

The trunk popped open with Dick right behind it like a jack-in-the-box. Chief Wheat was ready. He grabbed him by the hair and pulled his head back at a vicious angle.

"Perhaps we should have a civilized chat, laddie," the Chief said, with a jolly tone.

"Get your hands off me, you fucking redneck," Dick gurgled with a choked voice.

Wheat responded philosophically, "I'm more of a well-read neck, really."

"You're going to rot in jail," Dick hissed. His angry face still oozed blood from the antler injury.

Wheat was not impressed. He glanced over at Farley and Beaner, chuckled a little, and then slammed his ham-sized fist into Dick's jaw. Dick sagged as his lights went out.

He pursed his lips as if considering his best option and then said to Farley and Beaner, "Be good lads and just take him around the back to the garage, will you?"

The pair obeyed without comment, but as they dragged Dick's limp form, they began snickering.

"Holy shit. This guy's gonna have a bad day."

"I know, right? I'd rather rassle a kraken."

Chief Wheat took his time. Slowly, grindingly, with righteous fury as his propellant, he extracted a full confession from Richard Dick. It took a while because Dick's ego was so gigantic that he could not accept blame, although the Chief had to admit that he was gifted at laying it at the feet of others.

He knew what had transpired; it was as clear as day. He proceeded with the attitude that this was retribution and he would mete it out using his level-headedness. He could not involve Vicar, for he might lose all control and too many lives would be ruined: Vicar's, Jacquie's, baby Frankie's. No, this was his duty and honour — he was the *Sergeant-at-Arms*, after all.

When Dicky Dick's denials and threats wore on his patience, he simply laid another round of pulverization on him, until he got what he wanted. There was nothing quite so delicious as forcing a propagandist to admit the truth. Wheat was all too aware the confession was coerced and cared little about it; he grimly but faithfully coerced Dick's filthy lying ass off. When Dick passed out, he got a cold jet from the garden hose.

It seemed probable to the Chief that, even if this dreadful man was convicted of his crimes, his sentence and treatment would be humane. That was unacceptable. He had, after all, nearly burned Vicar and two little children to death, pushed Vicar to the edge of ruin, badgered him cruelly, angered a whole town, and damaged the finest pub known to humanity. *His local*, goddamn it. His name was on a plaque to prove it.

Dick's mouthy protests slowly petered out. It was getting harder and harder to argue in his own defence as he gobbed up blood and even a couple of teeth.

■ ■ ■

A man taking his dog for a late-night tilt found Richard Dick, alive, barely conscious, on the grass in front of the walk-in clinic, left where he was sure to be discovered. He looked like a cardboard sheet that had been slid under a leaky old car, and his formerly pretty face was now hamburger.

Chief Hank Wheat returned home, got into pyjamas, and poured two beers into a huge pewter mug. He put a long straw in it, so to sip hands-free, pressed play on his Shanneyganock playlist, and plunged his aching fists into a cooler full of ice.

It would be some time and a large outlay of cash on dentistry before Double Dick would again influence lives and public opinion by lying into a camera. His typing fingers were going to need a long vacation, too.

Forty-Two / Ann Tenna Receives Signal

"The funny thing is that when the table and the bookcase fell over, I couldn't feel any heat or see any damage to the walls. There must have been some distortion of the structure from the heat that I couldn't see."

"Well, bookcases can be tippy ... How high was the table, Tony?" Ray asked, referring to the one that fell and launched a vase down the steps.

Vicar thought about it and put the edge of his hand around his mid-thigh and said, "About yea high." He glanced over to Jacquie, who had picked the table out herself. She agreed with his estimate.

Ray looked at both and asked in a quiet mumble, "Was it a pretty stable piece of furniture?"

"Yeah, it was narrow, but it had big round feet for good balance. You can't use dangerous junk in a hotel."

Ray scrunched up his nose and paused before speaking.

"It seems possible, um, *maybe* possible, that those things were knocked over — pulled down."

"Pulled down?" Vicar knew where he was going with this but was reluctant to be too open to it with Jacquie right there. Jacquie's brow furrowed; she knew where Ray was headed, too, and would never ascribe ghostly explanations to simple scientific solutions. She didn't like Ray's constant close shaves with Occam's razor. She was all too aware that Vicar didn't need this brand of encouragement.

Ray continued, "I just can't figger another reason why those two things fell over when they did." He felt there were invisible forces afoot. "Kinda freaky how they got you up the stairs just at the right moment, huh?" Ray wasn't mumbling for a change. "Almost like something was trying to get you up there."

They'd ruled out earthquake. A quick check on the government earthquake website showed nothing, and the structure was still holding together, even after being ravaged by fire.

Seeing an opening, Vicar cleared his throat and said, "I haven't told anyone about this" — he glanced apologetically at Jacquie — "but something really strange happened to me as I was bringing the kids down …"

Ray and Jacquie leaned in.

"We were trapped. There was no way out. The fire exit was fully engulfed, and the second-floor landing was an inferno. There was no going through it."

"But you got out …" Jacquie was wondering where this conversation was headed and was trying to put a line under it.

"Yes, Jack," Vicar responded. "Thank heavens. But I had help."

"Con-Con. And Annie," she said, tidily filling in the details.

Ray stayed silent and listened carefully, his lips pressed tightly together.

"No … This *guy*. A young guy — uh, he only had one sock on — he took my arm and guided me through the fire. There was no heat. We just passed through flames — they should have roasted us."

Jacquie looked at Ray, who sat in the corner of their living room; his eyes were now open wide with surprise as he felt the conversation shift to a tack that confirmed his suspicions.

"Some *guy*?" Jacquie challenged. "Where in hell would he have come from?"

"No clue. He just appeared and went back into the flames."

Jacquie quickly offered, "This sounds like cases where people can lift cars when their kid is trapped underneath. It's called hysterical strength."

Vicar replied doubtfully, "Hysterical fireproofing? I guess …"

She defended herself quickly. "People under extreme stress sometimes even say they've seen angels, or maybe a dead relative … It's a coping mechanism. It's well documented."

There, she thought, mentally patting her argument as if it were clothes folded in a suitcase, *cut and dried.* She had kept her cool and remained detached, safely above the hysteria. *Somebody has to drive this crazy train.*

■ ■ ■

Ann Tenna was still in shock, days after the fire. She was so keyed up that she finally broke down and took some tranquilizers that the doctor had prescribed. She didn't like taking pills — *that goddamn dope* — yet had no qualms about vast quantities of nasty white wine better used for cleaning the glass in her shower stall. But after three sleepless nights and being so withdrawn that she couldn't even speak with Poutine, something had to be done. *Just try it. See if it helps.*

"Am I addicted yet?" Her eyes were anxious saucers. Poutine looked at the clock. She had reluctantly swallowed two little pills not three minutes ago.

"Ya can't git addicted from two sleeping pills!" Poutine barked in frustration.

"Don't yell at me. I bin through hell and back." Tears formed in her eyes and she looked hurt. Poutine was out of his depth, thoroughly unable to respond appropriately.

"Now, little missy, I know yer upset but don' choo make me yer escape goat ..."

■ ■ ■

Poutine sat in an easy chair, sipping a coffee, engrossed in the fire log channel; stultifying, but at the correct price point. *Wheel of Fortune* wasn't on till seven and he'd lost some of his captivation for Vanna White after Annie had come on the scene; she gave him everythin' he wanted and he didn't need to buy no goddamn vowel, dere.

He had directed Jacquie, with baby Frankie in her arms, to Ann's bedroom. Thankfully they were at Ann's own house and not the ghastly tin shanty that Poutine called home.

Her kitchen was Swedish, but the rest of the house was forced into a Mexican vibe with vicious looking cacti everywhere. Jacquie passed through a doorway with a curtain of stringed beads that rattled and annoyed and led down the hallway where Ann's bedroom was located. She briefly imagined Poutine putting up with such an irritating doodad; she'd bet money he'd yank it down at the first opportunity.

"Ann? Annie?"

"Yeah?"

"I just popped by to see how you're making out." She lowered her voice as she entered the quiet room. A wan face peeked out from under the comforter; Ann had pale cheeks and very dark circles under her eyes. Jacquie gently plopped the baby down on Ann's bed and watched her gently touch Frankie's hand.

"I'm doin' better. I had a coupla bad days."

"I know, I know. Tony was in a state for a bit but now he's *mad*. Extremely angry. You know how men deal with fear …"

"Well, I don' cry much, but I sure did this time." Ann's hand was still shaky.

"You have to let it out. It's healthy to release your emotions." Jacquie was relieved to know that Ann was processing, however difficult it was for her. The fire might well have been the worst stressor Ann had ever faced. "But you were such a hero." She said it genuinely.

Ann just looked away and patted the baby's bum rhythmically.

"Tony was so stressed out during the fire that he had a hallucination."

Ann briefly glanced at her. "Really? Maybe I was that stressed out, too."

Jacquie wasn't sure what Ann meant but continued.

"Tony says, claims, well … He told me that some guy came to them through the blaze, walked them to safety, and then went back into the flames and vanished. It sounds like one of those stories you hear about on TV …" She bit her lip into a doubtful look.

"Jacquie …" Ann paused and cleared her throat. "That wasn't no hallucination. I saw that guy, too. That's zackly what happened."

Jacquie's mind came to a halt.

"Did Tony tell you about this? Did you hear him talking about it?"

"Nah. I saw with my own two eyes. The fucker *waved* at me. I didn't even tell Poutine. He'd say I was loony — he ain't too good with fancy thinkin' … But maybe it's true. Maybe I am a little over the property line."

Jacquie swallowed hard and felt her face flush. This was not what she expected at all, especially from Ann Tenna, Tyee Lagoon's Queen of Zero Nonsense.

The furnace had been turned on for the first time in a while and had a certain dusty smell to it. Jacquie sniffed and realized that fall was here; she lived in denial about its arrival every single year but eventually had to admit the long days were coming to an end. Tony would start a fire tonight, and they'd have one going in the wood stove almost every day now until spring.

She was so glad they had it. You just never know when you might have a newborn baby delivered to your door while the power is knocked out, during a blizzard, in the dark of night. She shook her head. *I wonder what all the normal people get up to.*

Good thing Tony was constantly fixated on thoroughly dry, "seasoned" firewood. If it were left up to her, they'd all be sitting in the arctic cold of the winter rain shadow, trying to burn wet wood, choking on the clouds of smoke it belched out, huddled together, utterly miserable, under a tarp.

Somehow, they had survived the year. The last few had been cyclones of chaos, but they had been Continental holidays with liveried servants compared to this one. She fought her habit to be shy of the future. After all, she appeared to be along for a very bumpy ride but so far had managed. Taking a page out of Tony's book, she told herself she wouldn't "borrow trouble" — his mother's saying. If she couldn't feel confident about tomorrow, he had said, she should focus on today, until her confidence returned. *Sensible advice*, Jacquie thought.

Poutine advised her, too. Trying to be fatherly, he said, ever-so-Poutineish-ly, "When ya dig down into the mattress of the heart, ya gotta leave yer worries by the waste side, dere." She twisted her head and grinned.

He finished with, "Fur all intensive purposes, ya can't worry about shit that ain't happened yet." Jacquie smiled at his cryptic wisdom and gave him a hug. Then drew back. Holy crap, he really did smell like a goat.

She was determined that they would open the Knickers again. As soon as possible.

▬ ▬ ▬

Taking a small notebook from her uniform pocket, Con-Con interviewed Handlanger, his leg in traction and his anger at full boil. He was going to have Vicar put in jail, damn it. Assault with intent to kill. *Throw the book at him.*

"I understand your anger, sir. But I must point out to you that you were on private property, surveilling the inside of his house with a camera. In fact, you were capturing images of Ms. O'Neil in the privacy of her bathroom."

"Who cares? That doesn't give him the right to try to kill me."

"Uhh …" She collected her thoughts for a moment. "My initial investigation has indicated no intent to kill — on the part of Mr. Vicar, at least."

"What kind of crooked set-up do you guys run up here? Are you in partnership with this guy?"

"It sounds as if you're accusing me of conspiracy, sir. That's a very serious charge."

"You're damn right it's serious, and I'll see you both in jail."

"Mmm … Perhaps we can have our cells adjoining."

The cameraman looked at her, uncomprehending.

"Y'see, the fire investigator has concluded that the hotel blaze was set on purpose. You, sir, are a suspect in that crime because we cannot rule you out. I saw you at the hotel when it was burning, and witnesses put you there before it started. *Numerous* people reported seeing you there. The arsonist responsible for the fire will end up in the jug for not only starting it, but for attempting to kill the occupants of the building."

Handlanger's throat went dry and he couldn't speak. He waved his hand as if to dismiss Con-Con, realizing that he'd blindly followed Richard Dick down a road that ended in his own downfall. Con-Con bowed graciously and backed out of the room, adding, "Thank

---

you for your co-operation." Then, almost whispering, "We have an extradition treaty."

— — —

Lying in his hospital bed, Richard Dick couldn't remember how he'd come to be there. He simply came to and racked his memory for missing information.

He could recall seeing the moose, which he still mistakenly believed was Vicar, in the golf course parking lot. He remembered being locked in the trunk of a car, getting dragged out of it, and being savagely punched by that muscle-bound drunk from the Knickers. His memory after that became very fuzzy.

The doctor explained that it might all come back to him, but then, he might never quite be able to fill in all the blanks. All he knew for certain was that he was in dreadful shape and needed some more painkillers. He had somehow known that this trip would be a mistake but couldn't have imagined it going this way. He was in too much agony at that moment to even be angry. No doubt his finely honed instinct for revenge would return but right then he felt utterly defeated.

Damn this stupid place. Just get me back to LA where life makes sense ...

— — —

Bouquets of flowers lay on the ground in front of the Knickers in an ever-expanding display of sympathy.

There had even been votive candles burning on one of the evenings immediately after the blaze, which Jacquie thought wildly inappropriate; Vicar simply saw them as another way to burn down what was left. When no one was around he blew them out and chucked them in a garbage can.

The internet had been abuzz with the reports of the devastating Agincourt fire, and one of Vicar's many fans sent a link that led to a newspaper database that contained a very old article of great interest.

The clipping, dated April 10, 1970, explained how a hotel guest named Lawrence "Lorko" B. Kaminski had died of apparent food poisoning; a coroner would confirm exact cause of death later.

The Agincourt Hotel was the location of his passing, and the terse report continued, saying that Kaminski had been found "after having expired during Easter weekend." His body was discovered by hotel employees "still in the hotel bed" on March 31, having died "perhaps 48 hours previously."

The sleuth had done further digging and found a very short death announcement in the local paper, as well as a long, sad obit in the *Star-Phoenix* of Saskatoon, Kaminski's hometown.

A few more mouse clicks and a couple of phone calls led Vicar and Jacquie to the little cemetery just outside Tyee Lagoon, the Salish Sea Memorial Garden, where the earthly remains of Larry lay, marked by his name on a simple stone that also read, *A beloved son, 1951–1970.*

The Vicar's Knickers now had a ghost with a paper trail.

▬ ▬ ▬

Enough time had gone by that the fear and guilt burying Serena had been sloughed off and forgotten, and she was rising from the ashes. All she could think of now was that Vicar had her baby, and by God, she would make it *their* baby. It was going to take some doing, but she would get what she wanted. Sooner or later she always did.

Forty-Four / My God, Jim

They stood on the curb in front of the burned-out hotel and looked again at the fire damage. The bottom floor and back corner were toast, like a nameless red-shirted Starfleet ensign.

Vicar broke the silence. "Since we have to rebuild it, I think it's the right time to rename it, too." A fresh start with a new name might be a good place to begin.

Jacquie wanted to set an optimistic tone and get dibs on the name before Vicar started getting "creative." She tilted her head in thought and replied, "You said you wanted to give it a better name, anyways, right?"

He nodded. *Agincourt*, never a great name, was now cloaked in negativity. They had to find a more upbeat name. Surprising Jacquie, Vicar suddenly blurted out, "We need to call it Hotel Valentine."

"Valentine ..." She drew the name out as she spoke.

"Yes, why the heck not? Our friendly ghost. Let's give him top billing. And by the way ... Frankie came to us on Valentine's Day. 'Member?"

Jacquie remembered well. She in fact remembered grumbling she'd have been happy with a box of chocolates. She had since changed her mind.

"Hotel Valentine sounds perfect. Spot on." She gave him a little peck on the cheek. She chuckled and said, "A lot better than Hospital Fish. Whatever prompted that awful band name?"

Vicar frowned. "One of the last dinners they served Mom in the hospital. Vile whitefish with a ptomaine-flavoured sauce, meant to bring despair to the terminally ill. I'm certain that's what finally killed her."

"Tony, that is incredibly dark ..."

"I know ... Super dark. I don't even understand it now." He paused and blinked as if he was trying to refresh his inner screen.

"Do you know that I gigged the night my mother died? I was doing the Elvis thing. *For fifty bucks.* I was at the effing Moose Lodge, so I missed her last breath. I started the band right after she died."

Jacquie inhaled sharply and said nothing, but her eyes were stricken. My lord, but Tony had nooks and crannies in his brain ... *Hospital Fish, indeed; he should have named the band Hair Shirt.*

He must have named it that and then plummeted downward into the dumpiest dumps afterward, punishing himself, surviving on Hospital Fish like a prisoner subsists on bread and water. Bringing a dead woman back to life, then? *Talk about overcompensating.*

For Jacquie another piece of the puzzle had fallen into place; this was über-weird and too sad for even Vicar to guffaw about, but at least it added up. She gazed upward at a flock of Canada geese honking their way southward in a long V and tried to soak it all in.

Vicar, not aware of her thoughts, breathed deeply a few times and looked at the fire damage before his eyes, surveying all the work to be done in the gutted hotel. He very deliberately made the decision that it was not a complete tragedy, not a punishing setback. It was certainly not the best outcome, far from it, but at least he still had his fighting spirit, his little family, and the best pub anyone had ever seen, wounded and fire singed, but eventually to rise again. The fire might have ruined the hotel, but it seemed to have taken some unwanted baggage along with it.

He squeezed Jacquie's hand and said, "Hotel Valentine … See? It takes me a while, but I can name things, too."

Forty-Five / Blowing in the Wind

It had felt almost dead calm as Jacquie and Vicar loaded little Frankie into the car, but when they arrived at the high promontory overlooking the Strait, the breeze was strong enough to make their coats flap. The wind braced as they hiked toward the sea; the horizon threatened while the sky above was clear and blue.

Jacquie carried a small box that contained the ashes of Frankie Hall and wondered if they'd even end up in the water or if they might just blow away, a cloud of dust vanishing like the life it had once embodied.

They had been meaning to sprinkle Frankie for a couple of years but could never seem to find a window of opportunity, or a moment of calm, when something wasn't going sideways. Poor Frankie Sr. had been left sitting in the bottom of the hall closet — and after all she had done for them.

Vicar had baby Frankie strapped to his chest a held on to two camping chairs. He unfolded them a sat down in one.

"Do you want to do it now?" Jacquie wasn't sure wh kind of ceremony he had in mind; they hadn't really dis cussed it. She'd just assumed they'd wing it like every thing else, but he might want to say a few words abou Frankie Hall.

"Uh, no, Jack. Let's just sit for a minute."

She knew there was something forthcoming but couldn't quite guess what was in store.

Vicar gazed out at the foreboding horizon and the washed-out view of the distant mountains and said wistfully, "This seems like a nice place to rest ..."

"Yeah, beautiful. Just perfect." Her voice was quiet now, somewhat reverent.

"I never mentioned it because it seemed like too much. But ... when I was trying to get out of the fire, Frankie talked to me; I could hear her voice, pushing me onward."

Jacquie did not respond. Tony's experiences had be-come so frequent and so real to him that they almost seemed normal to her now. She had been thrown into confusion about Valentine the Ghost, but now she didn't bother doubting him about the echoing voice of a dead mother figure.

At this point, if he were truthfully reporting real events, then her life would be awfully boring without exploring them along with him. It was too late now to

attempt "correcting" him. She had signed on for the voyage. *In for a penny ...*

"I have dreamt about Frankie a lot of times in the last couple of years. She's looking out for me. And then she came when I was losing it. She came. I needed help and she showed up."

Jacquie kept it light. "Well, why not. Everything she did helped us. Both of us. So, *hell*, I believe you." He certainly had experienced *something*, and that had to be respected.

"Good, cuz I have trouble believing me."

"Either start believing or stop believing. We're not running a *waffle* house ..."

Vicar turned to her and smiled. He appreciated her sincere attempt at a dad joke but she just didn't have enough corniness in her soul yet. *Why, if that ol' corn sat long enough it became sippin' whisky.*

He opened the little bag that had been over his shoulder and took out a small bouquet of carnations. During her life Frankie Hall had frequently put a fresh one in the combination vase and picture frame that held a photo of her son, Billy Jr. After she died, Vicar made sure to keep the photograph where it had always lived and changed the flower every couple of weeks. He could almost hear her voice: *I like carns because they last so long.* He knew she'd be thrifty, even in mourning.

There were five flowers in his hand: one for her late son Billy; one each for baby Frankie, Jacquie, and himself; and one for Valentine the Ghost. He gently tossed them in the ocean as Jacquie carefully sprinkled

Frankie's dusty remains on top, her tears flowing freely as the ashes billowed into ghostly shapes that drifted in the wind.

Vicar's face was wet, too, and he wiped it with his sleeve. He cleared his throat and said, "Goodbye, Frankie … Stay in touch."

Acknowledgements

Let's hear it for the band ...

Pete McCormack (*guitar/vocals/vegetable platter*) is first on the list yet again — my never-ending thanks to him and his family for decades of unfailing support. David A. Popovitch, Esq. (*bass/pierogies*) gave much guidance on Canadian law; Peter Winn (*wine/risotto balls/DJ Jazzy Pete*) explained death so fowl; Patricia Stirling (*market analysis/vinho verde*) and her arm candy, Zdravy (*MacGyver/Chicken Wings*), live on the road to 'Topia ...; Duke Thornley (*drums/steaks*) has yet again been mentioned in despatches; Geoffrey Kelly (*flutes/guitars/complimentary refreshment sourcing*) taught me about the paradigm-altering delights of mining "white gold," a.k.a. golf balls.

Denis Collins once again helped with *me Oirish*; Larry Morrison gave me a great boost regarding abandoned babies on doorsteps; and of course, Frau Lori Brienesse-Frank (*BG vox/bartending/go-go dancing after too much bartending*) provided valuable background illumination. Ronald SB Harder (*bass vox/tour bus driver/ cook/fluffer*) would get a shout out but he's such a selfish bastard that I withhold my thanks. Chris Churchill, Esq., as ever, provided legal insight and some dark and delicious humour.

I promised Terry David Mulligan I would mention him in the acknowledgements and fully expect a glass of fine BC wine in repayment. You would *NOT* believe the preposterous quantity of bingo rolling around his studio.

Darren Smith and Kenny Kruper both gave helpful input on construction, demolition, and dream castles. David Pankratz explained how fires get investigated. Cindy Labonte-Smith once again gave the manuscript a thorough beta read. Maureen Schuler helped me remember names of arcane and antique objects … no further comment will be forthcoming on the subject.

Derek Bieri and the Vice Grip Garage family — a fella thanks you for your insight.

Shannon Whibbs and Shari Rutherford scraped the crud off the story, banging the detritus loose with their stainless-steel quills, while Jenny "JMac" McWha held the garbage can under it and then wisely fled. Erin Pinksen picked up where JMac left off. JJ Martin has again called, advised, and suggested. There have been several Canadian musicians, authors, and journalists of note who have been remarkably supportive of my writing endeavours: Aaron Chapman and Jann Arden are two that deserve special thanks. My gratitude to all of them for understanding the sacred chain of "one hand up — one hand down."

Thanks, Colin Rivers — if only you could prescribe medication ... Ani Kyd Wolf is digging in the corners, taking names and kicking asses.

My family, a large group, getting larger, to all of you: Thanks. Sorry about the walleyed staring some days. Spirits, my other family, are more precious with every passing year.

Ollie and Sparky, the two most loving and hilarious kids I know, man, do we laugh ... To my wife Merm — who thinks I'm a hoarder and that I'm not aware she throws out my beautiful "previously loved" treasures — be warned: *I know where you hide your snacks.*

Hats and Nate — Congrats and Good Luck

Lulu: Still with me

Ellie Harder — RIP

About the Author

Vince R. Ditrich, semi-retired from a fifty-plus-year career in music, thirty of which he spent with Canadian favourites Spirit of the West, lives in a log cabin deep in the rainforest of Vancouver Island, set so remotely in the bush that the nearest Walmart is nearly twelve minutes away by mule.

He is now ensconced in the high-flying ranks of Canadian authors, his unerring instinct for financial profits from the Arts guiding him yet again.

His interests include sleeping in, schlumpfing around in old-man slippers, reading books about other people exercising, and being gripped by an artsy ennui that'd be fashionable if he weren't in that wretched bathrobe.

Vince is married to Merm, a lovely woman who often recalls the date she once had with a man in a toupée and Dacron leisure suit who has now climbed way up to middle management at the bottle depot — *stability had been right at her fingertips …*

Vince's previous novel, *The Liquor Vicar* did not win a Pulitzer, Giller, Gov Gen's Award, or even Best in Show. He has set his sights on a Nobel for this one. They gave one to Bob Dylan, for God's sake.